Death

Sarah Ward is a critically acclaimed crime and gothic thriller writer. Her book, *A Patient Fury*, was an Observer book of the month and *The Quickening*, written as Rhiannon Ward, was a Radio Times book of the year. Sarah is a former Vice-Chair of the Crime Writers Association, Trustee of Gwyl Crime Cymru Festival and an RLF Fellow at Sheffield University.

Also by Sarah Ward

The Birthday Girl
The Sixth Lie
The Vanishing Act
Death Rites

SARAH WARD
DEATH RITES

First published in the United Kingdom in 2024 by

Canelo
Unit 9, 5th Floor
Cargo Works, 1-2 Hatfields
London SE1 9PG
United Kingdom

Copyright © Sarah Ward 2024

The moral right of Sarah Ward to be identified as the creator of this work has been asserted in accordance with the Copyright, Designs and Patents Act, 1988.

All rights reserved. No part of this publication may be reproduced or transmitted in any form or by any means, electronic or mechanical, including photocopy, recording, or any information storage and retrieval system, without permission in writing from the publisher.

A CIP catalogue record for this book is available from the British Library.

Print ISBN 978 1 80436 678 3
Ebook ISBN 978 1 80436 681 3

This book is a work of fiction. Names, characters, businesses, organizations, places and events are either the product of the author's imagination or are used fictitiously. Any resemblance to actual persons, living or dead, events or locales is entirely coincidental.

Look for more great books at www.canelo.co

Printed and bound in Great Britain by Clays Ltd, Elcograf S.p.A.

For Sarah Tarlow

Thou shalt not suffer a witch to live.

Exodus 22:18

1

It was only while knotting the red thread that he realised the woman he'd slaughtered was still breathing. She made a small sound, a slight release of air, and across the room he watched as her eyelids flickered. She was dying. He knew it and so, surely, did she. She was without any hope of help – even her dog had high-tailed it into the night. That had been his first mistake. Nowhere in her online presence had there been evidence of a pet. People who spent their days posting on social media usually couldn't resist a photo of their animal, but this woman, for reasons he couldn't guess at, had chosen to keep the little French Bulldog a secret. The focus of her Instagram account had been her house and garden. That had been her mistake.

She lived in a single-level duplex built in the 1930s before real estate boomed and developers crammed three-storey townhouses into postage-stamp-sized plots. He'd been able to sketch a rough floor plan of her home based on her Instagram posts. There was a corner that he hadn't been able to identify until last week when she'd revealed a photo of her revamped bathroom. Once he'd completed his sketch, he turned his focus to her garden. One shot in particular of rhododendrons in bloom had revealed the insubstantial latch she used to secure her yard gate. Only a quick drive-by was needed to ensure what was in his head matched reality. Then, it had been a case of checking calculations and biding his time.

The waiting had been the hardest. Once you've killed, he was discovering, you wanted very quickly to do it again. He forced himself to remember that there was an order of things and he had to be careful his baser senses didn't threaten to undo all his meticulous plans.

In the distance, he could hear the damn dog yapping. It was only a matter of time until a neighbour woke and recognised it as belonging to this house. He had to get a move on. The fact the woman was alive wasn't a problem. It was his second error of the evening but easily rectified. The key was to ensure the significance of the carefully chosen items remained unnoticed by the police when they finally got here. The woman had been a drinker. Nothing wrong in that, he supposed. Many of her 'look at me I'm relaxing in the evening' photos had featured a glass of red wine. The goblet didn't interest him, but the bottle did. It was perfect and he didn't even need to touch it. It sat open on the table with the cork next to it and would serve its purpose.

The woman was also a quiltmaker and had been keen to show her creations in her photos. Patchworks of colours – she'd liked cornflower blue set against crimson with splashes of green. Very New England, but it was what was in the background he'd been interested in. The spools of thread and a hedgehog pincushion. Cute. He sat with her sewing box on his lap as he tightened the knot.

When he was ready, he checked everything was in place and finished the task he'd failed to complete earlier. Then, going to the kitchen window, he pulled out the etching knife he'd bought in a hardware store two weeks earlier. He'd made sure it was an item among innocuous purchases. A couple of lightbulbs and a new garden hose. He'd also paid by cash and was pretty sure no one would remember him. It was one of those old-fashioned places without security cameras. He also didn't think for a minute anyone would notice what he was now sketching against the glass in the bottom right corner, hidden by the fold in the drapes. The dog was silent, which worried him more than the barking. It suggested someone was comforting the animal. He sped up the task and, when it was finished, slipped out of the side door, the one this householder had helpfully photographed with the locks in full view.

The night was silent except for a muted thud from the neighbouring property. A light was on in the hall; he was certain the house had been in darkness when he arrived. He hurried on, his sneakers squeaking on the frosty pavement. He allowed himself to relax when he saw his car down the alley. It was only as he was driving away that he realised his third mistake. But that was okay. He was certain no one, absolutely no one, would see that mark until he was ready.

2

The atmosphere was stifling as state medical examiner Erin Collins began her external examination of the cadaver. The air conditioning was doing battle with the heat of an unseasonably warm week and losing. Erin would have preferred to wait for the maintenance contractor to come and have a look at the unit before she started the autopsy, but no one could give her a time when that might happen. Personnel shortages, according to the woman on the phone when Erin had chased it up. In desperation, she'd set up a fan in the corner of the room and gritted her teeth. At least the woman lying on the table, ready for her last ever medical examination, was in decent shape. It could have been a lot worse.

Erin's colleague Scott, one of the office's medical investigators, had visited the crime scene to do an initial assessment at the victim's house. Only in movies could the medical examiner be in two places at once. Tasks were delegated. A suspicious death would first be attended by one of her investigative colleagues before a decision was made as to whether an autopsy was appropriate. At seven that morning, she'd been having her coffee, checking through emails and hassling the maintenance department before her day began. Scott had called her at ten past the hour. This one needed a post-mortem.

There were no signs of a break-in at Jessica Sherwood's house, but her dog had been in the garden at four a.m., which was unusual. Either she'd let the animal out and collapsed in her living room or someone had entered her home, with or without an invitation, and played a role in her death. Erin had shuffled her workload around while she waited for the body to be brought in. The teen who'd hanged himself in his uncle's garage and the farm worker who'd accidentally shot herself with a hunting rifle would wait until tomorrow when, hopefully, things would be a little cooler.

'Sure you want to do this one by itself?' Jenny, her assistant, was finishing her photographs, beads of sweat on her forehead as she bent over the body. It wasn't unusual for Erin to complete two autopsies at the same time on busy days. She could do the initial external exams together, moving from one cadaver to the other – it helped speed things up. Erin shook her head.

'Just this one, please. I'm in no mood to rush around today. It's too hot.' She looked at her notes. 'So, we have a Jessica Sherwood here, aged, according to her driver's licence, sixty-two. A former kindergarten teacher who still helped out occasionally at the local day care. Discovered lying on her side on her living room floor. No medical information yet, but her neighbour says she was fit and well.'

'A mystery.' Jenny lowered the camera and began to flick through the digital images. 'You like those. Jericho's very own Quincy.'

'Every time, although you're too young to remember Quincy.' Erin, who had been marking up the autopsy report, noting marks on the body, stopped when she reached the woman's neck. 'Jenny, will ya take a photo of this.'

With the post-mortem finished, Erin picked up the phone and called in the results to one of the investigating officers. She knew Detective Charlie Baros of old. Prickly and easily offended, talking to him was never a straightforward task. She kept the summary brief. He listened in silence as she outlined her findings.

'Appreciate the quick work, doc,' he said and cut the line.

The admin out of the way, Erin went to the women's cubicle and stripped off her scrubs, hair covering and mask and balled them up into a disposable bag. Naked, she crossed to the shower and let the hot water cover her body. Jessica Sherwood had died from asphyxiation caused by strangulation. The mauve bruises visible on her neck told a partial story; the cerebral hematoma and neck muscle contusions confirmed the external evidence. The dog in the garden hadn't been let out by its conscientious owner. It had escaped as life was being squeezed out of its mistress.

Homicides were rare in the state. Maybe twenty a year. OK, so not that rare, but everything's comparative. Killings were *comparatively* rare. Strangulations she saw less often, at most one or two a year. There were no defensive wounds on Jessica's arms and hands, which suggested she'd been taken by surprise. Her attacker had asphyxiated her and left her lying on the floor. The victim – early sixties, homely looking, no indications of having borne a child – reminded her of her Aunt Connie. Most likely it was a burglary gone wrong. It wasn't her job to make that call, but it had made for a bad start to her day. What she really didn't want is women who looked like Aunt Connie strangled in their homes by panicking thieves.

Erin wrenched the shower off and grabbed the towel, glancing up at the clock she'd had installed, to everyone's amusement, in the women's restroom. Well, what the hell? Time didn't stop even when she was taking a pee. The day had started and not a minute of it was her own. Erin retrieved her cosmetics bag from her rucksack and began to rub moisturiser into her face. Thank God it was summer. During spring and fall, she was committed to two afternoons a week at Jericho College. A new initiative encouraged by the Mayor's office, keen to forge links between the prestigious college and law enforcement. Within a month she'd be run off her feet. A new term, new colleagues, and that damned mentoring programme she'd been coerced into joining. Worse, a sea of new students brought up on a diet of TV who thought forensics was the only way to solve major crimes. The murder clean-up rate in Jericho? Previously ninety-five per cent, now down to sixty after a couple of bad years. That would give them something to think about in their first class. Solve that, Sherlock.

3

Carla, jet-lagged and disorientated, stared in dismay at the room that was to be her temporary home for the coming weeks and wondered if she'd made a terrible mistake. She shook the thought away – late summer, after all, is a terrible time to judge a place. Residents are away holidaying, and an influx of seasonal workers and visitors swell a town on the tourist trail. It had been the case in Oxford, and Jericho was no different. She was in another country, yes, but one that Carla had longed to work in. She loved the thought of New England, brought alive in the books by Edith Wharton and John Updike, and wanted to embrace the small towns that retained their settler feel, the changeable seasons each with their own dynamic and the academic excellence offered by Jericho College. It had been time for a move, a change from the lassitude that she could not shrug off. A way to escape the ennui of grief that had dulled but not disappeared.

She'd found temporary accommodation in the attic wing of a brick townhouse and even that hadn't been easy to locate. The summer season stretched into late September, by which time the semester would have started. Eventually, Patricia, a fellow parishioner of the church attended by her new boss Albert Kantz, had been prevailed upon to house Carla on the understanding that she'd look for somewhere else during the autumn.

Standing in her flight-grubby clothes in the large garret room, she remembered once more that you couldn't run away from your troubles; you just packed them up and brought them with you. Perhaps her mood would improve when she got onto campus. She missed the busyness of a September start of term inundated with emails, invitations to meetings and disputes over office space.

Carla eyed the modern double bed, wondering if it was as comfortable as it looked. The exterior of the house gave off gothic vibes and she'd had visions of sleeping on an ancient iron bedstead infused with decades of other people's sweat and skin. Her landlady Patricia had promised her the mattress was only two years old, which Carla guessed was the average lifespan for a bed in a hotel room. The other pieces of furniture were older – a bleached pine chest of drawers and a matching thin wardrobe with a mirrored door that creaked as Carla hung her clothes inside its pleasant, closed fustiness. She'd brought three suitcases with her, wincing at the extra luggage allowance, and was determined to make do with what she had. Anything missing, she would buy locally, from a goodwill store if necessary. Her Oxford flat, with its painful memories, had been cleared and rented out.

Carla crossed to the window and looked out over the town. The college, she knew, was over to the east, beyond the river and out of her sightline. In the fading twilight, she could see the white spires of two churches, one Episcopalian, the other Latter-day Saints according to Patricia. Her landlady, while showing her the room, had paused, offering Carla the opportunity to offer up her own religious affiliations. It was too early in their relationship for Carla to admit she had none. Patricia, she gathered, was an expert on religion, stray animals and quilt making. It made her sound more twee than the stocky, no-nonsense mother of five she was. Carla turned at the sound of a knock and Patricia came in with a tray.

'You didn't need to carry that up for me. I'd have come down for tea.'

'I doubt my tea-making skills are up to English standard. I've brought you hot chocolate and cookies. It's your first night and you'll be tired.' Patricia put the tray on top of the chest of drawers as the smell of cinnamon filled the room. 'My son will be bringing a table over from his basement tomorrow for you to work on. Will you manage until then?'

'Of course. It's kind of you to go to this effort for this temporary arrangement – I'm not sure what I would have done if you hadn't come to the rescue.'

'Rescue?' queried Patricia. 'I'd hardly call it that and, if you don't mind me saying, you look the competent type.'

Carla smiled. 'I guess I am, but it just feels so strange. I mean, I've travelled around the world on digs, but I've never managed to shake off the unfamiliarity of first days.'

'Digs? You're in the same field as Albert then?' Patricia perched gingerly on the bed, careful not to disturb the smoothness of the home-made quilt.

'He'll be my new boss. Do you know him well?'

'Well enough. He and his wife Viv are regulars at the church, their kids less so, but you know what it's like for youngsters these days. Plenty of other things to occupy their time. You know she's a cop?'

Carla started. 'A cop? No, I didn't. I don't actually know much about Albert as I was interviewed over Zoom.'

Patricia snorted. 'That's the way everything is going these days. Working remotely. Not much use for an archaeologist though, is it?'

In fact, quite a lot of Carla's work had moved online over the last couple of years, but Patricia ploughed on, not expecting a response.

'I have to say it sounds an exciting life. I think if I'd had a choice, I'd have wanted to be an archaeologist too, unearthing the past and all that. Don't tell me it's nothing like I imagine because I won't believe you.'

Carla laughed and picked up a cookie, sure that the sugar would help lift her mood. She bit into it, savouring the burst of flavour in her mouth.

'I'm a bit of an outlier when it comes to my profession, if truth be told. It's not enough for me to excavate the sites and build a picture of the lives of the people I'm studying. I want to understand the feelings behind what I find. I call it the archaeology of emotion. It's what my reputation is built on.'

'The archaeology of emotion? I like that. People don't express their feelings as much as they should.' Patricia held her gaze, a flicker of understanding in her eyes. 'I heard you were a widow, so I was expecting someone a little older. You're young to be so unfortunate.'

Carla swallowed her biscuit dry in her throat and took a swig of hot chocolate. Unfortunate? She'd not been described as that before, but it wasn't a bad adjective. 'My husband died after a long illness. It's a been a while, but you could say I'm still excavating my own emotions.'

'Well, my advice, for what it's worth, is don't expect change to produce miracles.'

Carla, suddenly near to tears, turned back to the window. 'I think I'm beginning to appreciate that. Still,

Jericho is beautiful tonight, a bit like the Oxford I left behind. Through this window it looks as if I'm in a fairy-tale town.'

Patricia grimaced.

'Did I say something wrong?' asked Carla, thinking of Oxford's seedier side and the occasional bouts of city centre violence.

'Oh, I don't know. You're actually not that far wrong. Fairy tales have their dark side as well as happy endings.'

'And does Jericho have its underbelly?'

Patricia hesitated and pulled a wisp of grey hair behind her ear. 'All places have the wrong side of the tracks. We're just better in Jericho at hiding it. You just take care. Not thinking about dating again?'

'Not at the moment.' Carla hid her surprise. In fact, she had no intention of seeing anyone, but Patricia's question had prompted her to hedge her bets. Wasn't this a scene from a Victorian melodrama? The part where the matriarch of the house warns against male visitors. She saw Patricia relax at her reply.

'That's all right then. We have our problems like anywhere else. I have to say, I appreciate having company in the house. The town's got an odd atmosphere. I've noticed it for the last year or so. Anyway, don't mind my fancies. You'll settle in well, I'm sure.'

4

Erin sat opposite Charlie Baros, trying to ignore his insolent gaze as she outlined the results of Jessica Sherwood's blood and tissue sample analysis. These tests often threw up curveballs and were part of the process of determining the cause of death of the people who passed through the facility. Erin stood by the initial findings of her post-mortem. Jessica had been strangled and the cause of death was asphyxiation. The problem was that her blood analysis identified the presence of potassium chloride, a favourite drug for suicides due to its rapid absorption in the body. Jessica hadn't killed herself. The imprints of the fingers on her neck were of a larger hand, probably male. It was definitely a homicide. The blood results, however, revealed a more complex chain of events leading to the woman's death. Her attacker hadn't killed her at the first attempt and had injected the dying woman with a drug to hasten her end. The detectives were furious. It's hard to sustain the theory of a burglary gone wrong when the killer is carrying a hypodermic syringe.

'Perhaps he kept it on him for such a scenario,' suggested Erin.

Detective Amy Perez shot her a sympathetic look. Unlike her partner, she wasn't naturally combative, and she knew they needed to extract every last clue from the post-mortem. There was no obvious motive for the killing. Jessica's house and modest savings were to be inherited by a sister in Ohio, who had been ruled out as a suspect. There had been no similar homicides, although there had been a slew of house break-ins because of the hot weather. Just as they were filing it as a burglary gone wrong, the blood results had come back.

'The lieutenant wants us to go over everything again. See what we've missed.' Baros slammed his cup down on the table, its contents slopping around on the dark wood. 'What I'd like to know is what you missed. Because I don't see any mention of a needle mark in your report.'

Erin cast her mind back to the autopsy conducted in the clammy heat. Jessica had been found lying on her side in a state of livor mortis. Without a beating heart, her blood had followed the laws of gravity and settled on the lowest portions of the body. The resulting purple marks on the skin would have made a puncture wound difficult to spot, but Erin had examined the skin to the best of her ability. The question she was asking herself, however, was whether she'd returned to examine the body the following day. By then lividity marks began to fade and the skin returned to its pale waxen hue. When she was still unsure of the cause of death, she'd often take another look at the cadaver to see what new marks could be identified. But she was pretty sure she'd not revisited the body of a woman she'd already identified as a homicide victim. It was a mistake, but surely not a career-ending one.

She swallowed, desperate for a drink to moisten her parched throat. 'I'm going to look again at the autopsy photos, but I saw no sign of a puncture wound,' she told the detectives.

Baros swore and Perez placed a restraining hand on his arm. Erin, tired after a long day, snapped. 'If I recall, there was nothing actually stolen from the victim's home. How does that agree with your burglary gone wrong theory? Don't thieves usually steal something during break-ins?'

Baros didn't react. Perhaps he was used to women standing up to him. His boss was the legendary Viv Kantz, and Perez didn't come across as a walkover either. Instead, he folded the report and tucked it under his arm. 'Let's all of us see if we can restore our reputations.'

After they'd left, Erin looked at her watch. She should go home, get something to eat, watch a film. Anything to relax. Instead, she went to her office and pulled up Jessica Sherwood's file on her computer. Image by image she began her examination of the photos taken by Jenny.

5

'Doctor James?'

Carla had been about to give up and return to Patricia's house to fire off an irate email. She'd arrived on campus and no one was expecting her. Albert Kantz had sent her a message the previous evening with the location of her office and promised that the department secretary was aware of her arrival. He'd catch up with her at the office once he'd got a meeting out of the way. He'd forgotten, however, that for her to even reach the Department of Archaeology, she needed a pass to access the campus and, in a moment of daring, she'd eventually slipstreamed behind a student who'd looked a little affronted at her presence close behind him as he opened the door.

She entered a wide, panelled corridor where muted voices could be heard behind closed doors. There was nothing to identify where the department secretary might reside, but each door had the letter A followed by a number nailed to it. Carla followed the trail to A15, the office identified for her by Albert, amused to note there was no number thirteen on any of the doors. When she tried the handle, she discovered the office was locked. So much for New England hospitality. She dug in her bag and tried to connect her mobile to the university's Wi-Fi to send a message to her boss.

'Max Hazen.'

Carla jumped at the voice so close to her ear and looked up. A tall man wearing a cream linen suit held out his hand to Carla. His curling grey hair was clipped close to his head with the rawness that suggested a recent cut. Relieved that someone was finally talking to her, she grasped his fingers, noting the calloused skin and faint outline of an old scab. Max, as if conscious of her scrutiny, rubbed his palms against his jacket.

'Perils of the job – I spent the summer on a dig in Europe. I've been looking forward to meeting you.'

Carla had looked up the academic staff before leaving England, trawling through the college's website deliberately aimed at catching the eye of parents of wealthy New England freshmen who wanted an exclusive education for their offspring. There were around ten in the department, so she had no excuse for not getting to know the research interests of her new colleagues. Max had given little away about himself on the website, which was unusual. Your academic profile was a place to boast of your qualifications and publication history. Even a few words about your areas of study gave the department a more human face. Max's began: 'I am an archaeologist with an interest in Roman settlements.' Hardly the most dynamic of statements and the link to his curriculum vitae hadn't been working.

'Call me Carla.' She turned, looking down the emptying corridor. 'I don't suppose you know where I can get a key for my room. Professor Kantz sent me a message to get settled into the office.'

'He's put you in A15?' Max stopped, a flush creeping across his face. 'Well, that's just typical of the lack of respect around here.'

'Is there something wrong?' asked Carla. 'I'm pretty sure this is the office Albert told me to find.'

'Sorry.' Max folded his arms, not looking sorry at all. 'Ignore me, I'm sure it *is* the right place. A spare key is kept with the programme administrator. Give me five minutes.'

He walked away without waiting for Carla's reply. He wasn't happy about her being in this room and she hoped this wasn't the start of a feud over office space. The annual shuffle to accommodate new staff and changes in programmes often resulted in fallings out. As the newcomer, she should be bottom of the heap, but it looked like she'd been given a prestigious room away from the entrance. Great start. Carla leant against the door and watched the students file past her.

For the first two days it was newcomers only who looked as disorientated as her. Returning students would be allowed back the following week, allowing freshmen to familiarise themselves with the campus and register for classes. She watched as three students passed her wearing jackets and ties.

'Business school,' Max whispered to her as he returned, noticing her gaze. 'They're the only students who wear suits.' He held out the key to her. 'They were waiting for you to pick it up. I don't suppose you got the message to go to the office?'

'Professor Kantz didn't—'

Max smiled. 'Albert gets a little forgetful sometimes. Don't worry. I'll sort you out.'

He put the key in the door, an old-fashioned courtesy that set Carla's teeth on edge. She wanted to assure him she was perfectly capable of opening a door herself. Taking a deep breath, she followed Max into the room and stopped. 'Oh.'

Inside the high-ceilinged space, someone had either already settled in or never left. Carla dumped her shoulder bag on the chair and looked around. It was obviously a female space; she took in the pinned pictures of a desert dig showing a woman in khaki shorts, and the bottle of hairspray next to the oval mirror. The air was stuffy, overlaid with the aroma of rotting fruit. Carla bent down and pulled out the trash bin from beneath the desk. Empty.

'I can't believe it's not been cleared out yet.' Max's voice was shaking with anger. 'What the hell are they playing at? I'm really sorry about this.'

'It's fine. It's not the first time this has happened.' Carla, despite herself, glanced in the mirror. Her pale face still showed the traces of the jet lag she was finding it impossible to shrug off. 'Whose office is it?'

'Lauren's. I mean Doctor Powers's.' Max went over to the window and forced it open, letting in a whisper of cooling air.

'And is she coming back for her things?'

'No.' Max's gaze met hers. 'Lauren was unfortunately involved in an accident. She died this spring.'

'Died?' Carla's heart sank as she looked round again at the room, taking in clues to the woman's personality. Among the fieldwork papers was a Snoopy coffee mug and a pot of banana-flavoured lip balm. 'That's terrible. What happened?' She stopped, aware of the abruptness of her question. 'Sorry, you don't need to tell me if it's too painful. I find it hard to shrug off my perpetual curiosity.'

'As we all do, I'm sure.' Max paused. 'She drowned while swimming. It was a shock to us all. Lauren was one of a kind and a highly respected member of this department. I offered to go through her effects after she died to send her personal stuff back to her family in Maine. No one came back to me, so I assumed it had been done.'

'I'm so sorry. Please don't worry about the office.' Carla swung round the high-backed chair behind the desk, wondering if it would be tactless to sit down to take the edge off her exhaustion. She regarded the empty seat and noticed Max too had his eyes on it. 'If someone can get me some cardboard boxes, I'll clear the desk at least. I can work around the other stuff.'

Max, still unsettled, nodded. 'I'll send an email to the coordinator. She should have sorted all of this out for you.' He made for the door but lingered at the entrance, reluctant to leave her in the room. 'I'm really sorry about this.'

When he'd left, Carla flopped into the chair and closed her eyes. Max's reaction had unsettled her more than she cared to admit. More death, this time of a well-liked colleague. This room was a reminder that it wasn't just her who suffered from loss and grief. Her family must surely be waiting for Lauren's effects. Among all the academic papers and knick-knacks there might be well-loved mementoes of field trips. Someone would want the photo of the smiling woman pinned to the cork board. Carla pushed her chair over to the photograph and scrutinised the woman who grinned down at her. She was around her age, maybe a little older, with an air of good-humoured competence. A woman Carla would have liked to have been meeting on her first day of semester. She wondered, not for the first time, whether it was better to die gradually as Dan had done, aware of his mortality but able to make his own decisions about his death, or suddenly like Lauren with no time to be disappointed in what life had dealt you.

Carla was reaching out to touch the image when the door opened and Albert Kantz stood at the entrance. Part of his seniority, thought Carla grumpily, was that he hadn't felt the need to knock first. At the Zoom interview, she'd noticed that he had an unnerving resemblance to a young Hugh Grant, and this was confirmed in the flesh. She'd expected someone older, as Albert was a name she associated with those born in the early twentieth century. Her new boss was in his early forties, his dark brown hair turning grey at his temples and a network of creases radiating from his eyes.

'Sorry I'm late. Problems at home. My wife was called away and I needed to take Zoe, my daughter, to her shift at the local bar.'

'It's no problem.'

Albert's eyes widened as he took in the room. 'Jeez, they haven't even cleared this place. I don't believe it... Look, give me a day, will you, to make a complaint. They'll get the cleaners in, although I'm not sure given the amount of personal stuff...'

'Max said he'd offered to collect her effects.'

'You've met Max? That's good. I haven't completely left you stranded here.' Albert picked up a paperweight. It was a piece of stone, its chiselled edges suggesting a worked tool. 'Max knew Lauren well. He'd be ideal to supervise the packing. I'll talk to him about it.'

'I'm sorry for the loss of your colleague.' Carla was intrigued by the reactions to the room. Of course, it was an administrative blip, but Max had shown anger and distress at the presence of his dead colleague's possessions. Albert, despite his confidence that he would be able to get the room cleared, was looking in distaste at the object he was holding. Perhaps he had hoped the university would make a better impression on its newest member of staff.

'Max said there was an accident...?' Carla saw her question was unwelcome but was unable to stop herself. Part professional curiosity, part morbidity caused by the death of her young husband. The need to find companionship amongst the bereaved.

'Yes, down by the river.' Albert stopped. 'I'm sorry, but can I leave you for the moment while I sort a few things out? It's a difficult day for me. You'll be contacted sometime this morning by your mentor.'

'Mentor?' Carla's heart sank. 'I don't think I need a mentor.'

'I'm afraid every new member of staff is assigned one. You'll like Erin.' Albert paused for dramatic effect. 'She works in the mortuary.'

6

By lunchtime, Carla had seen no one. No mentor, no programme administrator, no Max or Albert. She did, however, know a little more about her dead predecessor. Unable to help herself, Carla had made a mental list of the objects on Lauren's desk but found nothing remarkable. It was the space of someone with too much stuff and not enough time to keep it tidy. The thought depressed Carla. Poor Lauren. With her spirits depleted, Carla needed an atmosphere more invigorating than Lauren's office, which was encouraging her to brood about the randomness of sudden death. Gathering her courage, she locked the office and headed down the stairs, looking for the coordinator's room. She found it tucked at the end of the corridor. Like everywhere else she ventured, it was empty. As she turned to leave, she careered into a tall woman dressed in black jeans and a polo shirt.

'Are you the programme coordinator?'

The woman took a step back. 'No, I'm damned well not. If you find her, tell her to answer her phone.'

Carla laughed. 'I wonder if she actually exists.'

The woman snorted. 'I'm thinking the same about Doctor Carla James.'

Carla froze. 'What do you mean?'

'I've been ringing her room all morning and can't get any reply.'

'My office phone never rang once.'

'Oh. It's you. Thank God for that.' The woman, unabashed, smiled broadly. 'I'm Erin. Your mentor. Full title, if you care about these things, Doctor Erin Collins. A proper doctor too, none of this academic stuff.' Again, the wide smile.

Carla held out her hand, unable to resist rising to the bait. 'You work in the mortuary, I believe.'

'Who the fuck told you that?'

Carla dropped her hand. 'A colleague.'

'Male, I suppose. I'm a state medical examiner. Work in a mortuary, my ass. You carry a spade for a living, I suppose.'

'Trowel actually.'

Erin started laughing. 'Don't mind me. I've had one of those mornings. Fancy a coffee?'

Erin took Carla off campus to a Greek coffee shop.

'Slightly more privacy for us. Slightly.'

'The campus is a hotbed of gossip, right?' Unlike Erin, who had perched effortlessly on the bar stools, Carla – a good five inches shorter – found herself wriggling up onto the leather seat. Erin pretended not to notice as she handed her a menu.

'The coffee's good, as are the pastries. Or we could have an early lunch.'

'Coffee and pastries are fine.'

Erin ordered for them both and looked around. 'OK,' she said in a mock whisper. 'First impressions of Jericho.'

'The town? Pretty, very New England, a little touristy. The fringes look more ordinary, but that's just the impression I got in the car from the airport.'

'OK, I meant the college, but you've nailed the town. What do you think of our fine institution?'

'Um,' Carla bit into a spun sugar confection. 'Everything feels a little haphazard. I can't get a feel for who does what.'

Erin snorted. 'I'll explain. The way this college is run is that the head of department is accountable for everything. And I mean everything. The rest of you do as you're told. I'm a little different as I have another job. Two days a week I lecture on campus, teaching a new generation of students the processes of pathology work and trying to persuade them that working alongside the dead can be as interesting – no, strike that – more interesting than dealing with living patients. Working in a morgue, as your colleague charmingly put it. The thing is…' Erin paused and stirred her coffee. 'It's a little traditional here.'

'That's pretty much what I was expecting.'

'This place is all about reputation. Staff are warned that under no circumstances should their behaviour bring the college into disrepute. That's in relation to their private or professional lives. They're hot on equality and diversity here, at least in theory, but I sometimes think the toll is on the female staff.'

'What do you mean?'

Erin glanced over her shoulder and lowered her voice. 'My advice is to keep your head down. I'll explain more another time. You like Professor Kantz?'

'He seems nice.'

'Well, you should be fine. His wife is the lieutenant at the police precinct – a big cheese – so as well as holding down the job, he does a lot of the childcare. No big deal, but he's a little, well, absent.'

'He seemed distracted this morning. Said he had to drive his daughter to work as his wife was busy.'

'Really? As I said, the majority of childcare falls to him. Nothing dramatic on the criminal front has gone on in the night, take it from me. If there's a fatality, I'd know about it.'

'A quiet morning then.'

'Let's hope so.' Erin grinned at her. She clinked cups with Carla. 'You and I will get on great.'

'Can I ask you something?' Carla was beginning to feel invigorated, down as much to the conversation as the coffee.

'Go for it.'

'I've been given the office of a colleague who died.'

Erin whipped her cup back onto its saucer with a clank. 'Don't tell me they put you in Lauren's room?'

'You knew her?'

'Not well. Just to smile at in corridors. I undertook the autopsy after her death, which was a little unusual as I rarely know the cadavers I dissect.'

'Max Hazen said she drowned.'

'Yes, I'm afraid so.' Erin bit into her own pastry and kept her eyes on Carla. 'She killed herself.'

Carla winced.

'I'm sorry.' Erin reached over to touch her arm. 'I got the bare bones of your story from Albert. I thought I should tell you rather than you finding out in passing. Do you want to talk about your husband at all?'

Carla shrugged. 'Not really. It was three years ago, although some days it feels like it was only yesterday. Dan was ill for a long time before he took his own life and, in some ways, it was a blessed relief, although I have to be careful who I say that to.' Carla stopped. 'You say you got my story from Albert. How does he know?'

'I told you, people like Albert make sure they know what they need to. It wasn't prurient gossip if that's what you were worried about. I had a catch-up with the prof when I was matched with you as a mentor, and he mentioned it. I'd have thought they'd have been a bit more fucking sensitive than putting you in Lauren's room though.'

'Max told me it was an accident.'

Erin rolled her eyes. 'Perhaps he was trying to spare your feelings too. Who goes swimming at ten o'clock at night, especially in the river?'

'Did she leave a note?'

'No. Did your husband?'

Carla shook her head. 'No need.'

'There you go. As I said, who goes swimming at night? Still, the absence of a note means there was some reasonable doubt. But it was a clear case of drowning. Nothing to suggest foul play.'

'They've left all her stuff in my room. I feel like I'm inhabiting the office of a dead person.'

'Right.' Erin wiped her hands on her trousers. 'That's what I'm here for. You don't want a mentor; I saw it on your face when we met and I'm not really the nurturing sort. When it comes to practical stuff though, I'm your gal. Leave it with me.'

'You sure?'

Erin frowned as her phone rang in her pocket. 'Give me a moment, would you?' She took the call and listened in silence. Carla took the opportunity to glance around the cafe, trying to separate the academics from tourists. As in Oxford, it was pretty easy to do – an innocuous pastime, although she wondered what Patricia had meant about the dark side of life here. Nothing here in this cafe to suggest Jericho was anything but a well-heeled campus town.

Erin cut the call and swallowed her coffee in one gulp. 'I spoke too soon about it being a quiet night – there's been a death and I'm needed at the scene.'

Carla slid off the chair. 'Of course. Don't worry about me. I'll get back to my office and track down my access pass. I need it all sorted before I start teaching next week.'

'Finish your coffee first,' said Erin. 'I'll sprint back to the campus and pick up my car. Take your time.'

'Sounds urgent,' said Carla, settling back down. 'I hope it's nothing too terrible.'

7

Erin smelled the stink in the air before she opened her car door. The stench of scorched flesh crept through the air conditioning system and into the car. She fought the desire to retch and fumbled for the face mask she'd stashed in her back pocket. She was in Silent Brook, a piece of scrub near the town's railroad. It also had a darker history, but she wouldn't think of that now. You had to go through an underpass to reach the land where the homeless would light meagre fires even in the summer. It attracted the criminal and the dispossessed and this wouldn't be the first body who'd arrived fresh from Silent Brook, ready for her examinations. There was a huddle of uniformed personnel – paramedics, firefighters, a city ranger and, of course, police officers. Scott peeled away from the group and walked towards her.

'I got the call half an hour ago. It's clearly suspicious and they want you to take a look in situ before the autopsy. You'll soon see why.'

Erin nodded and walked towards the crime scene tape, her eyes all the time on the charred shape lying on the floor. On the way over, Erin had steeled herself for the scene of death. Burnt cadavers weren't the worst that she had to deal with; drowning victims with their seal-grey skin made her want to retch even after all these years. Casualties of fire more closely resembled the casts she'd seen on a visit to Pompeii on her honeymoon, charred shells of people who had once been living humans. Victims of fire in enclosed spaces were often found in a procubitus position, their faces to the floor as they'd attempted to crawl away from the fire. Here, in the open air, the victim, a woman possibly, judging by size, was sitting upright with her legs bent and arms crossed to her chest, elbows out, a classic pugilistic pose, although thermal heat had robbed the deceased of her hands and feet.

Erin eyes travelled down the cadaver, and she swallowed, wishing she hadn't eaten anything with her coffee. The abdominal cavity had ruptured, possibly a result of the fire, and exposed the organs of the victim. Even from here, she could see the shrunken and split uterus. Definitely a woman then, and Erin was suddenly reminded of a car crash victim whose unborn baby had still been visible within the pelvis. *Christ, get a grip*, she told herself.

Erin looked beyond the body to the scorched ground on which the victim sat, noting that the fire hadn't spread far through the tinder-dry grass. It suggested a fierce sudden blaze, possibly helped by an accelerant. She bent down to step through the tape when she felt an arm jerk her back. It was Perez, nearly her height but at least fifty pounds heavier. 'You can't go in there yet. There's stuff around the body we need you to look at.'

'There's always paraphernalia around the victim.'

Erin glanced at Scott, who shrugged. 'Not like this there isn't. Lean forward and look for yourself.'

Erin stepped in the direction of the body and took in the small yellow flags laid by the police next to the objects. There was a beer bottle filled with a yellowish liquid, probably urine, two syringe needles, a piece of pale blue glass and a leather boot at least a size thirteen, so unlikely to belong to the woman. Near the victim's feet was a brown mass of organic matter that looked like animal fur. The usual detritus. Erin glanced around the waste ground. It was a dumping place. Hidden from the road, an area where you'd come if you wanted to abandon a litter of puppies or discard an old sofa.

'I don't understand why they've been flagged.'

'Take a closer look at the ground.'

Erin squatted and took in the scorched grass which crept underneath each object. If the ground had been burning, the shoe and plastic syringes should have melted, and the glass objects would show signs of thermal shock. The intact items had been placed next to the body after the fire.

'What are your thoughts on this, Amy? I don't think I've ever seen anything like this before.'

Perez scratched her thigh. 'Working hypothesis is that either people came down and had a party around the burnt body or the killer put the objects there after the fire had burned out.'

'Damn.' That sounded like some weird shit and beyond Erin's remit. *Focus on the body*, she told herself. *That's why you're here.*

'I know. And here's the lieutenant now.'

Erin turned as Viv Kantz stepped out of the car. Only half an hour earlier she'd been sitting in a coffee shop with Carla, talking about the cop's domestic arrangements.

'Does she normally come down to scenes of crimes?' asked Erin.

'Nope.' Perez nodded at Baros, who was sharing a joke with a paramedic. 'Baros updated her by phone, and she wanted to take a look. Regular party this is turning out to be.'

Viv reached them, panting slightly. She was either seriously unfit or under the weather. Her olive skin was flushed from the exertion and Erin could see she was making an effort not to look flustered.

'Perez,' Viv acknowledged her colleague with a nod. 'Give me a few moments with the doctor.'

Perez rocked on her heels and left them.

'You've taken a look?' Viv asked Erin.

'I've seen what I need. I'll do the autopsy today back at the facility.'

'Two kids found the body. Brothers.' Viv wiped her face. 'Can you imagine that? They'd decided to skip school and they gravitated here.'

Erin made a face. 'This place has a nasty reputation. Do you have an ID?'

'No purse or wallet apparently. Not even signs of melted plastic as far as we can see. The killer probably took her bag away. Did Perez show you the items scattered around the body?'

'She did, although I'm not sure what they're supposed to signify. Perhaps the syringes were put there so we'd assume the victim was an addict.'

'It's a good guess but nothing more. This type of shit's beyond both our remit. Look,' Viv paused, lowering her voice, 'how about I call Albert and get one of his lot down here. The syringes are one thing, but there's a hank of hair near the woman's feet.'

'From the victim?'

'I'm not sure, but your colleague Scott reckons it is, so I'm thinking ritual, which is way out of my area of expertise.'

Erin glanced over at Scott. 'Ritual? Not my area either.'

'Well, the archaeologists love it, I've heard. No harm in asking for another opinion, is there? Get a member of Albert's team down here to give the scene a once-over before we move the body. What's your opinion?'

Erin thought of Carla. Clever, professional and at a loss what to do this week in the unfamiliar town. 'Albert's got a new colleague who's at a loose end until term starts in earnest next week. She's stuck in a mire of office and personnel issues. How about I give her a call so she can get her brain working on something other than admin? Her name's Carla James. I think she could do with occupying herself this week.'

'The Brit Albert told me about? Why not?' They turned to look at the body. 'Be a nice mystery for her to solve,' continued Viv. 'Welcome to Jericho.'

8

With Erin gone, Carla ordered another coffee and used her phone to search for used car showrooms. She'd meant to ask Erin for a recommendation, but her mentor had shot off as if the soles of her feet were on fire. Carla knew that look, had felt it herself. The scent of the hunt, although she didn't personally like the analogy as she was opposed to animal sports. But still, Erin had left with that glint in her eyes. Carla found a used dealer lot near her lodgings in Hoyt Lane and flicked through what they had to offer. She wanted something compact and not too expensive to fix if anything went wrong. They had a couple of small Japanese cars that seemed to fit the bill and she would drop by to see them on her way home that evening. Jericho, she had decided, was a place where you needed your own transport, a marked contrast to her life in Oxford where her trusty black bike had conveyed her around the city. Carla missed her bike, and she frowned trying to remember if it was in storage with her other things. It must be, although she couldn't for the life of her remember wheeling it into the container.

On the way back to her office, Carla managed to find the IT department to get her email account set up and was issued with a pass that would allow her to come and go around campus. The sensation of the lanyard around her neck made her feel less a newcomer, probably also helped by her chat with Erin. Interestingly, her mentor had given little away about herself. She was in her mid-forties, Carla guessed, with striking red hair which showed no signs of grey. Carla had checked out Erin's hands but spotted no ring to suggest she was married. That was as far as her detective skills took her.

Back in Lauren's office – it was impossible to think of it as anything else – Carla opened a cupboard, found an empty space and cleared the drawers of her predecessor's desk and then the biros, academic journals and various items scattered on top of the desk. When the movers came in, they'd just need to put everything into boxes to send on to the woman's family. One side of the cupboard she saw was filled with notebooks. Like Carla, Lauren had favoured spiral pads and there must be around forty in there. Lauren had numbered them and scribbled on the cover page the dates that each notebook covered. Carla grabbed one at random and flicked through the pages. It detailed a dig in Arizona and on the pages, parched white from the sun, Lauren had noted the results of each day along with suggestions for the next. Lauren had been a good sketcher; amongst the plans and site outlines was a drawing of a dog. Carla shut the book and placed it back among the others.

As she moved her laptop to plug it into the charger, Carla saw an envelope had been placed underneath the computer with her name on it. She lifted the flap and saw it was an invite to a cheese and wine soirée in Albert's room in three weeks' time. RSVP to his secretary Lizzie. Carla tapped the envelope on the desk, thinking. Whoever had placed it on her desk had a key to the room. Whatever the etiquette was here, she wasn't happy about people coming and going as they pleased. She wouldn't have left her laptop here for a start if she thought people could access it. She doubted that it had been Albert who had placed the handwritten invite. His manner had suggested he'd be busy all day. Perhaps it was Lizzie herself who'd entered while Carla was out.

Envelope in hand, Carla slung her bag over her shoulder and set off to find Lizzie's office. After a few minutes of fruitless knocking on doors and receiving no reply, Carla gave up and went to find the refectory, suddenly hungry. At least it was around lunchtime, which was good news for her jet lag. She'd woken up ravenous around three in the morning the previous night and had scoffed a packet of biscuits she'd bought at the airport in anticipation of this event.

The refectory, she soon realised, was called the cafeteria in Jericho and was a cheerful room with white walls and exposed brickwork. Few tables had been taken, another lull before the students arrived in earnest, and Carla ordered a bowl of bean soup, having long ago realised that liquid was a good thing when tired and dehydrated. She took the tray to an empty table and dipped her spoon into the broth, savouring its tomatoey richness. She was on her second spoonful when a voice in her ear made her jump.

'You'll get better fare at the party. Excellent Californian wine along with European cheeses, although that'll be less of a novelty for you.'

Carla turned round and regarded a man around her own age wearing a wool jacket over a black roll-neck jumper. His curly hair was cropped short at the sides but longer on top with a side parting, giving him an air of Dylan Thomas. He had his eyes on the white envelope she'd placed on the tray.

'You made me jump. I'm—'

'The new prof. I know.' He walked around to the other side of the table and pulled out a chair. *Be my guest*, she thought. 'I'm Jack Caron. I spotted you across the cafeteria and thought I'd come and say hello. This is only my second year, and I can remember my first week vividly. It felt like I'd landed on Mars.'

Carla put down her spoon, glad of someone to talk to. 'Not just me then wondering if I've made a big mistake.'

He frowned, pulling the wrapping off his own sandwich. 'Seriously? I'm sorry to hear that. I hope you've been given a mentor?'

'Erin Collins.'

'The medical examiner? Lucky you. I was given a physicist in his sixties who I saw once and who then refused to answer my calls. You've come from Oxford, I hear?'

'Yes. You?'

'I did my doctorate at Yale.'

'Your accent, though.' Carla frowned. There was an inflection in his voice she couldn't place.

'My father's family are originally from Montreal. Well spotted, by the way. I thought I'd lost the accent.' He sounded annoyed, his lips pinched as he looked around the room.

'You like it here?'

'I do.' Jack took a bite of his sandwich while switching off his buzzing phone with his free hand. Carla saw he was wearing an expensive-looking watch and his whole attire confused her. His look was half beatnik, half preppy. 'The atmosphere's a little rarefied for me, but where there's money there's opportunities for funding, which is what we're all chasing. Where were you over the summer?'

Clearing out a flat and wondering if I lost my marbles by upsetting my regular lifestyle, thought Carla. She shrugged. 'Making arrangements to come here. I intend to spend next summer in the field to compensate. I'm hoping to write another book.'

'*The Archaeology of Loss.*'

She glanced up at him. He'd done his homework. 'That's right. And you're the expert on seventeenth century New England, I believe.'

He paused and Carla got the definite feeling he didn't want to discuss his work. 'Sure. Oh, hello, Professor Kantz.'

Carla turned to see Albert walking towards them, his manner distracted.

'You seem to be making all the friends around here,' he said, his eyes also on Carla's envelope.

Jack saw his gaze. 'We were just talking about your cheese and wine party.'

'Good, good.' Albert hesitated. 'I won't sit.' He looked uncomfortable as he caught Jack's gaze. 'Do you think you could give us a few minutes alone?'

'Of course.' Jack got up. 'See you both at the party if not before.' He got up and Carla saw he was wearing expensive brown brogues against his casual trousers. She liked to think she could read sartorial signals, but she was at a loss. She turned her attention to Albert, who was frowning at Jack's departing back.

'Sorry for the interruption. I'm glad members of the faculty have been introducing themselves. It'll be much easier after you've met everyone at the party. I like to leave it a couple of weeks after the start of term so it isn't dominated by quibbles over timetables and the like.'

'I'll RSVP to Lizzie to say I'm coming. Was it her who dropped off the invite?'

'She probably delegated it to the faculty office. They have a key to all the rooms.'

'I see.' So, the office wasn't going to be her private space. The lock was simply there to keep out students and others hoping to invade her time. 'What can I help you with?' She wished he'd sit down.

As if reading her thoughts, he took the seat Jack had vacated. 'I'm slightly embarrassed that early in our acquaintance I have a favour to ask of you. I'm not sure how you'll feel about it.'

Oh God, thought Carla, *I bet he wants me to pick his daughter up from work*. 'Go ahead,' she said. At least she could say she didn't yet have a car.

'The thing is there's been a suspicious death on a patch of wasteland to the east of the town. I don't think it's made the news yet, but Viv, my wife, called me about it.'

It wasn't what Carla had been expecting. She swallowed, her throat parched. 'A death? A recent one?' She couldn't imagine what help she might be.

'A burning apparently – it's not a pretty sight. My wife was down at the scene with the investigating team and medical examiner.'

'Erin?' Carla frowned, retrieving a water bottle from her bag and taking a swig. 'We were having a coffee downtown when she got a call.'

'She'll have been called to the scene. I'm sorry you two didn't get to chat for longer.' Albert paused. 'What do you think of her?'

'She seemed super smart. Very capable.'

'She is. You've clearly impressed her. She specifically suggested that you might like to go and take a look. Viv is keen to get an outside opinion.'

'Of a recent burning? I'm not sure what I'll be able to add to the forensic professionals.' He must know this. Carla couldn't understand why he was even asking her to get involved.

Albert picked at his jacket. 'This is a close community. We all help each other out. My wife occasionally calls me when a crime scene has some unusual elements. Not just murders, I hasten to add. Those are thankfully rare. Sometimes the landscape is of archaeological or historical significance, and I send along someone who might be able to advise on this.'

Carla relaxed. 'OK, I can see that. So, what is it about this crime scene that you think I can help with?'

'The victim was found with a number of objects around her body. Viv said they don't amount to much, but she feels they may have been placed deliberately to leave a message.' He paused. 'It's not going to be pleasant. I could ask Max instead if you prefer.'

Not on your nelly, thought Carla as she reached for her bag. She was well used to male academic colleagues getting the plum assignments and, in any case, here was a chance to prove her resilience to Albert, who had already commented on her widowed status to colleagues. 'I don't have a car yet. Can you give me directions?'

'I'll take you there myself.'

On the drive over, Albert was silent, which suited Carla as she wanted to take in the Jericho landscape. It had been an odd day, and she was rather looking forward to the slog of regular academic teaching. First, the shock of Lauren's room and news of her untimely death, and now she would be assisting the police with an investigation that sounded as if it was beyond her area of expertise. She'd excavated remains with pieces of soft tissue still clinging to the bones, but that was the extent of her experience – although given Max was an expert on Roman life, she suspected he wouldn't have had much of an edge over her. She hoped to God there were no forensic archaeologists already on site to mock her knowledge.

To calm her nerves, she concentrated on the world streaming by. The street of white university buildings, shouting privilege and tradition, changed to respectable family homes until they too petered out and the neighbourhood featured scratchy single-storey houses with threadbare yards. A lone dog took itself for a walk down the street, reminding Carla of the one in Lauren's notebook.

'The wrong side of the tracks, literally,' said Albert, noticing her scrutiny of the neighbourhood. 'The old railroad is behind those trees.'

'There's no station now?'

'It went about fifty years ago. I can't say the loss is responsible for the area's decline. I don't think it was ever prosperous around here.'

'Every town has its hinterland. Have you been living here long?'

'Me?' Albert turned briefly to her. 'All my life. My great-grandfather was one of the college's first students and the Kantz family have been here ever since.'

His voice held a note of pride and Albert was clearly the epitome of privilege, attending the college of his forefathers and rising quickly to head of department.

However, he was married to a police officer, not, she suspected, the usual choice of partner for an establishment academic who also had a formidable reputation as an archaeologist. He reminded her of the absent-minded academics Carla met at Oxford who cultivated a forgetful air to hide their competency. Carla continued to scrutinise the landscape, making note of the street names that often held clues to locations past. Summer Street and West Avenue were generic enough, but there was a profusion of English towns woven into the names: Durham Road and Lincoln Close. Finally, she noticed a pattern – the abundance of the name Franklin, probably reference to a family who had once owned the land. They turned down Franklin Drive and she wondered what the family, if they were still present in the town, felt about their name attached to such a depressing neighbourhood.

'Do you have much crime here?' she asked.

Albert hesitated. 'Not usually, but the place is changing. We've a couple of unsolved murder cases that are giving Viv sleepless nights. Ten, fifteen years ago that would have been unimaginable.'

'Are the killings connected?'

Albert shrugged. 'Apparently not. Viv has invited profilers, psychologists, criminologists, you name it, to scrutinise the deaths. There's no pattern and they're pretty sure they're a series of unconnected killings. The body you're going to be seeing now doesn't fit the other crimes either. The sensible thing for you to do is to look at the site and feed back anything of interest. Don't worry about the body. That's not your concern.'

'I'm looking forward to meeting your wife.'

'I'm afraid you've missed her today. She's back at the office taking charge, which is what she's good at.' He pulled into a parking lot and nodded to the group in the far distance. 'I'll leave you here. Viv likes my department to give their opinion occasionally but prefers me to keep out of her business. Feel free to chat anything over afterwards.'

Carla took in the expanse of grass and the large green electricity generator to the left of the group. 'What is this place?'

'Silent Brook. It's got a long history. The Dutch were the first to settle here. Not all took to the new land and there were a few suicides from that outcrop of rocks in the distance. Over the centuries a few unfortunates have followed suit.' Albert glanced at her. 'Sorry.'

'It's fine.' Carla shook away the image of Dan's body, folded over his sheets, the pile of medication he'd stashed and taken tumbling from the bedside tray onto the floor, and focused instead on sites with similar histories. There was one in Germany she'd spent a summer excavating as a student. She hadn't liked the place and concluded that the desperate had been drawn to the location precisely because of its inhospitable air.

'Don't worry.' Albert grimaced. 'This one doesn't sound like a suicide.'

Erin was easy to spot as Carla neared the death site. Her red hair shimmered in the heat as she made notes on her tablet while talking to a woman in a grey trouser suit. When Erin spotted Carla, she raised a hand in a wave.

'Glad you could make it down here. I want to introduce you to Detective Amy Perez.'

Perez shuffled her feet, keeping her eyes away from the crime scene tape. 'Glad that you could make it down here,

Professor. The boss said you'd be coming.' The detective didn't look happy, her manner radiating hostility. 'I'll take you forward to the vic. You need to brace yourself.'

Carla once read a paper on the smell of death. There were those who thought that two thousand years failed to eradicate the aroma of death, its scent clinging to the earth for centuries. Carla had been inclined to agree. Graveyards, burial mounds, excavated tombs often had a vegetal, musty smell that couldn't be accounted for just by the surrounding climate. Here, however, the stink was something else and it made Carla want to retch. She looked to the two women for their reaction. Erin, wearing a medical mask, was difficult to read. Perez had pulled her face covering down under her chin and looked as if she couldn't care less.

Damn it, thought Carla. *This isn't my day job.* She yanked her sleeve down over her hand and put it to her face. 'Do you have a spare mask?'

Perez passed her a paper covering. Inadequate, but better than nothing. 'The reason the boss wants you down here is that she's interested in the items that have been left around the body post-mortem. She's thinking ritual or maybe a message to us in law enforcement. She wants to see if you have any idea what's going on.'

Carla groaned. Ritual was usually hard to prove in archaeology and often the default position when you couldn't think of another explanation. She caught Erin's eye and received a wink. 'Just let us know your initial impressions,' she said. 'All the items will be sent to forensics for testing, so we're looking for an arrangement we might not be able to decode ourselves.'

Carla sighed. 'I'll look, but, believe me, you can see a pattern where there is none if you're not careful.' She ignored the look Perez gave her, which suggested she'd known calling an expert in would be a waste of time.

Carla decided she'd treat this spot as if she'd been called to a dig where she had no background on the project. An expert on a very specific aspect of the site and nothing more. She glanced at the body long enough to take in its condition, the blackened skin, gaping pelvis and rictus grin of the skull with its fathomless sockets. Ignoring the bile that shot up her throat, she turned her attention to the items around the body. Erin joined her. 'You'll see the objects are undamaged, so we're pretty sure they were placed after the fire.'

Carla frowned as she took in the scraps littered around the body. Her initial impression confirmed that there was little she'd be able to add to the investigation. 'The placement of the objects gives the impression of scatter. There's no discernible pattern.'

'Do you want me to go through each item with you? Perhaps that will spark some ideas. Number one: a brown bottle with a screw-top lid. I thought beer, but that doesn't fit. Perhaps a soda of some kind. There's no label.'

'Do you know what's inside?' asked Carla.

Perez joined them, unwilling to be left out of the discussion. 'Could be urine. Once we've got the all-clear from the doc here, we'll take it in and analyse it.'

A bottle of urine? It wasn't out of place in this scrubby wasteland. Carla felt two expectant pairs of eyes on her. What the hell could she say about a bottle of piss?

'Next item,' said Erin, pointing it out with her pen, 'is a man's left walking boot. We're saying male because it's a size twelve to thirteen. No sign of its pair.'

Carla felt on surer ground. 'Shoes are very personal items. Even in prehistoric sites, there's no evidence people shared footwear. They're not just to protect the feet but signal status, wealth, occupation.'

'Why only one though?' asked Perez.

Carla thought rapidly, keen to impress this sceptical detective. 'Occasionally a single shoe is placed in a house as a good luck charm. It's a long held custom but harmless.'

Perez snorted. 'Didn't bring our victim much luck. What about the syringes?'

Carla shrugged, feeling helpless. 'I don't know. Are they empty?'

'Looks like it,' said Erin. 'Forensics will be able to say if there are traces of narcotics in them. Over there is a shard of blue glass. Can't think where it's from, but it's thick. A window maybe.'

'Could be cobalt,' said Carla. 'First found in 2000 BC Mesopotamia. It's decorative, but I don't know of any significance in it.'

'Then there are some coins. Two dimes and a nickel. Maybe fell out of the killer's pocket when they placed the other objects.' Erin continued without looking at Carla. Perhaps she could sense her desperation. 'Final item is that clump over there. It's a hank of hair placed near the feet. My assistant Scott thinks it's from our victim. Although most of the hair on her head is burnt, what's left suggests a recent hacking.'

'Laying items at a dead person's feet can be an act of reverence. I haven't heard of anyone cutting off someone's hair after death, though. If anything, women are usually buried with their combs or hair jewellery. Cutting a woman's hair after they're dead is surely more an act of hate.' Carla felt a third person join them, the smell of expensive aftershave mingling with the burnt flesh stench.

'So, is it a ritual or not?' Carla swung around and saw a man sporting a crew cut, his grey-brown eyes taking in her long skirt and jumper.

'This is my partner, Detective Baros,' said Amy.

The man made no move to reveal his first name nor shake hands with Carla. She swallowed, her jet lag returning with a vengeance, or perhaps it was this cop's nauseating cologne. 'If it wasn't for the fact that the items have clearly been left after your victim's death, I'd consider them random detritus.' Carla reached into her bag and pulled out her notebook. 'I'm going to sketch the location of the items in relation to the body. It will give me something to research when I'm back at my desk.'

The man behind her gave a long sigh and left them. Perez peeled away and followed her partner without giving Carla a backwards glance. The attitude of the pair infuriated her.

'I can't just come up with something off the top of my head,' she said to Erin. 'It looks more like a crime scene than an archaeology site.' Her fury made her pen wobble in her hand. 'Are they always this friendly?'

Erin shrugged. 'I'm the medical examiner. They have to work with me. But yes, Baros's attitude is what you expect from him. Perez just follows suit.'

'Why?'

'Why what?'

'Why does she follow suit?' Carla squatted and drew an outline of the blue fragment of glass.

'Don't know. She's nobody's fool. Do you honestly have no suggestions?'

'None at all. It's as if someone has thrown random items around the body.'

Erin shrugged. 'It was worth a try. The detectives are pissed because their lieutenant wanted a second opinion and I suggested you. It's not your fault you can't make any sense of it. They're doing no better.'

Carla snapped her notebook shut and pushed it back into her bag, trying to shake off that lingering feeling of failure.

'Can I give you a ride back?' Erin asked. 'I'm done here. The autopsy will take place tomorrow.'

Carla, desperate to get the smell of burning fat from her nostrils, nodded. 'Please.'

9

He'd never had himself down as a rubbernecker. The others he'd slain and left, glad to get away despite the compulsion to stay and adorn the settings in the chosen pattern. He'd enjoyed the act of getting away without detection and picking up the threads of his ordinary, if privileged, life. Yet, here he was, watching law enforcement go about its business. He had a vantage point few knew about. He'd discovered it on a reconnaissance visit and it was here he'd returned to when he could keep away no longer. He could still smell the soap he'd used to scrub himself clean. He'd needed the shower as the killing had proved distressingly gory. Perhaps not as much as number three, but he could not stand the smell of burnt flesh clinging to his body. Even this far, when the wind took an ill turn, he caught whiffs from the body in the distance.

He'd disposed of his clothes from the previous night by burying them in the copse behind his house. It was a dank, unimaginative place. As houses had gone up in the neighbourhood, the arc of new roads had circled the clump of trees, developers too wary of the deep roots and watery pit to concrete over the patch. He would have liked to have kept the clothes. For the others he had simply washed what he was wearing at the highest setting, hoping the boiling eradicated any forensic evidence. But no amount of washing would rid them of that smell.

He wondered why he'd been so set on the burning. Any form of killing would have done. The pattern, as he'd suspected, had not been noticed and the flames had only served to bring himself into danger. He was, however, enjoying the puzzlement of law enforcement as they measured, photographed and pondered the site. He was also nearing the end and now was the time to show his cards a little more. There would be no satisfaction without a little reveal towards the conclusion.

He recognised the detectives, Baros and Perez. The pair were well known in Jericho even if they weren't particularly competent. The woman with the flame-red hair was also familiar, but he couldn't, from this distance, place her. He focused on a slight figure, probably a woman, making notes on a clipboard or notebook. She wasn't wearing the white overalls of the CSI team; probably a consulting expert hoping to make her mark by helping solve the case. He was so nearly there now it made no difference. He had nothing to concern himself with, but still he watched.

Sometimes, the women's ghosts came to visit him at night. He'd awoken the previous week with the familiar shape of number one, her face featureless as it had been that fateful night. He'd turned on the light and there had been no one there. His imagination was proving trickier to control than the women concerned.

10

Erin drove her usual route back to the campus, making a wide arc of the town, which took them over a bridge at a bend in the river. She saw Carla looking down into the brackish water. The current was sluggish but with the hint of a stronger undertow. A student had drowned leaping off the bridge during end of year celebrations and the college now stationed security guards during graduation days.

'Did Lauren jump from here?'

The question, so close to her own train of thought, startled Erin, and the car wobbled as she lost concentration. 'Jeez, you just come out with it, don't you? I thought I was blunt, but you take it to a new level.'

'Sorry. I was voicing my thoughts out loud. The only thing I know about the river is Lauren's suicide. I mean, I don't even know its name.'

'Didn't do much reading about Jericho before getting here, huh?'

Carla caught Erin's jokey tone. 'Guilty as charged. Actually, I looked up the university but, as for the town, I just thought I'd discover it when I arrived.'

'The river's called the Alford. No idea where it got its name.'

'There's a town in Lincolnshire with the same name.'

'That figures. Early settlers used names from the home countries. Made life a little easier, I suppose. Anyway, in answer to your other question, no, Lauren didn't jump from the bridge. It's a little exposed if you're intent on taking your own life. Too many passers-by ready to talk you out of it, even at ten p.m. Not every suicide wants to be saved. Lauren went in further downstream. There's a park next to a church around the next bend. Name of Suncook; it's an indigenous name. It's there she slipped in – she left her shoes on the bank, so we're pretty sure about the location.'

'Why there though?'

Erin took her eyes off the road and glanced at Carla. 'Why not?'

—

The body of the fire victim arrived at the facility at the same time as Erin. She immediately arranged for the woman to be sent for a CT scan. Its advanced state of decomposition meant she might miss the presence of foreign bodies such as a bullet and any fractures in the victim's bones. After Baros's scorn at her handling of the murder case of Jessica Sherwood, she was determined to triple-check everything. Fortunately, she had recent experience of autopsying fire victims and would use all her knowledge on this Jane Doe.

Giving the woman a name would be a first step. As a pathologist she wasn't just there to ascertain the cause of death. She was also a key link in the chain to identifying the victim. If the woman had sported a tattoo, it would now be unrecognisable on the charred flesh. Instead, she'd be relying on dental work and the identification of any burnt pieces of jewellery – a watch that might be recognisable to a member of the victim's family. Erin, however, wasn't hopeful. Silent Brook was a place the dispossessed gravitated towards. She wasn't banking on a local dentist having records for this victim.

'Did you manage to get any bloods?' she asked Jenny, who was wheeling out the body towards the imaging unit. The girl's black hair was pulled back into a severe ponytail.

'Are you kidding me?' she shouted over her shoulder.

Erin sighed. Goddamn it. That limited the possibilities for DNA analysis. She would need to rely on hard tissue such as bones and teeth to extract any genetic material and it would be hit and miss if any of it was successful. The woman's name, she thought to herself, was unlikely to come via the post-mortem. The detectives would have to, well, detect.

Erin sat down at her computer and put the name Silent Brook into the database. Over the last five years, eleven bodies had been found in that scrubland and brought in for autopsy. Six had been overdoses. Heroin, heroin in combination with synthetic opioids, methadone, methamphetamines. Three of the deaths had been from alcohol poisoning and two from hypothermia. Only a male in his twenties had been murdered; knifed in the stomach by a drunk who had soon been apprehended. Erin frowned. Not one of the earlier victims had been female and yet the place had a reputation for being a dangerous place for women. The main highway out of town ran past the land and the town's sex workers used an underpass to pick up trade. The place's reputation must be down to other felonies – rapes, assaults, non-fatal narcotic overdoses – rather than actual deaths. The dead woman, currently being scanned over on the other side of the facility, was the first female homicide at Silent Brook in the last five years.

Jenny came back into the room, peeling off her latex gloves. 'All done. I've put her back in the store. Results around ten a.m. tomorrow.'

'OK. Let's schedule the autopsy for midday. I'd really like to see those images first.'

If the CT scan failed to show anything, she'd be concentrating on the woman's lungs. Looking for soot inside the woman's bronchial tubes to suggest death from smoke inhalation. A quick conclusion as to cause of death would partially redeem her in Baros's eyes, although, from the look of the pair today, neither was thrilled at being given this death to investigate.

Erin looked at her watch. Time to call it a day. She felt as exhausted as Carla had looked and tomorrow was going to be busy, busy, busy. Carla was an intriguing one. Behind that tiny stature and defensive pose, there must be a formidable brain. People like Albert Kantz didn't bring people in from the outside – and Carla was definitely an outsider – unless they would add prestige to their department. Still, there was a vulnerability to Carla that brought out Erin's protective instinct. While she remembered, she fired off an email to Kantz's secretary, asking her politely to ensure Carla had a clear office by the end of the week. As she pressed send, she heard a clank coming from the corridor, the sound of a door shutting and something else. Footsteps? Erin rose and pulled open the door.

'Jenny, is that you?'

There was silence, only the sound of the clock above her desk ticking, reminding her that she had a life elsewhere. She'd go home and take a long shower and put on a movie. Ethan was at his dad's, so she'd have the place to herself. Who knows, she might even find a soap drama where she wasn't inclined to shout at the TV over their portrayal of medical examiners.

11

Back in her office, Carla logged into her Jericho email and a message popped up from building facilities informing her that its staff were busy. It would be a few days before the office was completely cleared of Lauren's effects. They were very sorry, but Carla would be sitting amongst her former colleague's things for a little longer. Carla leant back in her chair and closed her eyes, listening to her stomach rumble. She hadn't managed any food since the three mouthfuls of soup at lunchtime. She should force down a sandwich to keep up her energy levels while she looked over her notes. She was all prepped for her classes next week, so the body discovered at Silent Brook was her only distraction.

Her phone pinged with a WhatsApp message. Until she got a US sim card, she'd have to rely on the university's Wi-Fi to communicate with her family back home. As she expected, the message was from her mother, currently on a yoga retreat in France. Sylvia, at the age of seventy-three, was currently undergoing a late-life crisis as Carla and her brother had termed it. Always selfish, she'd left Carla's father for a man twenty years her junior whose job involved 'something in TV'.

'Perhaps he repairs them,' had been her brother Pete's only comment on the matter. He had refused to speak to his mother since, leaving Carla as the sole recipient of Sylvia's calls when she was feeling lonely.

'Call me when you can,' said the message. No concern about how Carla was feeling after the long flight. Carla rolled her eyes and turned over her phone. She needed to start setting some boundaries and her mother would have to learn US working hours when Carla would be incommunicado. She was feeling out of sorts, and it wasn't just her mother's message. The scorn of the detectives had got to her. Viv Kantz had asked for her opinion, and she felt she should have something concrete to feed back to the team. Carla pulled out her notebook from her bag and studied again the objects left around the dead woman. Weirdly the diagram didn't help at all. Carla was used to making rough sketches on site, but the amateurish strokes on her notepad failed to convey the horror of the scene. She hoped that oblivion had been quick for the victim. Women had been burned alive throughout history, although not, as many thought, in the witch trials that had affected New England. There the women had been hanged for their sins, although in Scotland and mainland Europe, women had been committed to the flames. There was also the Hindu custom of Sati, also known as widow burning, where wives were placed on the funeral pyres of their dead husbands. This was the most extreme example, but there were modern day cases, such as the still unsolved discovery of the murdered Isdal woman in Norway, burnt like this victim in an out of the way place with a lonely history.

Carla considered the objects, wondering if she could find a pattern, any pattern, in the choice of items placed around the body. In her professional experience, people were occasionally buried with drinking vessels. Frank

Sinatra, she thought, had been interred with a bottle of Jack Daniels. Not very helpful in relation to this victim as she couldn't even be sure that the bottle contained alcohol. The glass shard was a mystery, although cobalt blue glass, known as smalt when it was powdered, did have a link back to Ancient Egypt. An archaeological link, then, but nothing else brought to mind the ancient African civilisation. The syringes had looked depressingly modern and were perhaps an admonishment for a lifestyle badly lived. Carla moved on to the coins. Two dimes and a nickel, Erin had said. There had long been a tradition of putting coins on the eyes or in the mouth of the dead. Charon's obol, designed to bribe the ferryman taking the dead to the underworld. Surely, though, it would have been no hardship to place a coin in the mouth or on the eyes of the corpse. The killer must have stayed around long enough for the fire to retreat sufficiently for them to arrange the objects around the body.

With a sigh, Carla put down her pen. The detectives had been right to be sceptical. She could see no pattern. Perhaps once the victim's identity was known, the reason for the objects would become apparent. Time to call it a day and head off to see the car showroom, which was open until six. She locked up her office and headed towards the entrance. The twenty-minute walk to Hoyt Lane would clear her head and give herself something else to focus on. She only hoped that car salesmen weren't as sexist as they were back in England. The last time she'd bought a car, the rep had directed all his spiel towards Dan even though her husband had never been behind the wheel of an automobile. If she had no luck with this salesroom, she'd collar Jack, the friendliest of her colleagues she'd met today, and ask if he fancied accompanying her on a car-buying trip.

Outside the building, she ran into Max. He was searching in his leather briefcase and would have missed her if she hadn't called out to him.

'How's your first day been?' he asked.

'Not what I expected to be honest. I'd forgotten how much admin is associated with a new post, but,' Carla paused, remembering how upset he'd been at the discovery of Lauren's effects in the office, 'I think facilities are now aware of the state of my office.'

'State is the right word,' grumbled Max, pulling out his car keys. 'I hope tomorrow is more fruitful for you. When is your first class?'

'Friday. Actually, this afternoon was more dramatic as I was called to a crime scene down by the railway. It's certainly not my usual routine.'

'Crime scene?' Max frowned. 'Did Viv Kantz call it in?'

'I believe so. Albert drove me down there and gave me a brief history of Jericho en route.'

Max looked a little put out, closing his bag with a snap. 'I'm often the first port of call when they want an expert opinion. What happened?'

'A fatality. There were some objects around the body they wanted me to look at.'

'Anything worth noting?'

'Syringes, a urine bottle—'

'Oh.' He lost interest. 'That kind of death. We do occasionally get called to help. Sorry it happened on your first day. Do you fancy a drink? There's a bar downtown well away from campus. Before you think I'm hitting on you, I'm just being sociable.'

Carla wondered why he'd made the point of insisting it wasn't a date. Perhaps he was married and keen to display his 'taken' status. She doubted this was the case – married men, if they wanted to make sure she knew they were off-limits, usually made it perfectly clear there was a wife in tow. No, she suspected Max was single but uninterested in her as a prospective date, which was fine by her. Or maybe she'd got that wrong and was out of her depth in this complex social scene. Perhaps Erin would be able to explain the signals she was supposed to decode. 'Why not?'

The bar wasn't what she'd been expecting. Max presented an urbane if forbidding approach to the world. Morrell's was noisy and filled with office workers enjoying downtime after their day jobs. Carla supposed the attraction was the lack of college students, but the music thumping in the background set her teeth on edge. It was waiter service and at least they were efficient. A young woman dressed in tight black jeans and a checked shirt took their orders.

'Whiskey and rye for me.' Max looked across at Carla. 'What's your poison?'

'White wine.' Carla, dog-tired, was determined to make an effort. Max took off his jacket and she saw his white shirt was pristine after a day in the department.

'I hope you don't think my comment was sour grapes earlier.' Max made a face. 'We're not called into police cases very often and Albert does spread it around the department. I don't like you to think I was pissed at you going.'

Like hell, thought Carla. 'My mentor is the medical examiner, Erin Collins. I think she asked for me.'

Their drinks arrived and she took a glug of the cold wine. The noise from the other patrons was only just bearable and she wondered again why Max had chosen this place. Although he listened to her reply, she had the impression his concentration was elsewhere, and she saw him taking in the outfit of one of the servers whose jeans fitted tightly to her long legs.

'Do you come to this place a lot?'

It got his attention. 'You don't like it?'

'It's pretty noisy.'

'Hi, Max. Is everything OK?'

Carla turned and took in another of the servers, a suntanned girl with cropped hair. The severe cut chopped into her fair-haired, pretty looks, giving her a more interesting air.

'Fine, Zoe. This is a new colleague, Professor Carla James.'

'Another prof. This town must have more per square capita than any other.'

'Don't tell that to the Harvardians. Carla, can I introduce Zoe Kantz, Albert's daughter.'

Carla took a closer look at the girl and saw she'd inherited her father's laughter lines but little else. 'Good to meet you. Your dad mentioned dropping you off here earlier.'

Zoe made a face. 'He doesn't like me doing evening shifts. This place can get a bit rowdy after ten, so I've been allowed to take a job here as long as it's daytime only.'

'You're not at college?'

'Just graduated. Deciding what to do with the rest of my life. Mom's hassling me to choose sooner rather than later.'

'You don't fancy following her profession?' asked Carla.

Zoe made a face. 'Not likely. I don't have the stomach for it. I heard something was going on the other side of town today.'

Carla glanced at Max. 'At Silent Brook?'

'That's the one. God. Mom will be in a foul mood when she gets back. There's always something going on down there.' The girl had the exuberance of the young. She must be at least twenty-one to be working in a bar and graduated, but Carla felt old enough to be her mother.

'She'll be working late, I suppose?' Carla asked.

'I guess.' The girl's gaze drifted away from them. 'Mind you, two of her colleagues are over there. Do you know Charlie and Amy?'

The question was meant for Max, who shook his head. Carla's heart sank as she contemplated the back of Baros's head. 'I met them both today. I don't think they were thrilled to see me at the crime scene.'

Zoe hurried to a call from another table and, as if conscious of her appraisal, Baros slowly swivelled in his chair and caught Carla's eye. Frowning, he turned back to his companion and muttered something to her. Perez leant to one side to catch a glimpse of Carla, her expression neutral.

'Excuse me.' Carla slid off her chair and made her way over to the detectives, never one to let a slight pass her by. She saw in satisfaction a flare of alarm in Perez's eyes as Carla appeared at the table.

'Hi. I hadn't expected to meet you again so soon,' she said to them both.

Baros lifted a glass of beer to his mouth. 'Small town,' he said. 'Hard to stop bumping into your acquaintances. Even when you're trying to get some downtime.'

She ignored his rudeness. 'I guess the body's been removed from the crime scene. Was anything else discovered around the victim? Something I might have missed?'

'Nope.' Baros's words were swallowed into his glass.

Perez shot him a look but kept quiet. The attitude of the pair of them infuriated Carla. 'I thought you'd be working hard on the case this evening. Good you can spare time for a beer.'

Baros slammed the glass down and looked at her. 'What's that supposed to mean? What's there to investigate? Another dead hooker.'

'Another?' asked Carla. She felt Max join her, his tall presence just behind her as one male scented another.

Perez picked up her beer. 'It's not the first death at Silent Brook we've attended. Not that it's any of your business. We've strict shift patterns and we're off duty.'

Carla wanted to defend herself. Explain she was still jet-lagged and sensitive to their disdain of her. Instead, she smiled. 'I'll leave you to it.'

She heard Baros mutter something under his breath.

'What did you say?' asked Max, tensing. *Oh God*, Carla thought. *I don't need anyone fighting on my behalf.*

'Let's go.' She pulled at Max's sleeve, but he shrugged her off like an outraged suitor in a western.

'Would you like to repeat what you just said to Carla's face.'

'Thought she'd like to keep her own house in order before she started criticising us.'

Carla frowned, trying to decipher his words. He must be talking about Dan, which made it an odd comment given his death was now three years old. Viv Kantz would know her story and must have passed it on to the detectives when they'd returned to the station as there had been no comment on her status when she'd met them at the crime scene. That he would use Dan's death against her sent her into a fury, although she was also outraged at Albert's indiscretion. First Erin and now Viv. Was she to be discussed like a troublesome patient rather than a professional colleague? Time to nip this in the bud. She leant forward so her lips were close to his ear.

'It's the dead who have the most to tell us. Don't forget that, Detective Baros.'

He turned back to her, his face a visage of indifference. 'Sure.'

12

Carla's first class the following week was teaching a small group of second year students about post-execution death rites. It had been a popular subject in her last job and take-up for this semester had been good at Jericho. However, it soon became clear she was at a disadvantage because her class followed a lecture with Jack Caron. Jack's course on New England houses was bound to be popular – students from Jericho, after all, were largely pulled from the east coast states. Carla had never had a problem with well-liked colleagues, and she wondered why she felt the pinch of discontent at Jack's popularity given he'd obviously felt as ill at ease as she when he first arrived. Her students were mainly female, which might explain some of Jack's star attraction. As she pulled out her notes, she shamelessly listened to two girls discussing him.

'I bet Byron looked a little like him. It's the dark hair against pale skin. Shame he's teaching houses rather than poetry.' A girl with a fizzy fringe gave the other a knowing look.

'Oh, I don't know. We get the option of a field trip at the end of the semester. Think seventeenth century New England.'

'He brings his wife along, I've heard, or if not, she makes a guest appearance.'

'Shame.'

So, Jack Caron was married. He hadn't mentioned his spouse during their conversation. He'd suggested he'd been lonely during his first year at the college and now she was discovering that he had a wife.

'Right,' Carla cleared her throat. 'Welcome to the class. Tell me, what do you think happens to a body after execution?'

Over the course of the following hour, Carla's spirits rose. The students were bright and motivated even if their buzz was a carryover from Jack's lecture. Towards the end of the hour, she saw a group of four students lingering, waiting to speak to her.

'Anything else?' She was dog-tired again and wanted to grab a coffee before her next class.

'We heard you went out to see the woman found at Silent Brook.'

'I did. Who told you?'

'Doctor Caron mentioned it in class. He was talking about locations that have a bad reputation. Did you know suicides used to gravitate there?'

Here was a group of students who, thank God, didn't know about her background. It was a relief to finally speak to people not walking on eggshells whenever suicide came up. 'It was mentioned to me. Why do you ask?'

'Do you believe that places are inherently bad? I mean, you talk about gibbets and their locations. Crossroads, summits of hard-to-reach hills. They must have been chosen for a reason. Do you think an area's poor reputation is inherent or developed over time?'

It was an interesting question. Carla's scientific brain rebelled against any mystical belief in the inherent nature of a place's atmosphere, but she'd worked alongside colleagues who absolutely believed that stones held onto their history. 'I believe reputation develops over time, possibly a result of its location and geographic profile. The reputation, once developed, can stay in people's memories. Why so curious?'

The student with the frizzy fringe shrugged. 'Just interested. I mean, Shining Cliff Wood also has a mean reputation. Jericho's lovely, isn't it, and forest landscapes aren't inherently bad? So how come poor reputations attach to certain places?'

'Have you been to the wood? Can you feel anything?'

'Nothing beyond the fact I'm walking down a path surrounded by densely planted trees which are a little overwhelming.'

'There's part of your answer then, isn't it? The vegetation of the area has contributed to its reputation.'

Carla saw she hadn't convinced the girl, and the group were still discussing inherited memory as they wandered away. She left the building and crossed the courtyard towards her office. To the right, a gaggle of boisterous students exited the door of a building with 'James Franklin Wing' emblazoned above the door. It looked newly built — so the family were still big in town, she assumed. She must ask Erin to tell her more about James Franklin.

Back in her office, Carla saw she had an hour before her next class on the archaeology of human sacrifice. Once she'd checked her notes were good to go, she drummed her fingers on her desk, wondering how to occupy her time. She sniffed the air, trying to identify who had been in her office again. Lizzie, Albert's secretary, had left no trace of perfume when she left the invitation on Carla's desk, yet here was a light musky smell, difficult to identify whether the wearer was male or female. Carla had decided to cart her laptop and shoulder bag to each lecture, which meant at least her belongings were secure but, once again, she was uneasy at the thought of someone in her office.

She was unlikely to find any answers today and, to distract herself, she picked up the phone and dialled the local police station, asking for Detective Baros. Carla was a little miffed that, having been brought into the investigation, her lack of ideas meant that she was no longer of any use to the team. A woman had died, and she cared enough to want to know if they'd managed to identify the victim. The local press was subdued about the matter, which was strange given that Jericho was considered to be a relatively safe place to live. She wondered if the story had been deliberately supressed now that term had started, but she was loath to subscribe to conspiracy theories. Baros's desk phone rang unanswered and went to voicemail. She left a message asking for an update on the woman found at Silent Brook and tried Erin's phone. At least she had her mentor's mobile, but that was switched off.

With a sigh, she glanced around at Lauren's things still languishing in her space. The office was due to be cleared later in the week, although she'd got used to the messiness of the room. She felt a connection to the dead woman who'd got so low she'd entered the river to allow the waters to take her to her end. She wondered if Lauren had left a bottle of her perfume on a shelf or perhaps a scarf where the scent lingered on. Picking up her bag, she wandered down the corridor, looking for someone to talk to. She'd been given no guide to the building and had been forced to orienteer herself. Her knowledge of the campus now consisted of the toilets, coffee shop and her seminar rooms.

The door to Jack's office, further down the corridor, was closed, but when Carla glanced through the window, she saw he was sitting at his desk, talking on the phone. Even through the closed door, she could hear an argument taking place, although the words were indistinct. He was expansive as he made his point, gesticulating at the person on the other end of the line.

Carla slunk away before Jack could catch her gawping at him, her already low mood inflamed by what had sounded like a marital tiff. Towards the end of his life, she and Dan had argued bitterly, Carla shocked by the extent to which her husband resented her zest for life while he was withering away. Now that it was all over, she worried about the lost time spent on these disputes. Carla had been a widow-in-waiting for a long time. Perhaps she would have a chat with Erin, who presented as both sympathetic and worldly. Was it time, even after the trauma of the last few years, to dip her toe into the dating scene?

13

Erin dropped by Carla's late on Wednesday afternoon after a morning of lectures. She'd had a difficult post-seminar meeting with a student who'd used an essay writing service the previous semester and was in danger of being thrown off his course. He gave her a sob story about the stresses of academic life, which was all well and good, but how would he cope once he entered the medical profession? In the end Erin had promised to write a letter to the academic standards lead, but she personally thought her student was on his way out. Fancying a bit of light relief before going on to the facility, she texted her son Ethan that she'd be late home from work and headed to Carla's to see how she was settling in, conscious that her mentee had left a plaintive message for her on her mobile, asking for an update on the woman found at Silent Brook.

On the road outside her address, Carla was tinkering under the bonnet of an automobile. She lifted her head to grab a rag as Erin approached and gave her a wave.

'Got myself a car, as you can see.'

'Neat.' It was a small Yaris. Ethan wouldn't have been able to get his long legs into the passenger seat, but she could see it suited Carla. 'Nothing wrong with it, I hope.'

'Just checking the oil. They said it was topped up, but I wanted to make sure myself.' Carla slammed down the lid. 'Everything OK?'

'Just checking up on you. I sent an email about your office. Have they got back to you with a date when they'll clear it out?'

'It's happening Friday, but what I really want is an update on the woman we saw together last week,' Carla said. 'Let's go inside.'

Erin followed Carla up the wooden steps and into a room to the right. 'This is nice.' The kitchen smelled of fresh apples and flour, although Erin couldn't picture Carla baking a pie. She watched as Carla filled a kettle and put it on the stove.

'Coffee all right?'

'Sure.'

'You know, I've kind of got used to having Lauren's things around me. I'm not sure what the office will feel like when her stuff is gone. The only thing I've done is put the photos of her on the bookshelves face downwards. I had a horrible feeling it was going to take weeks for the office to be cleared and it felt strange having a woman I never met staring at me.'

'Makes sense. I'm sorry about the delay. Everything moves at a glacial pace in Jericho,' said Erin.

'Surely not in your work?'

'Don't you believe it. I know medical examiners in the big cities who autopsy four corpses a day. It's two max for me and that's rare.'

'So, what about the burned woman?'

'I'm not sure how much I'm supposed to tell you given you're not officially part of the investigative team.'

The kettle whistled and Carla filled a jug with hot water. 'You don't seem the type to worry too much about the rules.'

Don't I? thought Erin. Well, Carla had her wrong there. She had a good job, a teaching position and a son to bring up. She was also watching her back after failing to spot the syringe mark in Jessica Sherwood's dead body, so if Carla thought she was going to break the Hippocratic Oath based on a shared liking for each other, she was in for a shock. What she could tell Carla was the cause of death which would be on the official death certificate, a public document.

'She died from a combination of incapacitation by barbiturates and poisoning by carbon monoxide.'

'She was poisoned then set alight,' said Carla, making a face.

'Exactly. I found soot in her lungs, indicating she was alive while she burned. Her bloods and stomach suggest she'd consumed around twenty sleeping pills along with alcohol. If there had been no fire, I'd have said suicide, no problem. But even if she set herself alight, she didn't then put those objects around the body. So, it's a suspicious death.'

'What do the detectives say?'

'They've put the victim down as an itinerant from out of town, maybe a sex worker who's upset a client. No local women have been reported missing.'

Carla frowned. 'Sex worker who upset a client? That's a little harsh, isn't it? How about a victim of a sexual predator who preys on prostitutes?'

Erin folded her arms. 'That's what I said. Okay, okay I get your point. I wasn't implying any fault on the sex worker's part.'

'Sorry, but language matters. Prejudice against prostitutes is endemic, isn't it? You say no one's disappeared and they focus on the sex workers. Is that sensible? Surely the women themselves would be able to tell you if one of their colleagues is missing.'

Erin shrugged. 'It's a place to start at least.'

Carla glanced at her, unimpressed. 'All right, if you say so. What about suspects?'

'Silent Brook is close to the main highway, so we get a lot of drivers passing through. The only potential eyewitness we have is of a girl climbing up into a truck around midnight. It might fit. The trucker picks up a girl, has sex with her in his cab, something goes wrong, he panics and sets the girl alight.'

'Where do the pills come in?'

'Before sex, after sex. Who knows? The detectives don't care. The working hypothesis is that neither victim nor killer is local, which slows everything down.'

'Jesus. Don't they even want to identify the victim?'

'I've taken impressions of the jaw and teeth, so we may be able to make a match if we have a possible victim. I've also taken samples from her bones, so fingers crossed they can extract DNA from that.'

'But no likely victim means there's no one to compare DNA to.'

'Exactly.'

'I just don't believe it. I saw detectives Baros and Perez in a bar the afternoon after we found the body. They showed no interest in the death at all.'

Erin took in Carla's anguished expression. 'Look. Forget all those cop shows you see on TV. Murder cases take time. Years even and not every one gets solved. Detective Baros is a dick. Agreed?'

'Agreed.'

'But Viv Kantz isn't. She runs that place like clockwork, I promise. The burnt woman is in the system and is being investigated. It'll be done properly, but don't hold your breath for any instant results.'

'Fine.' Carla dumped the coffee in front of her.

'Did you get anywhere with those things scattered around the body?'

'I can't see any pattern whatsoever. I suppose there's always the possibility another person distributed those items after the woman died. Someone other than the killer.'

'There are plenty of wackos around Silent Brook, that's for sure.'

Carla sat down opposite Erin at the pine table and took a sip of her coffee. 'I might try to speak to Viv Kantz direct. Just explain that I couldn't find anything. It'll at least give me some closure to that day.'

'Why not? I wouldn't bother the detectives if you have nothing to report. They're savage when it comes to any perceived incompetencies. Take a woman, Jessica Sherwood, who died in her own home. It was the cops who had decided it was a burglary gone wrong, but it's me who gets the flack when blood work, which we always have to wait for, suggested that the killing was planned.'

Carla looked up. 'Was it a recent death?'

'It took place in late summer, and I have to say it got to me. Jessica was a woman in her sixties who reminded me of a relative. All right, I can see it looked like a break-in gone wrong, but it seems she was finished off with some potassium chloride, which doesn't fit the modus operandi of your average burglar.'

'Police are more interested in her case?'

'A long-time resident of Jericho asleep in a house one evening who ends up killed? You bet they're more interested in her. Passing killers preying on the sex workers is one thing; a perpetrator breaking and entering to murder elderly residents is something else.'

'Was it a lone attack?'

'Appears to be, which is how we want to keep it. It was a place near here actually, Penn Street. No need for you to worry, of course, but best to be aware. Your landlady will know all about it, for sure. She's not mentioned anything?'

'She's said nothing to me at all, but this situation is only temporary. I need to start looking for a place to live as soon as I can.'

'I'll keep my eyes peeled. Not always easy to find somewhere in Jericho. I'll let you know if I hear of anywhere.'

Back in the medical facility, Erin could still feel Carla's disappointment in her, the detectives, the town. Carla was an idealist. The wonder at discoveries in her work – the emphasis on how people felt – blinded her to the inconsistencies of human nature. Detectives Baros and Perez were doing what people the world over had always done. They were prioritising their limited resources and concentrating on what would most likely cause shock waves through the society within which they operated. This meant focusing on Jessica Sherwood's murder and not the woman lying still stinking in the mortuary.

Erin took a sip from a sports energy drink bought to revive her flagging energies. That and the coffee Carla had made her should keep her buzzing for the next hour while she ploughed through some admin. She called her son, Ethan, and told him to order a pizza and leave a couple of slices for herself. She worked methodically for the next ninety minutes until she looked up and saw it was gone six. Time to go home for a cold beer and even colder pizza. The conversation with Carla continued to niggle at her. It had been the discussion about Jessica Sherwood – the killing that she couldn't forget.

The autopsy snaps, which she'd examined time and time again, simply reinforced her opinion that the needle mark would have been found on the underside of the woman's body where the blood had pooled after death. Erin hadn't been able to see it and this omission wasn't a reportable offence as far as she could see. She wondered if the killer knew more about human pathology than they suspected and had known a simple needle mark would prove impossible to find on the livor mortis marbled skin of the corpse. She would have to put up with Detective Baros's scorn for the foreseeable future, but so what? It was she who'd ordered the bloods to be taken, which had identified the presence of potassium cyanide. One up for the ME office. *Sorry, Baros, but we did our job.*

14

Carla hadn't been able to sleep after Erin's visit, the injustice of the woman's fate gnawing away at her. Of course, inequality in the treatment of female victims of violence was the same the world over. A respectable retired homeowner killed within her house was going to attract more attention than an unidentified possible sex worker. But Carla thought things had changed in the twenty years since she'd entered the workplace. Weren't we all a little more clued up about the rights of women, whatever the background? She expected Erin would have called her naïve, but then Carla hadn't had to harden herself to the images of victims of violence. Even the brief glance she had given the body had made her realise the dead she had unearthed as part of her job was nothing compared to the horror of a recent violent death. No wonder her dreams were fractured.

If she was honest, she was also a little put out at the detectives' attitude towards her. She was used to being a respected authority on the archaeology of loss and her colleagues treated her with sometimes embarrassing reverence. She had little experience of dealing with the police and couldn't imagine a situation back in England where she'd be called in with half an hour's notice to assist in an investigation. The devolved nature of law enforcement out here was something she was still getting to grips with, and things felt a little loose. Carla preferred to be in control and one of the hardest parts about coming to Jericho was surrendering all feelings of comfort. All she could do was follow her own ways of working, which had got her so far in her career. She would call Viv Kantz, but only after she had satisfied herself that she hadn't missed anything.

Rain bounced off the baked ground at Silent Brook as Carla stepped out of the car. She put up a huge umbrella she'd purchased off a street seller and surveyed the spot. All that remained of the place where the woman had burned was a large patch of scorched grass and imprints of boots made by first responders. Carla took out her sketch and checked each spot where the items had been placed. She couldn't make any sense of why they had been arranged in a particular way, but she was now beginning to think a ritual of sorts might be behind the pattern – not necessarily to do with the objects themselves, but the act of revering a burning corpse. People who were attracted to these kinds of places were those struggling with addictions and meagre lifestyles and ritual was often one way of seizing control of a desperate situation.

Behind her, Carla could hear the rumble of trucks. The detectives were right that the place had an itinerant community but, other than a statement from a witness that they had seen a woman climbing into a cab, there appeared little to link truckers with this death. It was odd that she was automatically assuming the killer was a man, which, really, only went alongside the fact that everyone was assuming the victim was a sex worker. *Think wider*, Carla told herself. She took off her jacket and threw it into the back of her car along with the sopping umbrella, took out a waxed coat she'd worn on many digs, and set off, the rumble of traffic turning into a scream as she neared the road. Rain dripped from her hood into her eyes as she surveyed the patch of land separated from the highway by a row of scrubby conifers. Carla looked in vain for an opening and, not sure what else to do, squeezed herself through a gap in the trees. She landed on a strip of concrete close to a pickup whose shocked driver leant on his horn. To the left she could see the overhead signs directing traffic past Jericho and onto Maine. On her right was an underpass, which must be where the sex workers congregated. She didn't much fancy walking along the road, especially as she was following the flow of traffic and she wouldn't be able to see anyone pulling up behind her.

She braved the trees again, feeling happier walking in the puddles forming on the grass. She also had sight of her car, the place she'd make for if she sensed trouble. When she neared the thick concrete of the underpass, she saw a space in the trees, the likely route through which the sex workers brought their clients into the field. Carla slipped through and saw two figures standing beneath the underpass. One was talking through a car window. Agreement reached, she opened the door and the car sped away. Carla watched as the other woman scratched something on the concrete pillar.

At Carla's approach the woman turned, her expression little friendlier than the detectives when they'd first seen her. She had pale hair spun like candy floss that had been teased into a mass of curls. Through the light, Carla could see the girl's scalp.

'Sorry, could I have a word with you?'

'Where you from? SWARM or the outreach project?'

Carla shook her head. 'Neither – I don't even know what they are. I'm from the university.'

This got the girl's attention. 'What do you want? I'm taking part in no study. We're not animals in the zoo to be stared at.'

Carla lowered her hood. 'Nothing like that. I was called out the other day to the woman found burnt in that field.'

The girl turned her face away. 'You heard about it?'

'I saw the smoke.'

'You saw the fire? What time was this?'

'About one a.m. I just thought it was the drunks keeping warm.'

A beige car slowed down but, after taking in Carla, sped off again. 'Look, I've gotta work. He'll be back on another circuit soon and I know him, so if you could make yourself scarce.'

'I'll be quick, I promise. The police have a theory that it was a working girl who was killed by her client. Have you heard of this?'

'News to me.'

'But the police have questioned some of you, haven't they? I mean, you saw the fire, so the death must have taken place while some of you were working.'

'No one's said anything to me.'

'But they have questioned some of your colleagues, haven't they?'

The girl shrugged. 'Not that I've heard.'

A car drew up and deposited a woman in her forties under the bridge. The driver screeched off without looking at the pair chatting.

'How's it going, Lucy?' The woman's eyes were wary.

'It's all right. She's from the university. Asking about the burning woman.'

Carla felt the woman's gaze shift to her. 'Not a cop then?' asked the woman.

'I'm working alongside the cops.' A white lie. 'I was saying to Lucy that the current theory amongst the investigating team is that she was a sex worker killed by her client.'

'Bullshit.'

'Have you heard whether the detectives had been down here to talk to you?'

'They haven't.' The woman crossed her arms.

'Dallas is our union rep,' said Lucy. 'She'd know of any police questions.'

Carla felt a surge of anger. The police hadn't even visited the women before coming up with the prostitute theory.

'So, no one's gone missing from you recently?'

'Didn't say that.' Dallas stopped talking as the beige car, true to Lucy's prediction, approached the underpass once more.

'This is my one,' said Lucy and she left without a backwards glance.

'One of you is missing?' asked Carla.

'No, dead. But not from the other night. Two years ago; January time when it was cold. Her name was Stella, fifteen years old. A client took her to the Franklin shopping mall and the next day, she's found in the car park.'

It was that name again. Franklin. 'How did she die?'

'Strangled by a scarf. Killer must have brought it with them unless she was dumb enough to be wearing one. Girls learn not to wear shit like that. I mean, why present a client the means of hurting you?'

'Did they find the killer?'

'Nah. Where you from?' Dallas reached into her bag and brought out her vape, taking a deep puff.

'England. You?' She felt stupid asking the question and the answer came as no surprise.

'Dallas. But in case you're thinking I'm Dallas from Dallas, or some asshat thing like that, it's just my working name. I took it when I started dancing in the bars and it stuck.'

'And you're the union rep?'

'That's it.'

'So, what you're saying is that three years ago Stella was killed by her client and then there's another killing this month close to where you work and not a single detective comes to see if you're missing a girl?'

'You got it.'

'And you're absolutely sure you're not missing a colleague?'

'I don't think so. Word of mouth is strong here. Stella had only been here a few days, but we knew her all right. Fifteen and chasing her demons, so she fit in well enough here. If the burnt victim was one of us, we'd know.'

'Police say they saw a woman climb into a truck about midnight.'

Dallas snorted. 'You'd see the same any night. That tells you nothing.'

'But still, no local woman has been reported missing. It must be someone from out of town. Any ideas?'

'No.' Dallas was beginning to lose patience.

'Is the shopping mall where Stella died near here?'

Dallas shook her head. 'That's the weird thing. It's about five miles away. Whoever heard of a john taking someone that far. Stella must have known she was in trouble within a few minutes.'

'Even though she was so young.'

Dallas shrugged. 'She'd been turning tricks for a while, I think. We do our best to keep people safe.' Dallas pointed at a pillar. 'We write down the car plates of clients who pick us up along with the date. Not foolproof because they know we do it, but it helps.'

Carla felt the stirrings of excitement. 'So basically, the car registration number of Stella's killer could be written on the pillar.'

Dallas nodded. 'Come take a look.'

As Carla approached, she saw the concrete was covered in thousands of scribbles, not all dated.

'You think the police care enough to go through every number plate on that pillar?' asked Dallas. 'I can tell you for nothing that some of our clients are serving officers.'

Carla frowned at the numbers. 'You know, I think I might go over to the Franklin Mall anyway.'

'What for? I told you the death was a long time ago.'

'Just curious. It's my superpower.'

Dallas smirked. 'You don't want to hear about mine.' She handed Carla a card. 'Come back and tell me if you find anything, OK?'

15

The first killing was the hardest. When the idea had begun to awaken in his mind, unfurling like petals from a daisy, he had wondered if he would be able to initiate his plan. He personally had nothing against sex workers. They performed a valuable function for the townspeople of Jericho, or at least those who were inclined to use their services. He'd never picked up a girl himself. He'd had no need or desire to go near the underpass near Silent Brook, but when he saw the three girls shivering one December night, an idea had come to him as to how he could finally get things going. He'd had to reconnoitre the place first. Driving past at different times of the day had given him a feel of the quiet times. He'd been surprised that mornings, although less busy than the nights, were still marked by a steady stream of girls getting into cars.

Night time had held the appeal. He was still nervous back then and in the January winter, darkness had descended by five p.m. He'd wanted to pounce soon after. The regulars didn't come on until after seven and traffic had been busy, meaning his car was likely to go unnoticed. However, it had been the location that was key, and the mall didn't shut until eight p.m. So he waited, spinning endless trips around the highway until, just after midnight, he had spotted a lone worker. She'd walked towards him, young and confident, and had slid into the front seat once she'd negotiated her fee.

'I know a car park. It's a few miles away, but we'll have privacy there.'

'Sure.' Stella King had shrugged.

She hadn't even bothered to hide her real name. Another myth smashed, although he suspected she was too young to have formed a fresh identity for herself. She'd fiddled with the radio in his car, finding a station which pumped out tunes he couldn't identify.

Deciding how to kill the girl had taken him almost as long as finding the right victim. He'd been squeamish and had dreaded having to use the knife he carried. He'd parked up in the lot, away from the lamps which shone neon onto the asphalt. Of all the locations, this was the one which he was most proud of. The one he'd had a hand in creating. She'd no sense of danger as he leaned across her. Only as his hands had gone to her neck had she opened her eyes, in those final moments realising that Jericho wasn't to be the new life she'd prayed for. God knows why she'd chosen this town. Stella King didn't belong here but not for the reason that had killed her.

His presence that night had gone undetected, which showed his plans were sound. How much effort had gone into finding Stella's killer had been difficult to gauge. He'd made a few discreet inquiries and discovered detectives were looking for an out of towner. Idiots. He'd finally allowed himself to relax and consider number two.

16

'I've got a lead on the identity of that fried woman.'

Erin closed her eyes. She was at least spared having to look at Baros, but she was discovering he could be as irritating over the phone. 'Go on.'

'Hotel over at Southside known as the Lake House. Know it?'

'I've heard of the place.' Ethan had mentioned his father going there with his new girlfriend, but she'd certainly never been treated to such luxury during their time together. 'You're telling me they've discovered a guest missing? How come they've only noticed now?'

'Did I say guest? One of their staff, goes by the name of Tiffany Stoker, has disappeared. She was a seasonal employee; arrived in April and due to finish end of October. On Sunday she put in a last-minute request for leave. Wanted a few days off, which was refused as there's a two-week rota which is pretty much fixed. When she didn't turn up Monday, they thought she'd decided to take the days off anyhow. She was getting fired when she returned on Wednesday.'

'Not much incentive to come back then. Why do they think she might be our victim?'

'Someone finally took the initiative and opened up her room. Purse and phone are still there. It looks like she never left or she took off in a hurry. Either way, it's suspicious enough for us to start digging.'

'You think she's a strong possibility?'

'She's the only recent missing person we have.' Baros sounded bored. An itinerant hotel worker was no doubt adding to his sense that this wasn't a case worth his trouble.

'Not a sex worker then.' Erin couldn't resist the dig.

'Don't you believe it. It's not unknown for hotel staff to turn tricks on the side. I'm not ruling anything out.'

'Does her room give any clues to what might have happened?' Erin paused as Jenny came into her office with her iPad. Erin signed off the autopsy note and showed her assistant who was on the line. Jenny rolled her eyes.

'On my way over there now. Fancy the ride? I've got little to go on from your autopsy to help me with an ID. Maybe you'll be able to spot something.'

Erin looked down at her desk. Its tidiness masked the endless emails waiting for a reply and she had a full teaching day tomorrow. She'd promised herself an afternoon clearing the messages. While she had a vested interest in identifying the woman, there was a grieving family waiting for answers after their son had thrown himself from the attic room in their house. She, as ever, owed her allegiance to the dead.

'I'm not sure I'm going to get away. Look, her phone still being in the room is weird, but there might be other stuff that needs decoding. I'm not an expert at sifting through possible crime scenes; you might want to bring someone on board who is confident about semiotics of location.'

'Semiotics of location?' Baros snorted and stopped. 'You don't mean… No way. That prof's worse than useless, and anyway, if it's a crime scene, we got our own experts. Anyhow, I got a mouthful of dirt from her in Morrell's the other night. According to her, I'm not allowed to go for a drink after a shift.'

'Carla's a little intense, but she has good ideas.' Erin felt a little guilty putting Carla's name into the mix. As her mentor, she should be easing the first few weeks, not using her as a distraction. But Carla, she thought, was sharp and had appeared genuinely outraged that the burnt woman at Silent Brook wasn't being given the priority she deserved. 'Besides,' Erin gave a long pause, 'you're not dealing with a sex worker from out of town now, are you? This Tiffany might not be a permanent Jericho resident, but she'd been here for a while. Tourists will hear hotel worker and wonder if their accommodation is safe. This zooms right back to priority.'

'Still no. I didn't like her, and she came up with fuck all. I don't want my time wasted.'

'All right. You look at the room yourself and see if you can decode it for insights into our Jane Doe's death.'

She had hit a nerve and she heard Baros sigh. 'OK, you call her and tell her to meet me at the Lake House in half an hour. If she's not there, I'll do my stuff and go. I'm not waiting around for her.'

'Understood.'

Erin spent the next ten minutes trying to call Carla, but her mobile rang unanswered. She shut down her computer and shoved her laptop into her backpack. She'd read the report at home later and give the dead boy's family a call in the morning. The emails would go unread for another day. At the very least she could report back to Carla what she'd found.

The rain was shooting needles on the asphalt as she picked up her car. The woollen coat she was wearing leaked the smell of lanolin into the car and she turned up the heater to dry herself off. The sound of the fan at first masked the sound of her phone ringing. Carla was calling her back.

'Where are you?' shouted Erin into the Bluetooth speaker.

'Driving back from Silent Brook. I was going to visit Franklin Mall.'

'Well, sorry to interrupt your shopping trip, but Detective Baros has called. We think we've got an identity on the dead woman. Her name's Tiffany Stoker, a hotel worker who hasn't returned from some unofficial time off. He's agreed that we can meet him there. Actually he's expecting you. As you weren't answering your phone, I was going to go myself.'

'Which hotel?'

'It's called the Lake House. Your GPS should get you there. It's in a district called Southside, just outside the town.'

'I'll be there.'

Erin cut the call and increased the speed of the wipers. So, Carla had gone back for another look at Silent Brook. If she'd known, Erin would have insisted on accompanying her. Jericho's air of gentility belied its dark underside. She wouldn't let any of her staff – male or female – undertake lone visits to certain parts of town. Silent Brook was one of them.

Turning off the main road, she followed the well-maintained track to the hotel. Visitors wanted rural, but they also demanded comfort. The lighting, however, left something to be desired. More show than use, the lamps cast a weird orange glow into the rain. Erin slowed down to a crawl. Baros had said he'd give Carla half an hour to get there, but if he saw Erin arrive, he wouldn't feel the need to hang around. She wanted to give Carla time to catch them up. She sped up when a pair of lights appeared in her rear-view mirror. Baros or Carla, it was too dangerous to carry on at the snail's pace.

At the car park she spotted Baros's car. He had a distinctive old Mustang, and, from the steamy windows, he must be enjoying a coffee inside. She flashed her lights at him and drew up beside him, followed by Carla. Carla was the only one of them with an umbrella, which she offered to Erin. Baros ignored them both, hunching his shoulders as he ran into the portico entrance. Erin hurried after him, leaving Carla with her umbrella, looking in through the window into a brightly lit room.

'Hurry up, you'll get soaked,' shouted Erin.

'I wasn't expecting a delegation,' said Baros, showing his badge to the receptionist. He turned and smirked at Erin's bedraggled appearance. 'I do the talking, OK?'

They were expected. A buzzer was pressed, and the manager came hurrying out sporting a gold badge engraved with the name Clyde. He was an anxious-looking man, in his fifties, with a thin moustache. His ex-military appearance wasn't what Erin had been expecting in the rustic setting.

'Miss Stoker, Tiffany, lived in one of the worker's rooms. I can take you there now. We've not touched anything.' He gathered them up like a mother hen, keen to get them out of reception.

Erin and Carla followed the two men down a passage and out through a side door, clearly meant for staff. Unlike the white stucco of the main building, the staff were housed in a brick annexe entered by a door secured with keypad lock. The corridor had a brackish smell and there was a notice on the wall warning any damage to the building or its contents would be taken from employees' wages.

'Looking after its workers,' Carla whispered to Erin.

'Always,' she replied.

Tiffany's room was spartan. She'd kept her meagre belongings tidy, and on the pine bedside table was a bottle of water and a mobile phone plugged into its charger.

'It's locked,' the manager said. 'There'll be missed calls from us since Monday. I was furious when she didn't turn up for her shift.'

'Any idea why she wanted time off?' asked Baros.

'She wouldn't give a reason, which was why I refused her request. I appreciate staff have family emergencies, but Tiffany couldn't even be bothered to think up an excuse. She said she needed to get away for a few days.'

Baros made a face. 'You said her purse is still here.'

'Over there. It was on the floor when I first came into the room. When I realised her wallet was still in the bag, I called you.'

Tiffany's bag lay on the bed. Snapping on a pair of gloves, Baros rifled through it and extracted a wallet and set of keys. 'You last saw her Sunday evening; is that correct?'

'At around nine p.m. She came to my office asking for the time off.'

'Do you have lockers for staff to leave their belongings?'

'There's a rack at the back of this building, but many don't bother; they just leave their bags in their rooms. I tell them not to do it. It's not as secure as the lockers but...' The manager shrugged.

'So, you're saying that if she was abducted while working, she wouldn't have her phone or purse on her,' said Erin.

Clyde looked shocked. Exposing the hotel as a potential location of a kidnapping had not been his intention.

'Who was the last person to see her?' asked Baros.

'I'm pretty sure it was me.' Clyde's expression turned glum. He'd probably watched too many police dramas where the last witness is the chief suspect. 'She was working the bar. Her shift started at three p.m. that day and she'd served afternoon tea with another member of staff then helped at dinner. Her shift wasn't due to finish until eleven, so she used a break to come and see me.'

Carla, Erin saw, was looking around the room, but Erin thought they'd be hard pressed to find anything interesting in the girl's things. On the table by the window was a single cheap magazine, a small bag of toiletries and a bag of apples. Baros opened the doors to the wardrobe and a few pieces of clothing in muted colours filled one end of the small space.

'What do you know about Tiffany Stoker?' asked Erin.

'I have her resume, which I've forwarded on to Detective Baros. She was in her early thirties, an itinerant worker. I got the impression she didn't settle at anything.'

'And that didn't bother you as a potential employer?' asked Erin.

The manager shrugged. 'That's the type of worker we get for these roles. She came from the Chicago area but appeared to have gravitated to Jericho. I telephoned her previous employers myself. She had good references.'

'Any boyfriends?' asked Baros.

'No idea.' The manager pursed his lips.

'Where did she go on her days off?'

'Again, I don't know. She kept herself to herself and the other staff can't tell me anything.'

'Any theories, Professor?' Baros raised his voice. *Here we go*, thought Erin. Carla didn't react immediately, her gaze fixed out of the window. She swung round to face Clyde.

'Have you had a window broken recently?'

'Window?' The manager looked at Baros as if to check he was allowed to answer random questions.

Baros shrugged and put away his notepad. 'Answer the prof.'

'Not that I'm aware of. I'd notice in this weather and, besides, a guest isn't going to put up with a cracked window.'

'I don't mean like this here.' Carla pointed at the mean plain window which looked out onto a gravel courtyard. 'I noticed the downstairs windows of the hotel have small panes of coloured glass at the top.'

'They're from when the house was originally built. They're an art deco design, an important feature of the building.'

'And have any of those broken?'

'No.'

'Are you sure? Can we take a look? It'll only be the downstairs rooms.'

Clyde shot a desperate look at Baros. 'That's a lot of windows.'

Baros shrugged, enjoying the manager's discomfort. 'I'm in no hurry.'

Erin wondered if it was the weather that was temporarily mellowing Baros or if he wanted to see Carla flounder once more. Probably the latter.

As they made their way to the main hotel, Erin leant into Carla. 'What the hell's this about the windows?'

Carla shrugged. 'Could be nothing.'

The manager led them through the front rooms consisting of a large sitting room and a bar. At each window Carla inspected the intact panes. Erin had noticed Baros had gone quiet and was helping with the inspection. She wondered what she was missing. They passed through a large function space and the dining room, which was being laid for dinner.

'The kitchen is a modern extension with plain windows.' The manager was itching to get back to his office. A sheen of sweat covered his face.

'What rooms haven't we covered?' asked Baros.

'The orangery at the back has the same glass, but it's shut off for winter.'

'Open it up,' said Baros.

They stood outside the entrance to the garden room, a cold draught shooting under the gap between the door and the ground, as the manager left to fetch the keys. Baros, Erin noticed, had his eyes on Carla. Clyde returned to open up the room and Erin saw he'd taken the opportunity to wipe his face. The air was icy inside the space. It would be unheated in summer and locked up when the weather turned cooler. Even so, it's temperature was well below what she'd have expected. Wind whistled through a gap in one corner where blue glass met the brick surround.

The manager stared at Carla. 'How did you—'

'It's the same glass as found around our victim's body,' said Baros quietly. 'The killer must have knocked out a pane and taken it with him.'

'You mean this is an act of vandalism.' The manager was furious. 'The Jericho Building Preservation Society will have something to say about that.'

Erin bit a retort. An employee lay unrecognisable in the morgue and all he cared about was the decor.

'How did you guess?' Erin asked Carla. 'I walked right past the window.'

'I saw the colours. The rain and the outside light were refracted off the glass and the blue pane immediately brought to mind the glass fragment found beside the body. The glass must have shattered when the killer knocked out the pane. If you look outside the building, you might find the remaining shards, but if blue glass is important to the killer, he's probably kept them.'

'So the killer was here.' Baros turned to the manager. 'Do you have any security cameras?'

'There's no need. This is Jericho and we're out of the way here. Any trouble, and there isn't much of that, is confined to the odd drunk guest and pilfering from staff.'

'You didn't suspect Tiffany of that?' asked Baros.

'She seemed pretty straight to me.'

'And you're sure she didn't say who she was planning to spend her days off with?'

The manager, still looking unhappy, shook his head. 'Is it too much to ask that you keep this quiet? We've had a tough time since the pandemic. Bookings are only beginning to pick up.'

Baros shrugged, itching to get away. 'Don't know. If you're concerned, give my boss Lieutenant Kantz a call. She might be able to put a lid on things publicity wise.'

As Baros and the manager left, Carla continued to stare at the window. 'What is it?' Erin asked.

'Why blue glass?'

Erin frowned. 'What do you mean?'

Carla turned. She looked exhilarated. 'I need to think things through. Thanks for getting me out here.'

17

Carla saw Baros was itching to get away. The connection between the hotel and the chunk of glass found next to the body confirmed that Tiffany Stoker was the likely victim found at Silent Brook. She'd have liked to ask him why he hadn't interviewed any of the prostitutes who worked their trade so close to the murder site, but she supposed it didn't matter any longer. He was in a hurry to update Viv Kantz that he had an ID on the dead woman and cover himself with the glory. Carla doubted her role in discovering the broken window would make it into the report.

Erin stared after him with a rueful expression. 'Oh, well. At least he allowed us to tag along. I guess we should be happy with that.'

Carla shook her head. 'I'm surprised I'm even here. Did you suggest I come along?'

'I did, but I thought you'd be able to help with any pattern present in the victim's room – spotting a connection to the stuff left around the body. Which you did, of course, but not from what was in Tiffany's personal space. Have I redeemed myself?'

'What do you mean?'

'I rather thought you were disappointed in me given Tiffany's death wasn't receiving the same attention as Jessica Sherwood's.'

Carla made a face. 'I wasn't blaming you. I appreciate it's the system – let's call it patriarchy – and it's been proved once more. There's a strong possibility that the killer was here and Baros couldn't wait to high-tail it out of here.'

Erin took a deep breath, wondering why she was bothering to defend Baros. Perhaps it was a reminder that she was on one side of law enforcement and Carla the other. 'It's late. He'll have had a long day. If it's important, he'll bring a team out in the morning. We're under-resourced here. You heard the manager say there are no security cameras.'

'But he could interview guests.'

'That's a huge undertaking and he'll need permission from Viv before he starts knocking on doors. If it was a guest, and I seriously doubt it, they'll be well gone by now.'

'Why don't you think it was someone staying here?'

'You have to pay by credit card these days. Even if they gave a false name and address, they still need to pay. They'd leave too much of a trail.'

'So you think the killer was local?'

'Could be. Look, I've gotta go. I've a mountain of paperwork to get through. Call me if you need anything.'

On the drive back to Hoyt Lane, Carla had played the scenario repeatedly over in her head. Tiffany's killer had been at the hotel and had managed to lure her away from her shift or waited until it ended at eleven. She'd got into his car or pickup and he'd taken her, willingly or not, away to Silent Brook. Perhaps they'd shared a drink in the car park, Tiffany unaware that she was about to embark on her last ride. Mixing pills and alcohol could have been one way to subdue Tiffany. This suggested it wasn't a random meeting of killer and victim but that she had known her abductor and had got into the car without a struggle. Carla wasn't convinced Erin was right to rule out the guests, especially with the discovery of the broken glass. Presumably before taking Tiffany away, her killer had spotted the coloured window panes and decided to make it fit their plans. There must be a reason or pattern. It was the only thing that made sense. She'd been so dismissive of ritual when she'd been called into the case, but she was now fascinated by the idea of the killer selecting the glass. It suggested they were willing to embrace opportunity, although its significance remained hidden.

Carla found a space on Hoyt Lane and parked up the car. Although the rain had stopped, she felt damp around the edges and was desperate to change into dry clothes. She tried sneaking past the kitchen, but Patricia was waiting for her.

'Everything all right?' Patricia shouted from the kitchen. 'I've just dropped the pies I made at church ready for the sale in the morning. Don't look so forlorn; I saved one for us.'

Carla hesitated. Perhaps food laced with sugar would cheer her up and she could let off a bit of steam with Patricia. In the kitchen, her landlady held up a pie, its dark golden pastry arranged into a lattice pattern.

'Fancy a piece now? I could make some coffee.'

'I think I've had my caffeine quota for the day. Pie would be nice though.'

'Right you are.' Patricia cut two generous slices and put one plate in front of Carla. 'I'm out of cream, I'm afraid.'

Carla nodded and gave the thumbs up, a piece of the fragrant apple pie already in her mouth.

Patricia fiddled with the tea towel, looking embarrassed. 'You feeling all right? One of the women at church said you'd been involved in looking at the woman who died over at Silent Brook.'

Carla swallowed the pie and picked up another slice with her fork. 'Involved is a little strong. I work with the husband of the lieutenant involved and she asked me to take a look.'

'Viv Kantz. Well, she's nobody's fool. Was it someone local?'

Carla hesitated. Whatever she said, it was bound to get back to the members of the church and she had to remember that Albert and Viv belonged to the congregation.

'It's possible she's been identified. A hotel worker from out of town.'

Was it her imagination or did Patricia relax? 'That's sad. We get a lot of seasonal workers and I like to think we look after them. They often turn up at church, for example. We're still a close-knit community despite the expanding town.'

'My mentor, Erin, said that a woman died near here in the spring. Did you know her?'

'Jessica Sherwood? That was a terrible tragedy, although I'd never heard of her until she died. She was a retired teacher but not at the school my lot went to. Why do you ask? I keep this house secure. You don't have anything to worry about.'

Carla frowned. 'Jericho's generally safe though, isn't it? I mean it's no more dangerous than anywhere else?'

'No more, I suppose,' agreed Patricia, slicing a piece of pie with her fork. 'Perhaps because we're such a small community, murder is always a shock. I never expected it to impact on me personally though.'

'You?'

'One of my goddaughter's friends, Madison Knowles, was killed two years ago. She was in her second year at college, and it was such a senseless murder. I don't think I've felt truly safe since.'

'She was a student at Jericho?' The pie stuck in Carla's throat. 'What happened?'

'She was knifed in her room at night. For a moment we thought we had a Ted Bundy here, but there were no more attacks.'

'She was living on campus?'

'In a sorority house with three other girls.'

'Were they attacked too?'

'They didn't hear a thing. The four of them watched a movie together, two stayed up chatting for another hour while Madison took a shower and went to bed. Her alarm went off at eight a.m. the following morning, but it rang and rang. One of the other girls went to check what the problem was and found Madison dead. They think she put up a fight, God bless her.'

'That's terrible.' Carla felt like throwing up her pie. She should have agreed to that coffee. 'Could I have some water?'

Patricia crossed over to the sink. 'There was blood everywhere. A slaughterhouse. The girls had done everything right in terms of security. It was a hot evening,' continued Patricia, 'but all the windows were shut and doors locked by the time they went to bed.'

'How did the killer enter?'

'Forced open a door, apparently. This guy must have hated women, right?'

'Right.' Carla considered. 'Maybe someone she knew – an ex-boyfriend, for example.'

'He was out of town and his alibi checked out. We've been on tenterhooks ever since, waiting for the next victim.'

'If it was two years ago, then maybe he's left Jericho. A college student moved elsewhere.'

'I hope you're right, although that still makes it someone else's problem, doesn't it?' Patricia sat heavily back in her seat. 'You know, I hate to gossip, but we've talked and talked about the case in our craft group. Did you know one of the staff from Albert Kantz's department got involved in that case too? She was called to look at the scene, like you were at Silent Brook.'

'She? It wasn't Doctor Max Hazen?' He'd been keen to suggest he was the favoured choice of archaeological expert.

'Definitely a woman, but I don't think I ever knew her name.'

'Might it have been Lauren Powers?'

Patricia frowned. 'Maybe. Doctor Powers sounds familiar. How clever of you to guess.'

Carla made a face. 'No guess. Lauren is my predecessor and I'm now in her office. Did she discover anything?'

'Oh, I wouldn't know that. As I said it's just church and quilting gossip. We don't have anything else to do when we're together. I'll tell you what I do know, though. The case is unsolved and, if you ask me, they've run out of steam. Whoever broke into that dorm is nothing more than an animal and even that's being kind to him.'

'It could have been a woman.'

Patricia shot her a look. 'Right.'

Back in her room, Carla paced the floor. If her hunch was correct that Tiffany knew her killer, then it was possible he had struck before, but she couldn't understand why the police weren't connecting the cases. Just because other experts had been brought in and not found a discernible pattern, perhaps here was somewhere she could finally help. Admittedly the killings, while both ferocious, didn't sound similar, but perhaps it was worth a shot trying to link the two. Jessica Sherwood's killing was probably unconnected to Tiffany's death, but there was something about the savagery of Tiffany Stoker and Madison Knowles dying that suggested a link. If it was Lauren who had attended Madison Knowles' crime scene, then it would be interesting to learn what she'd been able to contribute, but there was no way to discover her observations unless she'd written something in one of the notebooks Carla had found in the cupboard. She sat down on the bed. What time had the movers said they were coming in the morning? She knew it was early, but how early – eight a.m.? Tomorrow would be too late. She could get in before they arrived – say, leave here at six – but she had no idea how long it would take to find the right notebook. The only option was to go in now and look through the hoard.

Carla loved deserted buildings. Not for her the fear of the liminal and abandoned. These spaces were food for her soul and, as she showed her pristine pass to the night security, she felt her spirits lift. It was darkening outside, and she could see the other offices in the corridor were empty from the blackness seeping underneath their doors. The sensor lights came on one by one as she walked down the corridor and opened up her office. In the room, there had been a subtle shift in the atmosphere. There was that musky smell, not unpleasant but alien, and now she was sure definitely male. She looked for another note but found nothing that a colleague might have left for her. The office was otherwise as she'd left it, her jacket still slung over the back of the chair. She picked it up and shoved it into her bag. If she took away everything that belonged to her, she could leave the movers to go about their business tomorrow.

Feeling a little guilty, Carla locked herself in the room. If anyone else happened by, it would give her a chance to get her story straight. She was removing her own effects ready for the movers tomorrow. She opened the cupboard and saw it was untouched since she'd jammed it full of the objects on Lauren's desk. The notebooks were the type you could find in any stationers or supermarket. Simple spiral pads, some purchased in situ on digs based on the language on the covers and the price stickers: Euros, Pesos, Canadian Dollars. Carla lifted them out and tried to decipher the system of dating the pads. Number 36 straddled the end of 2020 and slid into the following year. As she read through dig notes, lecture jottings, shopping lists and random thoughts, Carla felt her heart ache. Dan had left similar notes, and they were now in a brightly lit storage facility outside Oxford. He'd been an archaeologist too and had understood Carla's passions. She'd have loved to discuss the case with him and see what insights he could bring. Carla shook away the thought and continued her task.

Notebook 36 ended in April without any mention of Madison Knowles. Carla hunted for the next book and found 38 without any difficulty. Number 37, however, was not there. In frustration, she pulled out every notepad and put them in order. As far as she could see the only book that was missing was 37. Damn. She didn't know an exact date, but Patricia had said it had been hot, which suggested summer. Carla grabbed the notebook with 38 scrawled on it and saw, in dismay, that it began in October. She checked each page, but the jottings revealed nothing about Madison Knowles. Carla leant back against the wall. Where the hell was the missing notebook? She raised herself to look through the shelves and began to remove journals and books at random but knew it was a thankless task. Perhaps Lauren had handed her notes over to the police.

Picking up the two remaining notebooks covering the current year, Carla idly flicked through the pages. In the most recent, she spotted the name Detective Baros in a sea of doodles and also the name she kept seeing around town: Franklin. The page was packed with notes in Lauren's distinctive spidery handwriting. At the top were a list of names with numbers against them – the results of student essays she'd been marking. Further down were random scrawls; they looked like little flames in a row, then three numbers and the name Detective Baros. The digits meant nothing to her, but she would show them to Max, who had known Lauren, and see if they made sense to him. She slid the book into her bag. The family would get the rest of Lauren's effects and if Carla got an attack of the guilts at some point in the future, she'd send it to them at a later date.

Back at Hoyt Lane, Patricia was waiting up for her, calling Carla into her sitting room.

'I heard your car leave and I was worried. Perhaps it was our conversation, but I don't like you wandering around after dark. Look, don't rush to find somewhere else to live. Stay until Christmas. I just don't need a full-time lodger, but I can see you're the quiet type. Stay for a few months.'

'You sure?' Carla felt a rush of relief at the thought she could stay in this homely room a while longer.

'Why not. It's nice to know I have company. Let's celebrate with a glass of sherry.'

Patricia removed the stopper from a glass decanter and poured two small glasses.

Carla took a sip of the amber liquid, resisting the impulse to wince at the cloying sweetness. 'Can I ask you a question? If you saw these numbers, would they mean anything to you?'

Carla pulled out Lauren's notebook and showed the page to Patricia, who frowned. 'They're too long to be phone numbers. Do you have any ideas?'

Carla shrugged. 'They mean nothing to me.'

Patricia frowned in concentration. 'You know, they're kind of familiar. Maybe ask my son; he's good with numbers. Who does the notebook belong to?'

'My predecessor, Lauren, the one we were just talking about. Given the figures are next to Detective Baros's name, I wondered if I should hand it over.'

'He might know what the numbers are.' Patricia stopped. 'Any clues in the doodles?'

Carla peered at the page filled with tiny flames. 'Nothing significant, I don't think.' She snapped the notebook shut and picked up the glass of sherry. 'Cheers.'

18

The weekend yawned in front of her when Carla woke on Saturday morning. She didn't think Patricia's hospitality extended to her mooching around the house and she would have to find something to occupy her time. The week's teaching had given her a buzz – it was great to be back in the saddle with motivated students. The time had sped past so quickly she realised she hadn't rung her mother back as promised. *Shit.* Looking up at the clock, she saw it would be early afternoon in England unless her mother was still at the French yoga retreat. With a sigh, Carla called her mother via WhatsApp and listened to it ring.

'I thought I'd been forgotten here.' Sylvia was in fine form, Carla saw immediately.

'Hasn't Pete been in touch?' asked Carla, knowing full well her mother preferred to hear about her brother Pete's job in the big firm of London's accountants than Carla's academic achievements.

'So what if he has? He's not my only daughter, is he? I knew this would happen,' her mother huffed.

'Knew what would happen?' asked Carla, confused. Her mother had taken the news of her daughter's relocation to New England coolly. There had been no mention of holiday visits or how Carla was finally spreading her wings after the tragedy of Dan's death.

'You'd leave England and us all behind. Don't you owe us something after everything that happened?'

That was her mother's euphemism for Dan's death: 'everything that happened' and, not for the first time, Carla saw how monstrous her mother's attitude was.

She took a deep breath, determined not to rise to the bait. 'I was ringing to see how you are.'

'I'm stressed,' snapped her mother. 'The bathroom light keeps...' Carla went into a reverie as her mother droned on about her domestic woes and she doodled on a pad, her sketches reminding her of those made by Lauren. She remembered the confident smiling face in the photos and thought it pretty certain that Lauren wouldn't have put up with a mother attempting to undermine her confidence at every turn. By the time the call had finished, Carla was desperate for some fresh air, and she had a specific destination in mind.

She made a coffee, poured it into a flask and set off towards the river in the watery sunlight. She had formulated the plan at three a.m. when she had been wide awake, her mouth parched after two glasses of Patricia's sickly sherry. Patricia she liked and Erin she admired, but it was with Lauren that she felt an affinity. She could understand desperation and loss, but Lauren had also had something Carla prized most of all: a curious mind. The numbers, Carla was sure, would mean something to Charlie Baros. Lauren might even have shown him the page of jottings. She just had to discover a way of finding out what they meant before speaking to him as she was sure he'd refuse to share any intelligence he had with her.

The oak and elm trees were turning yellow, and the sharp wind would soon sweep the leaves on the floor. It was a fifteen-minute walk to the river as she passed dog walkers and joggers enjoying the brisk morning air. When she reached the bridge, Carla stopped and looked over the ledge into the green-brown depths. Why drowning? Carla wasn't much into romanticising death. Forget the images of Ophelia or Maggie Tulliver sinking into watery depths after heartbreak. The reality, as Erin would surely agree, was pain followed by oblivion and a bloated corpse for an innocent bystander to discover. Nevertheless, it felt a female way to kill yourself. None of the drama of hurling yourself under a train or jumping from a height. Here, you'd wade into the Styx-like darkness and allow the undertow to sweep you off your feet.

Lauren had been an archaeologist whose photos in her room shouted her love of landscape. This spot, for all its dankness, must have had a terrible attraction for the woman. Carla turned her back on the river and glanced at the town around her. Stretching away to the right was a thin path leading to one of the churches she could see from her bedroom window. Erin had mentioned Suncook Park next to a church as the spot Lauren had chosen. Carla began to trudge towards the building, keeping her eyes away from the water.

The residents of this Jericho suburb were still waking up. If Silent Brook was the wrong side of the tracks, this was the right one. Three huge colonial-style detached houses, two of them sporting the American flag, gave way to an expanse of manicured lawn. This strip of greenery must be what Erin referred to as the park. At the top of the slope was a square glass building, its mirrored windows providing privacy for the occupants. Set against the white houses, its modernity was shocking, and she wondered what the town planners had been thinking when they agreed to its design.

More of an effort had been made towards the river. Round flower beds were cut into the closely clipped grass near the bottom of the incline and filled with dog roses and box hedging. Carla moved on towards the adjacent church. St Luke's proclaimed itself as Episcopalian. Perhaps the proximity of a place of worship had provided some comfort to Lauren when she'd decided to enter the river here. She'd chosen the place well. The water swept into eddies away from the bank, the current hurrying downstream. Once you'd made the decision to enter the water, all choices were likely removed.

Carla watched as a golf cart came meandering down the hill. A tanned man in his fifties pulled up against one of the flower beds and began to snip at one of the rose bushes. Carla hesitated, trying to gauge the worker's friendliness. He lifted his head and gave her a nod of acknowledgement which made up her mind. She walked towards him, her shoes sinking into the damp grass. 'I'd been admiring the roses. You obviously take good care of them.'

The man gestured with his secateurs. 'Mr Franklin is particular about his roses.'

Carla followed the direction where the man was pointing. 'Mr Franklin? I keep wondering about the family. Who are they?'

The man frowned at her. 'Where you been? You never heard of James Franklin?'

Carla shrugged. 'I'm new to the town.'

He turned back to the roses, unimpressed. 'You see any new building in Jericho, James Franklin is responsible. He wants to double the size of the town.'

'And that's a good thing?'

'Bringing a lot of prosperity. It's keeping local folks in work. Who am I to complain?'

'What about the college? That must bring people in.'

'Temporarily.' The man's tone was downbeat. As in Oxford, there must be a tension between town and gown.

'And is that building the head office?'

The gardener rolled his eyes. 'It's an office hub. People can rent space by the month. The Franklin HQ is the other side of town.'

'Not Silent Brook?'

The man gave her a scornful glance. 'Of course not. You'll find the HQ on the other side of his mall.'

Of course. Franklin Mall was where Stella King's body had been found. James Franklin, it appeared, had stamped his name all over town.

'You're asking a lot about Mr Franklin.'

Carla smiled, wondering if curiosity was discouraged in the town. 'I was just being nosy. I'm still trying to discover the town.'

'Work in the college, do you?'

'How can you tell?'

'You don't sound like a local and you don't look like a tourist. They're all still in bed.'

'I am a professor in the archaeology department.'

'Like that one who drowned.'

Carla stiffened. 'You knew Doctor Powers?'

'That her name? I watched them fish her out of the river.'

'But she just entered the river here, didn't she? The river is fast flowing, so she surely would have been swept downstream.'

'Had weights in her jacket. Didn't want to go far, I guess.'

So, Lauren had put stones in her pockets like Virginia Woolf to speed her death. That suggested she had every intention of not being pulled out of the river alive. Hardly a cry for help when you've weights to pull you down.

Carla studied the flower beds, noting the sweeping arcs in the planting. 'Did you design the beds?'

The man snorted. 'Me? Everyone has got a role here and that ain't mine.'

He reached into his tool bag and a bottle spun out onto the glass. The label said 'Grasshopper Beer' and both of them regarded it for a moment.

'In my bag for after work,' the man said finally.

Carla shrugged. 'Makes no difference to me.'

'Drinking on the job is a sackable offence according to Mr Franklin.'

'Well, you're not drinking it while you work, are you?'

The man relaxed. 'Suppose not.'

Carla looked at the bottle. 'That a local beer?'

'Sure. Brewed nearby. First liquor I ever tasted.'

'Can I look?' Carla reached down. It was made of thick clear glass with a metal cap, nothing like the one found next to Tiffany Stoker's body.

'I have one a day,' he confided. 'Goes nice with the cheese sandwiches my sister makes me.'

'You live together?' asked Carla, handing back the bottle.

'Sure do. She works for Mr Franklin too. Has a good job working at HQ.'

Carla heard a clank as he replaced the bottle in the bag. He grinned at her. 'Empty from yesterday.' He held up another of the clear glass bottles in which he'd shoved an apple stalk and an empty packet of crisps. Something shifted inside Carla.

'Witch,' she whispered, and watched his face fall.

19

Stupid. The answer had been in front of her from the beginning. When she'd first looked at the items placed around Tiffany's body, she'd remembered that shoes were often used as a means to counter witchcraft. The significance had eluded her as they were often kept in hearths or boundary walls to protect the occupants of a house. A boot in an open piece of land had no in situ meaning and as an archaeologist, that was what she'd been looking for. If, however, she removed setting – so hard for her – the other objects had a force that united them. They were also objects she might find hidden in fireplaces or tucked into hard-to-reach places encased in a ceramic flask or glass bottle. Witch bottles, as they were commonly known. Bellarmine jars from the continent had been popular receptacles in England and Wales, but Carla wasn't sure if they'd also been exported to New England. The items found around Tiffany's body were modern day equivalents of what a witch bottle might contain. A syringe needle instead of pins. Modern day coins. A hank of hair. Whoever had killed Tiffany Stoker had scattered items to imply she was a witch.

The mild, sunny day darkened before Carla's eyes, and she wondered if her imagination was running wild. Witches were, of course, associated with New England, but she'd discounted any connection with the burning woman as those unfortunates had been hanged, not put to the flames. And yet, the witch bottle theory made sense – a pattern only those familiar with the objects would be able to discern. Carla looked at her mobile. It was too early to call Erin and tease out her theory. Erin surely didn't work on weekends, and she was allowed time off from what must be a stressful job. Baros and Perez were out of the equation. She wasn't going to meet those mocking grey eyes again without having fully thought through the connection.

She sat on a bench while the gardener carried on with his pruning, now ignoring Carla after her outburst. Carla shivered, drawing her thin cardigan around her shoulders. Tiffany's killer had likely picked her up from the Lake House the evening of her death. It suggested a personality who was prepared to take chances, but she wasn't sure this would necessarily make it an opportunist killing. There was a degree of planning – from the blue glass knocked out of the window, to the possessions scattered around Tiffany's body. He could have picked up the syringes, a bottle of urine and the old shoe from the wasteland, but taking the time to spread them around her corpse could hardly be spur of the moment.

The detectives and assorted advisors had considered the possibility, but the question was, would other consultants have looked for items with ritualistic significance in relation to other murders? There had been the other deaths in the last few years: Jessica Sherwood, who may have been the victim of a robbery gone wrong, Stella King, the sex worker killed in a mall parking lot, and Madison Knowles, the Jericho student. Jessica Sherwood, according to Erin, had died a relatively painless death, which didn't immediately tie in with Tiffany's brutal killing. Tiffany didn't appear to be a sex worker, despite Baros's mean comment about prostitutes using hotels, which made a link with Stella King less likely too. It was the murder of Madison Knowles, the death that Lauren had consulted on, that most bore the hallmarks of a violent killer. Carla looked around at the sleepy town that was coming to life. It was hard to imagine a killer operating in this environment and yet Patricia had talked about Jericho's dark side. Perhaps this was it.

On impulse, she dialled Albert's number. 'Do you think your wife would mind if I gave her a call?'

'Viv?' he asked. 'Is something the matter? You know we have our own security on campus if there's an issue there.'

'It's not so much that. I just wanted to chat through an idea I had about the death I attended at Silent Brook. I know she was looking for any clues as to ritual and I do have an idea I wouldn't mind talking to her about.'

'Hold on. She's at work; she can't keep away from the place. I'll call her using the house phone.'

Carla looked at her watch. 'I hadn't expected her to be at the precinct. I can call her there.'

'The receptionist is a Rottweiler. She probably won't put you through. Give me a minute.'

Carla heard the phone being placed on a hard surface and footsteps receding. She stood at the edge of the river and glanced across its depths. Viv Kantz had a reputation with a capital R. Carla really hoped she wasn't about to make a fool of herself. Immersed in her thoughts, she didn't hear the phone being picked up.

'She's got a space at midday and can spare you ten minutes max. That suit?'

She could have hugged him. 'Works for me fine.'

Carla was a little disappointed when she finally got to meet Viv Kantz. Given her reputation, she'd expected a more imposing figure. She was around Carla's height but thicker set with soft wavy hair which settled like a halo around her head. She was sitting in a huge director's chair which swamped her small frame.

'Sorry I missed you at the crime scene. I had to get back here and update the deputy chief. You know how it is. My detectives said you didn't discover anything of interest in relation to the items around the body.'

'I didn't while I was at the site.'

Viv tapped a pen on the desk. 'Don't let it get you down. It was just an idea that someone from Albert's department might be able to help. I like the community to feel I'm doing everything I can when something terrible like that happens. Detective Baros tells me you attended the search of Tiffany Stoker's room at the Lake House. That's above and beyond the call of duty.'

Carla felt the sting of the reprimand. 'Erin – I mean Doctor Collins – thought I might be able to help.'

'Which you did. I gather you made the connection between the blue glass discovered at the scene and the window pane.'

Baros had at least credited her with that discovery. 'There's the possibility the killer was in the hotel unless Tiffany broke the window herself.'

Viv shrugged. 'It's possible, although either scenario doesn't really explain the glass present next to the body.'

'I think I might have a theory that I wanted to run past you.'

'OK, I'm all ears but, you know, you could have mentioned it to Detectives Baros or Perez. They're leading on the case and they have my full support.'

Carla was conscious of Viv's scrutiny. Any negative comments about Baros would clearly be unwelcome. 'I'm not sure I've endeared myself to your team. I was surprised to see them in the bar the evening of the killing. I think they thought my words were a criticism.'

'Morrell's? It's where most of the cops go to unwind. I hope they weren't indiscreet. They're under strict orders not to talk about cases in public.'

'Our conversation was brief. I also met your daughter.'

'Zoe? She didn't mention it.' Viv didn't want to discuss her family. 'So, tell me about your theory.'

'It's going to sound a little strange.'

'Believe me. I've heard it all before.'

'Probably not this.'

Viv sighed. 'Try me.'

'OK. We think each item was left after the woman's death. Some we might associate with a junkie – the bottle of urine, for example – if that's what it was.'

'Definitely urine,' said Viv. 'And no, we can't DNA it because it's not a great source of nucleated cells. The killer probably knows this. It's on every CSI programme.'

'Others are more oblique though. The coins, glass, hair. But they do have a common factor. They're the items people used to put inside a witch bottle.'

'A witch bottle?' Viv looked amused. 'What's that?'

'They're bottles people used to place behind their fireplaces, up in the attic, behind plaster. They were designed to scare off evil spirits.'

'I think I know what you mean. I remember my German grandmother talking about protecting the house against curses, but I'm pretty sure these were shoes filled with charms.'

'Some societies used a shoe or boot.'

'Hold on, there was a boot found at the scene too, wasn't there?'

'Exactly.'

Viv ran a hand through her curls. 'You think we've some weirdo who's created, what, some deconstructed witch's bottle plus other charms to ward off evil?'

'That's exactly what I think.'

'Jesus. That's sick.' Viv leant back in her chair and regarded Carla. 'The problem, I suppose, is that it doesn't mean a killer did it. This town is full of the bohemian types. One possibility is that they came across the burning body and instead of calling it in as most normal people would do, they created this weird thing to ward off spirits.'

Carla's spirits sank. 'You think that likely?'

Viv shrugged. 'I have to consider all angles.'

'But what about the glass? We can link that shard to Tiffany's place of work. The killer must have picked that up the night of Tiffany's death or maybe just before.'

'Maybe.' Carla could see Viv was unconvinced. 'Why the hotel glass, though? Why not an ordinary blue bottle?'

'It was close to hand. Blue is a sacred colour in many cultures, including here in the US. The killer is someone who likes to play with imagery.'

Viv shook her head. 'I don't know. There's a lot of this case that isn't making sense. Any ordinary murderer would have high-tailed it out of Silent Brook after the killing. If your theory is correct, they could have placed the items away from the fire and the idea of a witch bottle would have still held true. Why stay and watch?'

'I'm not sure. I can't get any sense of the type of killer we're dealing with.'

Viv snorted. 'Join the club.'

'I got the impression,' Carla was choosing her words carefully, 'that the case isn't a priority for the department.'

'Who told you that?' said Viv sharply. 'That's certainly not the case.'

Carla wasn't prepared to drop Erin in it. 'I just got the impression that your resources were focused on the killing of Jessica Sherwood.'

Viv pursed her lips, fixing Carla with her gaze. 'There's been two killings in Jericho this year. Every person's death, whatever their status in life, is equally important. We're now sifting through every guest that Tiffany might have met while she worked at the Lake House. It's the end of the season. Do you know how many people that makes?'

'It must run into the hundreds.'

'Believe me, it does.'

'But the most recent guests are surely—'

'Don't tell me how to do my job, please.'

Carla, chastened, took a deep breath. 'And you're not connecting it to any other murder cases?'

'Others?'

'Madison Knowles and Stella King, for example. I also heard there was a recent death of a woman in her home.'

Viv flushed. 'You've clearly been doing your homework. The answer is no. Madison and Stella's murders are still open, but we believe that their killers, like that of Tiffany Stoker, have moved on. Miss Sherwood is different.'

'You think there's a murderer left in town?'

'Yes, I do.'

Jesus, thought Carla. The woman was cool. A killer in town and she'd admitted it as if it were a mild case of shoplifting.

Viv looked towards the door to show Carla her ten minutes were nearly up.

Carla said, 'I know my predecessor worked on the Madison Knowles case. Was she able to help at all?'

'She couldn't see any pattern. Like with you, we were grateful for her trying.'

'She didn't leave you a notebook on the case?'

'Not that I'm aware of.'

'Can you check? I'd be interested to see her thoughts.' Carla didn't mention she'd already searched through Lauren's belongings looking for the elusive jotter.

Viv sighed and got up to open the door, hollering at the busy office. 'Baros, Perez, get yourselves in here, would you?'

The two detectives, who'd spotted Carla sitting in the chair, walked toward the office as slowly as they could get away with. If Viv noticed, she gave no sign. She pointed at Carla.

'Remember Doctor James. Baros, you and she are almost pals, I believe.'

'I wouldn't say that.' His grey eyes narrowed as he took in her slouchy cardigan and pants. 'Has she got something for us?'

'She's asking if we have a notebook that Doctor Powers used when we consulted her on the Madison Knowles killing.'

The detectives shared a glance. 'She never shared any notes with us.'

'You're sure?' asked Carla. 'When I moved into her office, I found a more recent notepad with your name in it.'

She saw a gleam appear in Baros's eye. 'So?'

'If you don't have her notes from the time of the investigation, I was wondering if she tried to contact you nearer the time of her death.'

'Nope.' Baros put a stick of gum in his mouth and began to chew it. 'That all?'

'What about you?' Carla asked Perez, who shook her head.

They ambled out of the office with the same insolence as they had entered.

'Look.' Viv leant back in her seat, after they'd gone, her gaze on Carla. 'In some ways you've reassured me. Definitely no connection to my other cases. There was none of that weird shit with any of the other women. Forget Tiffany Stoker. I'm sorry you had to see her body like that, but you've got a good theory with the witch bottle idea. I'll get the detectives to see if there are any devil worshipers in Jericho. God help us, but it's worth a shot. Other than that, forget the other killings. My job is to keep Jericho safe and that's what I'm doing.'

20

'That prof you suggested wasn't much use.'

Baros was leaning on a filing cabinet, flicking through an autopsy report. A rigger at a construction site had been standing underneath a mobile crane when a metal joist disengaged itself from the load and crashed to the ground. The construction worker's body had been in parts when it arrived at the facility and Erin had put down the cause of death as severe head trauma. As in, it was no longer there.

Erin ignored Baros's statement. She hadn't thought for a moment that he and Carla would get on and she wasn't getting involved in any personality conflicts. 'Think the construction company is to blame for this one?'

Baros shrugged. 'Perez is down supervising the interviews now. The crane operator is an old hand claiming faulty equipment. Who knows? He may be right.'

'One of James Franklin's new developments?'

'A housing estate down near Cheetham's Pond. Franklin's design, but he's subcontracted all the work out. Not his problem apart from it slows down construction.' Baros tapped the report on the cabinet. 'I'll take this back to the office.'

'Be my guest. I'll be emailing it through to you anyhow. Any developments on the woman at Silent Brook?'

Baros made a face. 'No leads. My money's on that she was turning tricks as well as her bar work. It would suggest why the girls who congregate at the underpass hadn't heard of her.'

It sounded like he'd finally checked out the prostitutes as potential witnesses. Carla had been adamant the girls hadn't been spoken to and her opinion of Baros had taken a dive. Erin had suspected he'd eventually get round to it. Baros was lackadaisical rather than incompetent.

'She must have had a way of advertising her services if that's the theory. Got any ideas how she got her clients?'

'Perez is speaking to the union.'

And what, wondered Erin, *exactly are you doing while Perez does all the work?* Baros, however, wanted to talk about Carla.

'I don't know what it is with the lieutenant. Four, maybe five cases, she's got one of Albert's people to come down and take a look at the scene. What have they given us? Zilch. No leads, no suspects. Just some vague comments that anyone with a pair of eyes could have made.'

Erin had wondered the same. Viv had trained in Boston and had brought to Jericho some of the latest lateral working practices. A few, such as authorising the increased use of drones, had resulted in a sharp drop in petty crimes. But it was on Viv's watch that there had been unsolved murders and an increase in fear of crime in the community. None of this, however, was Carla's fault.

'She did what was asked of her. She came down, observed the objects around the body, made some notes. The fact she's not come up with anything might mean there isn't a pattern. A negative result in my job allows me to exclude certain elements.'

Baros stared at her, his cold eyes catching her gaze. 'I might have a lead on the killer of Jessica Sherwood. You know, the vic where you missed the needle mark.'

Don't rise to his bait, she cautioned herself. 'Go on.'

'Neighbour along the road was breastfeeding at four a.m., about the time Miss Sherwood was killed. She heard the dog barking but thought nothing of it. But she also says she heard the sound of a car starting. Not the same direction as the dog but nearer her house.'

'She didn't see anything?'

'Her curtains were closed, but the timings would be right. We think the victim was murdered around the time the dog was let out into the garden and the killer must have needed to make a quick getaway. He or she probably stashed their car in the nearby alley.'

'You think it might appear on surveillance cameras?'

'It's a possibility. There's nothing on Penn Street, but we're looking at surrounding areas.'

Erin kept the scepticism off her face. Security cameras were on the increase in Jericho, another of Viv's initiatives, but coverage was patchy. It would be a lucky break to capture a car and get its licence plates.

'OK. Well, good luck and keep me informed. Let me know of any progress.'

Baros, bored, buttoned up his jacket. 'I got the lieutenant giving me grief on this. I need concrete evidence from the medical examiner's office, not hypotheticals. It would help if Perez was focusing on the job.'

'Sounds like she's doing all the work.'

Baros's lip curled. 'Thank you, doc. I see the other side of things. She's got a bee in her bonnet about Stella King. Remember her?'

'The sex worker who died at Franklin Mall. Why's she relooking at that?'

'Guess.'

'Oh.' Erin resisted the temptation to laugh. *Good for you, Carla*, thought Erin. *Give them a kick up the arse for a change.*

'Perez spent time in vice. She's all sympathy when it comes to the girls. Plus Dallas, the union rep, has been giving us hell. Wants the lighting improved in the underpass since Tiffany died.'

'Is that your jurisdiction?'

'Of course not, but we have regular meetings with the union and we're the ones Dallas thinks can get things moving.'

'And what's all this got to do with Perez?'

Baros shrugged. 'As I said, she's got a bleeding heart when it comes to the girls. She thinks we might have missed something first time round.'

'And what do you think?'

Baros zipped up his jacket. 'I think your friend Carla needs to stay in her lane. Leave policing to the professionals.'

21

The first weeks of term passed in a blur for Carla. She had a sense she'd put the cat among the pigeons but wasn't holding her breath anything would actually happen. She tried to concentrate on life away from death and decay, but the weather wasn't helping. The leaves on the trees yellowed and, by the end of the month, had begun to drop onto the sidewalk, picked up every morning by collectors. Carla appreciated their efficiency but missed the sludge of leaves on her walk to college in Oxford. Autumn had been Dan's favourite season too. New terms meant new beginnings for both of them. The timetable at Jericho was teaching heavy. Research was encouraged in holidays or sabbaticals only. Carla got to know her students and whose classes they preferred. Jack Caron remained a favourite, Albert was respected and his classes well attended. Max appeared less well-liked, and a few students complained he marked essays harshly.

One Friday morning, she had a class titled 'The Criminal Corpse'. It was oversubscribed and Carla was surprised to find that the students attending had been selected by a ballot. It wasn't a process she'd had anything to do with and she wondered how the selection had taken place. The lack of transparency put her teeth on edge and she was determined to bring it up with Albert whenever she had her review. She began her course with folk beliefs associated with bodies of criminals, fictionalised retellings of hangings in literature and the magical powers associated with the corpse. Here, Carla was in her element as the dissection of emotion was what she loved. How simple it would be if the ancient belief that dead corpses would bleed in the presence of a killer were actually true.

The call out to Tiffany Stoker's body had given her a fresh insight into how much people were invested in hunting down the criminals in their own community. She noticed her class was mainly women, which was unusual. The other modules had a more even mix of genders and she didn't for a minute think men weren't interested in the subject. Once more, she was pretty sure the ballot hadn't been a fair one – had the male students been selected for more mainstream courses?

The death of Tiffany Stoker remained a shadow hanging over her. Details emerged in the local newspaper as the investigation, as far as she could see, creaked on. At thirty-four, Tiffany had not settled at any job, working in bars, hotels and restaurants to make a meagre living. She had parents in Chicago who had come to claim her remains and had offered no motive as to why Tiffany had reached such a tragic end. If she had a boyfriend, it was news to them. Carla heard nothing from the detectives and she hadn't the courage to contact Viv again. Albert's cheese and wine party was scheduled for that evening and she was glad it was now a few weeks into term. She was able to put names to faces and was beginning to get a grip on the bewildering bureaucracies of Jericho College.

–

Just as well I don't suffer from agoraphobia, she thought as she shoved her way through the throng of people inside

Albert's office. It was at least four times the size of her own room, which was cavernous now Lauren's stuff had been cleared. About thirty people stood in huddles, chatting while balancing plates of cheese and crackers and wine in old-fashioned balloon glasses. The room smelled of wood polish, stilton and expensive perfume. She spotted Albert on the far side of the room talking to two male colleagues, his manner expansive as he held their attention. A table near the window was laden with European cheeses, the sort of stuff she could have picked up in a supermarket back home but probably cost a fortune here. She put a piece of brie on a cracker and felt a tap on her shoulder. Max handed her a glass of red.

'I thought I'd bring you a glass. You're not a teetotaller, I take it.'

'Certainly not,' she said, taking the wine from him. He led her by the elbow to a corner of the room. 'Want me to point people out? I'll introduce you to anyone who sounds interesting.'

Carla wanted to shrug off his grasp, which was a little too proprietorial for her liking. Although she was new to Jericho, she was perfectly capable of sliding into a conversation in a social situation such as this.

'I'm fine, I promise. I do this sort of thing all the time.'

Before Max could answer, she walked away, her escape hindered by a huddle of men in tweed jackets who refused to budge as she squeezed past. She spotted Jack in the corner talking to an overdressed woman in silver heels. He waved her over and she pushed her way through the body of people.

'Carla. Just the person I wanted to see. I wanted to introduce you to my wife, Anna, who's a confirmed Anglophile. She spent a year at Cambridge and loved it.'

Anna was a tall blonde who wouldn't have looked out of place in a Hitchcock film. She looked Carla up and down, an assessing glance. Carla had dug out the only cocktail dress she'd thought to pack. It was black velvet, probably a bit dated, but its bias cut suited her petite frame. Anna was wearing a long silver evening gown which should have looked ridiculous amongst the books and papers, but she carried it off effortlessly. They made for an attractive couple, thought Carla.

She waited for either of them to make conversation, but they looked at her, clearly waiting for her to take the initiative.

'Which college were you at?' Carla asked, glancing at Jack.

'Girton. I'd go back there in a shot if I could. I absolutely adored the city and its buildings.'

'You're an academic?'

Anna gave a laugh. 'Me? I don't think there's room for two academics in a marriage, is there? It's like two writers living together. They'd drive each other mad.'

Carla shrugged, thinking of Dan and how they'd supported each other in their careers even when Dan had begun to sicken. She glanced again at Jack, who was watching her reaction. The pair radiated tension, as if they'd recently finished a row. She shrugged. 'It depends on the dynamics of the relationship, doesn't it? Do you have children?'

She saw Anna's face fall and realised it was the wrong thing to ask. She could have kicked herself for being so crass – she hated being asked the question and yet she hadn't been able to help herself, her curiosity about the marriage of these two overriding her usual sensitivity. She was saved by Albert, who descended on them, drink in hand. 'Ah, you've met the lovely Anna. A fine historian, but I fear we've lost her to the delights of Jericho's social circle. Seen Franklin recently?'

That name again. Anna smiled and fiddled with her bracelet. 'James is very busy as you can imagine, but Jack and I see him occasionally.'

Carla saw Jack frown as if he wasn't much pleased being associated with James Franklin. 'Is he a benefactor to the university?' she asked.

'He's a benefactor to the whole town,' said Albert. 'His family has been here a generation longer than mine and he never lets me forget it.'

There was no edge to Albert's words, another man happy with his place in the world. They were joined by Viv, who was wearing jeans with a spangly top. Viv made a few remarks to Anna and then pulled Carla to one side.

'How are you getting on?'

Carla wasn't sure if she was asking about police business. 'I'm great, thanks. I hadn't realised there would be so many people here.'

'It's department staff plus partners. It gets a bit hot in here as the evening progresses, but it's a chance for everyone to get together now the semester is in full swing. You said you'd met Zoe, didn't you?'

Carla glanced at the girl standing next to her mother. Away from the bar, she looked younger in her jeans and sneakers. 'Of course. We met at Morrell's.'

'Having a drink with Max.' The girl winked at her mother. 'Another college romance, maybe.'

Carla shook her head, embarrassed. 'Not likely. It was purely a get to know you chat.'

'Good idea,' said Viv. 'Don't mix work with pleasure. Zoe, go get me a glass of water. This red wine is giving me a headache. Check your brother's okay too.'

In the distance, Carla could see a dark-haired teenager with buds in his ears staring into his phone. Viv followed Carla's gaze and shrugged. 'No chance of a babysitter for Liam. He's fine.'

'I'd been wondering whether to call you to see if you had any updates on Tiffany Stoker.'

Viv made a face. 'It's slow going. The guests have now definitely been ruled out. The Lake House is a place for couples. It's not a business hotel for single men. If she had a paramour, he's not stayed at the hotel.'

'And might be still in Jericho.'

Viv gave her a sharp glance. 'I really hope that isn't the case.'

Carla swallowed. 'I don't want you to think I was interfering with your case. It's just I'm now in the office that Doctor Powers used. It's hard not to think about her work on the Madison Knowles case.'

Viv's eyes roamed around the room. 'I'm wondering if it's a good idea to call in experts from Albert's department. No offence to any of you, but I usually only need some initial thoughts on the crime scene. The wider picture – patterns, trends – need to be left to my team. It's number crunching and anything we find needs to get past the DA's office to ensure it ultimately stands up in court.'

'And Lauren found nothing at all after studying Madison's room?'

'Room, house, street. It was the first time I'd asked Albert to suggest one of his colleagues. The dorm house wasn't the most accessible on the street. It had locks on all the windows and the girls made sure to bolt the basement door every evening. Not everyone does that.'

'You think Madison was targeted?'

'I don't think so.' Viv checked no one was in hearing distance. 'The thing is, before the killer entered Madison's room, another of the girls said she heard the handle of her own room turn, but she'd locked the door. It suggests the killer tried her first and, after not having any luck, moved on. He was out for blood and any of the college students would have served the purpose. The other girl had a lucky escape.'

'Do you think the house was significant? I mean location is something I'm fascinated by and I wonder if the house was targeted in any way, perhaps because of its poor security.'

'That's what we thought, which is why we brought in Lauren. Her expertise is in early settlements in New Mexico and Arizona. A long way from here, but Albert thought, of all his staff, she was the once most connected to the sense of place.'

'And could she come up with anything?'

'Nada. Although...'

'What?'

'After Lauren died, we discovered she'd been back to the house twice to have a look around. The owner lives next door and as it was the end of term and some of the girls had already left, she was happy to give the keys to Lauren.'

'You've no idea why she went?'

'None at all.'

'You think I could take a look too?'

Viv froze. 'Sticking with the witch bottle theory? You know, I took another look at the crime scenes of my unsolveds after you left the other day. I like to think I'm always up for a decent idea.'

'See anything?'

'Nothing to see as far as Jessica Sherwood. Just a usual suburban house without any evidence of disarray. Stella King's crime scene had even less to excite me. Just a bare parking lot. Madison's photos are a harder look, but I saw nothing significant.'

'Do you think I could examine those photos? It's nothing personal, but I know what I'm looking for. Whoever left the items around Tiffany's body is interested in ritual protection. It's not my area of expertise, but I should be able to spot items traditionally found in these bottles.'

Carla thought Viv was going to turn her down. She picked up her glass and glanced towards the drinks table. 'Why not. If you can give me any clues over Madison Knowles, I'll be grateful. Her parents are devastated. It's affected the mother pretty badly. Ever heard the story of the lost child of Wachusett?'

Carla shook her head.

'It's an old New England story. Maybe I'm not the best person to tell you. Let's just say Madison's death has hit her mother hard. The scene was terrible, Madison fought for her life. However, if you're happy to put up with the gore, I'll ask the team to get the photos out for you. Just stop by the station when you have a chance.'

'You couldn't send them to me?'

Viv gave her a look. 'That's not how it works. I've enough problems with officers sharing stuff on their phones. I'm not having anything leave the building if I can help it. I'll ask Detectives Baros and Perez to get the files out for you.'

They both turned as Albert came over to join them.

'Like the wine?'

'Lovely,' said Carla, who'd hardly taken a sip. 'Just catching up on a few things with Viv here. She was telling me about the lost child of Wachusett.'

Albert smiled. 'A story that would be right up your street, Carla. Lingering emotions and popular imagination. I still feel guilty about sending you to Silent Brook though. Sure you're all right?'

'Fine.'

Albert looked down at his wife, who gave him a bright smile. There were some things, Carla realised, that the couple didn't share. Fair enough. She hadn't told Dan everything either.

She felt Viv's eyes on her. While Albert's back was turned, she leaned in. 'Want me to make that call tomorrow? Go via the station to see the photos and then on to Penn Street. You need to see the carnage that took place in that room and then visit the home. If you find anything, call me.'

22

Saturday at the precinct was noticeably quieter than when Carla had previously visited. She guessed detectives took the weekend off as in any regular job, with just a core team keeping things ticking over. One of the detectives on duty was Amy Perez. She was dressed in a blue trouser suit with a cotton shirt that was slightly too short in the body which she kept pulling down. Without her partner, she was less hostile, although she didn't look like she wanted to let go of the clutch of files she was holding.

'Lieutenant says you want to look at some photos. Hope you've a strong stomach. Here you go: Madison Knowles, Jessica Sherwood and Stella King. Maybe you want to leave Ms Knowles to the last.' She handed over three pink folders.

'Pink files because they're women?' asked Carla.

'Pink files for homicides. Male or female, you get a pink folder.'

Feeling foolish, Carla nodded. 'Thank you. Is there anywhere I can get some coffee?'

'There's a machine on the first floor. You can sit at that table over there. I need your mobile.'

'Excuse me?'

'No photos are to leave this building and that includes any you take yourself. The boss asked me to remove your mobile.'

With a sigh, Carla switched off her phone and handed it to Perez, who nodded. 'I'll be back in exactly one hour. You're welcome to take notes.' Perez stalked off, leaving Carla to take the files to the small office set aside for her.

She began with Jessica Sherwood, the retired teacher killed in her living room while her dog roamed outside. Carla had been anxious about looking at the images and had slept badly. To steady herself for the morning ahead, she'd needed to take some painkillers with a decent cup of coffee brewed by Patricia. Jessica's photos, however, had nothing in them to give Carla nightmares. Jessica died in her living room that she'd also used for her quilting work. Perhaps she'd liked to work in front of the open fire. She could well believe that police attending the scene thought Jessica had dropped down dead from a heart attack. A few weeks after Dan's death, Carla had fainted after a week of erratic eating and not enough sleep. She had come to on the floor of her sitting room, staring at the stain in the ceiling caused by a water leak from the flat above. Jessica lay in a similar position and there was an absence of violence at the scene. If Jessica had struggled, there should be signs of a disturbance, but she simply looked as if she'd fallen to the ground. There were no signs of staging when it came to the body.

Carla's gaze cast around the living room. It was neat as a pin with evidence of the woman's quilt-making skills on show. There was a bottle of red wine on the table with a glass next to it, suggesting Jessica had drunk a small glass of wine while she'd sewed. That was a little unusual. People, in Carla's experience, didn't sew and drink red wine. Quilt making was a long job and the fabric needed to be kept as clean as possible. A spill of red wine would be difficult to remove and heart-breaking to a dedicated sewer.

In the overstuffed room, sewing tools were piled onto one table and various mismatched ornaments crowded the mantelpiece. The fireplace had once been the focus of ritual house protection, representing a gap, like the door and window frame, where spirits could enter the house. Carla squinted at the ornaments but found nothing to suggest there was anything but a jumble of heirlooms and cheap knick-knacks. On the cream carpet, a spool of thread lay where it had fallen, possibly from when the woman had dropped to the ground. It had untangled a little and the end lay in a gathered mess. Another unwelcome splash of red.

Carla leant back in her chair and considered what she'd seen. Pins and nails were often found in witch bottles. The idea had been that urine would lure an evil spirit into the bottle, where it would become entrapped on the point of the pin. Carla wondered if red wine might suit the same purpose. Wine representing urine, needles and pins instead of iron nails. God, she was probably clutching at straws but, still, the crime scene chilled her. The innocuous setting alongside the devilish crime suggested a warped mind and emotions allowed to run unfettered by notions of natural justice or kindness. And, for her, that was a link to Tiffany Stoker's death scene. Something evil at play.

The file bearing the name of Stella King was the slimmest. The photos were time stamped and began with a wide-angled view of the scene. The car park lots were at angles to each other, creating a fishbone pattern. The weird whiteness of the images indicated the photos had been taken at night with spotlights on the asphalt. Stella King was lying in one of the bays on her side and Carla flicked to a close-up of the body, wincing when she saw the image of the girl's face. Dallas had been sure that Stella had been killed using a scarf; perhaps using your bare hands ran the risk of leaving a finger or thumb print on the skin. This was another strangulation – a link possibly to Jessica Sherwood – but this body had been dumped in the open air and Carla thought the detectives were right to have assumed the body had been rolled out of a vehicle. There was a disjointedness to Stella's repose. She was not lying where she had fallen but from where she had been thrown from the vehicle. Bastard.

Carla scanned the scene but saw no coins, needles or other objects that could be construed as witch bottle material. Carla rubbed her aching head. She had expected Stella to have been desecrated given the job she worked. Misogyny was usually articulated through acts of violence intended to shame and destroy, but here the strangling looked more like an execution. At least the girl's death would have been swift and relatively painless, unlike that of the burnt woman. Shit, no wonder the detectives weren't taking her seriously. The crimes were completely dissimilar.

Carla put down the file and went in search of Perez, who was making a show of typing fast as she stared at the screen.

'Can I trouble you for a moment?'

Perez sighed and lifted her hands from the keyboard. 'What is it?'

'Are you able to give me a list of the items found on Stella King's body?'

Perez shook her head. 'Wasn't given permission to hand that over.'

Carla looked at her watch. It wasn't even ten a.m. 'I can call the lieutenant if that will make things easier. Is it particularly sensitive information?'

'No.' Perez exhaled. She found the file quickly, far more readily than Carla had expected. 'Got a pen?'

'Um. Yes.'

'OK. Around two hundred dollars in cash, lipstick, tissues, hand gel, condoms, a horseshoe charm.'

'A charm?'

'You know, one of those nickel and dime keepsakes you can pick up at a beachfront store.'

'And it belonged to Stella?'

Perez rolled her eyes. 'It was in her purse.'

Carla put a large circle around the item. 'Is that it? Anything else that might be worth noting?'

Perez shrugged. 'She was wearing shoes two sizes too small. She'd had to jam her feet into them.'

'Why would she do that?'

'Maybe she borrowed them from another girl. Liked the colour – they were glittery silver – and didn't care they didn't fit.'

Shoes again. Carla nodded her thanks and went back to her office, conscience of Perez's eyes boring into her back. It struck her that while there were plenty of instances when fetishist killers removed mementoes from their victims, here was someone who was possibly adding items to the scene, although how she could prove the horseshoe charm didn't belong to Stella would be difficult.

Carla steeled herself to open the file of Madison Knowles. She'd expected a sea of red – Viv had been at pains to emphasise the gore of the room in the sorority house. However, the first photo was of a typical student room, its walls painted a fern green and covered in art posters. There was a table against the window that Madison had used as both a desk and dressing table. College papers fought for space with make-up and hairspray. It was the model of countless student rooms around the country. It was the second photo that revealed it as a space of two halves. The bed was opposite the window and the body lying on it unrecognisable.

As she'd done with the burnt woman, Carla gave the cadaver a quick glance, reflecting that in all her years of site excavation, she'd never seen anything so terrible. People's lives left behind traces and it was for her to fill in the gaps by studying the scant evidence she was able to unearth. Here forensics must have been overwhelmed by the amount of material they had to sift through. It reinforced her belief that she was no expert in modern death and any secrets to be yielded up by a body was Erin's territory, not hers. Complete desecration of a human. Carla sat back and closed her eyes, trying to put herself in the shoes of a killer. This is what she'd expect from the killer of a sex worker. It felt like there was a moral aspect the murderer was trying to convey. But poor Madison was a student with her life in front of her and, given the killer had already tried the door of another student, possibly not even the original intended victim. Viv said she had fought back. Carla could envisage how that might incense a killer, but to this extent?

The room, however, was where she was looking for clues. The spatter, as Viv had warned, was up the headboard and onto the wall behind and to the right of the single bed. There was a pine bedside table, a simple twodrawer unit with a single lamp and a book. Nothing else. Madison's rucksack was on a chair nearby and the contents had been photographed. Hairbrush, wallet,

EpiPen, lipstick, a scarf. Try as hard as she might like, Carla could make no connection to witch bottles.

She picked up the files and took them over to the detective.

'Had your fill?' asked Perez, not taking her eyes from the screen.

'How do you cope? I mean, attending a scene like that. I haven't been able to get the woman from Silent Brook out of my head and now this. It must have been horrendous having to look down at the body of Madison Knowles.'

Perez stopped typing but continued to stare at the screen. 'You disengage. You'd never do your job otherwise. By the time we got to Madison Knowles's room, the help she needed from us wasn't sympathy but our forensic skills in trying to find her killer. Letting our emotions get in the way won't help us achieve that.'

'I can understand that.'

Perez swivelled in her seat. 'Find anything?'

Carla shrugged. 'I'm not sure.'

She thought she detected a glimmer of sympathy in the detective's eyes.

'Try me.'

'It strikes me that there's no obvious connection between the victims except that they're all women.'

'We have male homicides too occasionally.'

'Any unsolved?'

'Nope.'

'OK, so we have four unsolved murder cases involving females over the last four years.'

'Correct. But, as you say, different ages, economic status. Jessica Sherwood never left Jericho and was comfortably off, Stella King had been here a matter of days and lived hand to mouth. She had no savings whatsoever.'

'I'm wondering if the women aren't the focus at all.'

'We've considered that. We brought in your colleague to help us when it was clear the killer had tried the room of another student before he hit on Madison's.'

'I know. Did she tell you anything?'

Perez shrugged. 'Not to us. For what it's worth, I think you're right about location being important for Madison. I'm not so sure about the others. If there's a link, we've not found it. The lieutenant said you thought witch bottles might be a pattern for Tiffany. We've a couple of satanists in Jericho, but they're law abiding. One runs the local organic cafe. Viv got Baros to pay him a visit.'

'How did that go?'

'He's written a letter to the Mayor complaining of police harassment.'

Carla winced. 'Sounds like I'm in trouble.'

'Don't stress yourself. The main thing is he's been eliminated as a suspect. The lieutenant said you wanted to visit Madison's house.'

'Is that OK? I'd like to have a look at the scene myself. I'm wondering if I can find a connection in the setting.'

Perez reached for the phone. 'The killing was nearly two years ago. The room's been cleaned and rented to one, possibly more, students. New locks would have been fitted. What's the point?'

The point, thought Carla, *is that I don't have anything else to do on a rainy day in Jericho.*

'I'd just like to take a look at the site.'

23

The houses on Wildmarsh Street were similar in architecture to Hoyt Lane. The place, nevertheless, had a more hip vibe, the cars parked – VW beetles and battered pickups – along with bicycles hooked onto gates and drainpipes, clearly shouting student. Beta Rho Sigma was an old sorority dating back to the Thirties. It rented some of the best houses in the district and must have employed a contractor to take care of the neat garden wrapping itself around the plot. On either side, two private residences squeezed up against the lawn. Space, it seemed, had always been at a premium here. The house where the murder occurred was set back from the road. A newer building, apparently also rented by the sorority, stood in what once must have been the house's garden. To approach the scene of the murder, the killer must have walked in the dark down a passageway passing the newer home.

As a sorority house, there would have been other students going in and out of the building, but police had still pinned the crime on an out of towner. Carla agreed with the detectives' theory that the house had been directly targeted. College girls held an unhealthy attraction to predators and if it wasn't for the building in the old front garden, Carla would have gone for a random attack on a student house. However, the more accessible building would equally have served the killer's needs. He had risked drawing attention to himself by making for the harder to reach house, although his reasons for doing so were unclear.

A girl sporting two braids answered the door with an air of anticipation. She was wearing a furry gilet along with sliders which Carla had an idea cost a fortune.

'Come in. This is very exciting.'

Not if you'd seen the photos, thought Carla, but the girl was just out of high school so deserved a little latitude.

The new tenants had been in residence only a few weeks and there was still an air of transience about the place. There was a rota tacked by the front door with trash duties for each student and a reminder that everyone washed up their own dishes. The tang of fresh paint was just discernible, as the place was probably given a fresh makeover at the end of each academic year. When her mobile rang, the student made her excuses and went out, leaving Carla with a dark-haired girl in oversized jeans and a cropped top who'd come into the vestibule.

'The detective who called said you worked at the university.'

'I'm in the archaeology department.'

'Cool. I'm Kaitlyn – I'm majoring in American Literature. It's my room where the girl died unfortunately. Do you want to follow me down to the basement?'

Carla passed a communal living room, small kitchen and a bedroom on the ground floor. The other bedrooms along with a bathroom and a small laundry space were down a steep set of stairs.

'How do you feel about sleeping in the basement, especially given what happened in your room?'

'I'm fine with it. They've massively increased security since the murder. We can shutter the windows, double bolt the doors. I feel pretty safe.'

Kaitlyn had only partially unpacked and clothes were strewn across the bed. From a quick glance, Carla saw the room bore no resemblance to the photos she'd recently seen. All the furniture had been changed and the walls had been painted a dark cream. Kaitlyn continued to chatter at her side.

'We knew all about the killing, of course. Rooms are in short supply, so we were lucky to get a place and none of us are really spooked about it. There was no trouble at all last year.'

Carla nodded, trying to hide her disappointment at the altered appearance of the room. 'I'll take a look outside if that's OK.'

As she passed, her eyes were drawn to the window where three dark marks had been seared into the old pine on one side of the frame.

'What's this?'

Kaitlyn moved forward. 'They look like burn marks. A candle must have been put on the sill. You can see the shape of the flame.'

These were the jottings Lauren had made into her final notebook; they were flames that she had been trying to decipher. Carla could only guess what notes she'd made at the time of Madison's death, but these marks had continued to gnaw away at Lauren. She had been doodling them as she noted down the three numbers and circled Baros's name.

'Can I take a photo?'

'Sure. They're only candle marks.'

But not where a candle would have stood. Someone, with a taper in their hand, had held the flame against the wood and a long-buried memory was stirring. Carla was itching to get on the internet and check out the marks but, job done, Kaitlyn was hurrying her from the house.

There was a huge ash tree in the garden with a seat surrounding its trunk. Carla sat down, feeling the damp seep into her jeans. The rustling of the leaves overhead should have been soothing, but Carla's eyes were focused on the surroundings. A killer had visited here with death on his mind and it was possible there was a link with Tiffany Stoker's death. Scorch marks had been used as house protection and if the killer was responsible for the marks, it suggested once again the use of ritual to ward off evil. Even if this was the case, however, it didn't explain why this house had been chosen. Grass, the ash and a picket fence. It presented to the world an ordinary Jericho home.

Giving up, Carla picked up her bag and went back to the car. The place made her jittery and she couldn't shake off that she was plunging herself into danger. She wondered who else Viv had told about her witch bottle theory, Baros and Perez certainly, and possibly Albert, although she had pulled Carla away from him to discuss the case. Her danger, surely, would not come from those three. Carla was so deep in thought she didn't notice that her phone, which she'd left in the dashboard drawer, was ringing. She answered it, fumbling at the screen.

'It's Jack. Jack Caron. Anna's got a fundraising dinner tonight and it's women only. I wondered if you fancied a drink at Morrell's.'

Carla paused, confused. Was that what married men did on a Saturday night while their wives were elsewhere?

'I thought we could have a catch-up. We could do coffee if you'd prefer.'

Carla considered the empty evening lying ahead of her. There appeared to be nothing underhand in Jack's invitation, but drinks alone might be misconstrued by a casual observer, especially in a bar as busy as Morrell's. 'How about dinner instead?'

24

Madison Knowles had been the only one to fight back. It had surprised him as he was good at picking out the passive and the vulnerable. The strength of a girl fighting for her life had shocked him, but he'd had no choice but to take potluck when it came to his choice of victim. He had considered changing focus to the more accessible front building. It would have been easier to stake out, but a design is a design, and it was not his choice to make.

The first door he'd tried had been locked. Lucky girl. He'd moved on down the dark passage, feeling his way by spreading his gloved fingertips on the walls either side of him. He saw light seeping under the door from the next room on the left, which wasn't a good sign. Surprise was his ally, and it suggested the occupant of that room was awake and alert. He moved on, his sneakers noiseless on the carpeted floor. The room at the end of the passage was in darkness, although he could hear the faint sound of music playing. The girl was either listening to the radio or had dropped off to sleep and left it on.

He was running out of options, so he took his chance. He pushed open the door and entered the darkness.

'Who's there?' The girl's voice was groggy. She *had* been asleep, but a primaeval sense of danger had caused her to wake up. He crossed to her and put his hand over her mouth, and she bit him. The shock had stirred a base passion in him too and he slapped her, keeping his hand over her mouth. She'd fought him; he'd give her credit for her resilience. He'd had to use the knife he'd carried with him since the beginning; a reserve in case things didn't go to plan. There had been mess and stink, which wasn't his thing at all.

When it was over, he'd turned his back on the girl he later knew to be called Madison Knowles. He'd looked for a candle and found one. What was it with students and scented candles? Lighting the flame, he'd held it up against the frame of the window and made his scorch marks. He'd been shocked at how long it took, and he'd been forced to remain at the scene longer than he'd have liked. The singeing had brought to mind earlier burnings within the home. Fire had been one of the few protective elements available to settlers and they had embraced it with a fervour which was now lost.

The killing on that hot June night had taught him a valuable lesson. He didn't like to improvise, and he didn't like blood. He'd made sure for the next deaths that he had a syringe filled with his drug of choice. In the end, he hadn't had to use it until he'd entered that house on Penn Street, but Jessica Sherwood had been almost dead anyway.

Standing at his own window, he touched the frame, feeling the ridges of the scorch marks. For the first time since he began, he sensed danger and wondered about its origin.

25

'To be honest, I thought Anna had upset you at Albert's party. She was a little spiky that evening.'

Carla waved away Jack's apology. He'd suggested a downtown French restaurant on the opposite side of the river to where Lauren had entered the water. In the distance, through the window, she could see the spire of St Luke's illuminated in the night sky. The street had a row of eateries, all of which appeared to be doing a decent trade. Inside the French bistro, Jack took a moment to look round at the diners. Perhaps he was checking to see if there was anyone he recognised. Satisfied, he guided her to a table in the middle of the room.

'What did you think of the party? We only had time for a brief chat and then I lost you. I saw you chatting to Viv Kantz, who's usually good value. Did you manage to speak to anyone else in the department?'

'I met a few colleagues, but I'm afraid I used the chance to catch up with the lieutenant as I'd been called to help the police. I don't know if you heard about it.'

Jack smirked. 'I heard about it from Max. I'm afraid his nose was a little out of joint.'

'He was trying very hard to hide his pique when I told him I'd been down to Silent Brook.'

Jack again cast his gaze around the restaurant. 'Find anything interesting?'

Carla regarded him. He radiated a certain amount of satisfaction at Max's resentment, but she also got the impression he was fishing for information.

'It was a terrible scene and I'm afraid I wasn't much help.' She watched his reaction. 'I don't know why I was asked. Viv Kantz comes across as very competent and I was dealing with a recent crime. I've come across the occasional old crimes in digs, but my skills aren't transferable. Have you helped Viv at all?'

'Haven't been asked.' Jack shrugged and pointed at a blackboard. 'If you like Moules Frites, I'd recommend them.'

'Suits me.'

Jack ordered a bottle of white wine and leant back in his chair. 'Despite what Max says we've only been called in a handful of times and I'm pretty sure this is only the second murder. Lauren was called into the scene of that freshman.'

'Madison Knowles.'

'Right. I heard about it when I came for my interview and it felt, you know, cutting edge being allowed in on an investigation.'

'But she didn't discover anything, did she?'

Jack shrugged, pouring them both a glass of wine before picking up his own. 'Maybe not.'

'You mean she did?'

'Not at the beginning, I believe. I never actually asked her about it once I'd started the job, but she seemed to rekindle her interest earlier this year.'

'What makes you say that?'

'I asked her one day where she was going, and she mentioned the sorority house. This was a long time after the killing, so I wondered what she was up to. I suppose it helped her take her mind off things.'

'What things?'

Jack frowned. 'You heard she ended her life, right?'

'I heard.'

'Well, she was having a difficult time in her personal life. She'd been seeing someone, and he finished it. I think she'd fallen for him hard.'

'Someone in college?'

'I doubt it. It's hard to keep anything secret in Jericho, although I might be wrong.'

She remembered Max's distress at her office still filled with Lauren's things. Hard, but not impossible.

'You know,' Carla frowned, 'relationships end all the time. Presumably this wasn't the first time Lauren had been dumped. Why the extreme reaction?'

Jack shrugged. 'I don't know. When you put it like that, it does sound odd, but every relationship is different. It might have been emotionally abusive, perhaps she had more expectations of this man than previous partners. I don't know, but she went from being dynamic and involved to a shadow of her former self towards the end of her life.'

Carla let out a stream of air. 'Why am I getting the impression that I'm only seeing the surface of what's going on in Jericho?'

Jack frowned. 'There is only surface in Jericho. That's the point. Funnily enough, you remind me a little of Lauren.'

'I do? In what way?'

'I got the impression she wasn't much impressed by Jericho either.'

Carla laughed, pleased. 'Where was she originally from?'

'Phoenix, which is a little different from here.'

'I saw lots of photos of the desert.'

'That was her specialism. Archaeology of New Mexico and Arizona. Her classes were popular because she used to organise summer digs in the west. I personally can't think of anywhere worse than the desert in summer but, as I say, it was popular.'

Carla thought how different the wide Arizona landscape would be to the refined society of Jericho. For different reasons, Lauren would have felt an outsider like Carla. Unlike her, however, she was lacking the survival instinct. Because she'd taken a night swim with stones in her pocket and Carla would never contemplate that, and not just because Dan had taken the same route. There was a flicker of hope in Carla that refused to extinguish itself however bad things got. She looked over at Jack. His French heritage was evident in his dark brown hair. She'd have liked to quiz him about his background, but this was a semi-professional dinner. Asking about his ancestry suggested an intimacy she didn't want to push.

The waiter brought two bowls of mussels, the salty steam filling the air. Carla realised how hungry she was and picked up her fork. 'Will Anna be late?'

Jack shrugged. 'Doubt it. She knew I was inviting you out for a drink, just in case you think this is a little strange. I think she was a little embarrassed how she spoke to you the other day. Jericho is a small town.'

And she sent you to make amends, thought Carla. 'What made you get into New England settlements, given you're from Montreal?'

He gave her an amused glance. 'The city's only two hundred miles away but, anyway, my mother's from Portland. I used to love visiting here. It's got a sense of hidden history that I adore.'

Carla remembered Viv's comment at the cheese and wine party. 'Do you know the story of the lost child of Wachusett?'

'Of course. A child, Lucy Keyes, went missing in the woods near the settlement of Wachusett. The parents went looking for her, but she was never found, and it sent the mother mad. She could be heard calling out the name Lucy for decades after. Why do you ask?'

'Viv Kantz mentioned her in relation to the parents of Madison Knowles.'

'Oh, that's sad.'

'You know,' Carla kept her tone neutral, 'another piece of New England lore I was thinking about was witch bottles. Do you know about them?'

'Sure. The tradition was brought over from England and there have been quite a few discoveries in old settlements. It's part of this region's history.'

'Right.' Carla frowned, taking a sip of her wine. 'So if, say, someone was wanting to repel evil spirits, what else might you find? Wasn't there something about graffiti?'

'Sure – there's the letter V inverted twice to make an M representing the virgin mother. Or people might immure a cat in a wall. There are examples of mummified animals found by buildings. Then doll charms – often with curses attached. To be honest, I could go on about this all evening. Is there a reason why you're so interested?'

Carla put down her wine glass and shrugged. 'I'm not sure. I think it's fascinating, but what I'm interested in is the emotion behind these items of house protection.'

'Emotions? How about fear and suspicion? You're talking about an era of child mortality and crop failure. Tragedies were blamed on the devil and people looked to the objects around their house to repel evil spirits.'

'You mention suspicion. This is where communities turn on each other.'

Jack put down his fork. 'It doesn't take much. Why are you asking?'

'I saw some burn marks recently in an old house. I'm sure I remember reading about them.'

'Taper burns? They're another ritual of house protection. Reeds dipped into tallow and deliberately held against wooden linters, beams, window frames. It's the idea of fighting fire with fire. We call it sympathetic magic.'

'Why sympathetic?'

'Basically, religion didn't object as it didn't explicitly contravene their own teachings. You'll find plenty of churches with apotropaic marks. You know daisy wheels, the Marian symbol, other unending patterns.'

'Fighting fire with fire, you said.'

'Sorry, are you thinking of the woman in Silent Brook? Let's change the subject.' He took a sip of wine. 'Where exactly did you see the taper marks? I'd be interested in taking a look myself.'

Carla forced a smile. 'A private residence. I'll ask the owner if I can show you sometime.'

26

After dinner with Jack, who had helped tease out some of the subtleties that Carla had forgotten, she was convinced that the unsolved murders were linked. She often warned her students against finding patterns where there were none, but from what she had discovered from the crime scene photos and from talking to Perez, there was a strong possibility of a link based on protective charms. Stella King had died with a horseshoe charm in her purse. Cheap and tacky it might be, but it represented a keepsake to ward off spirits. Had the girl bought it herself? Possibly. But it was equally likely that her killer had slipped it into her things. Once, the charm would be made of iron, considered to be a metal with magical properties. Enclosing a cemetery with iron railings was considered to encircle the souls of the dead. If Stella was the first death, and the horseshoe nothing more than a cheap trinket, then the killer had been playing around with substitution. The ill-fitting shoes might also have a role, but Carla couldn't yet grasp the connection. Her theory must be watertight if she was going to present it to Viv and she would need to mull on the significance of the glittery pumps.

The room where Madison Knowles had died showed the taper marks that mirrored those previously discovered in seventeenth and eighteenth-century houses. They served as folk magic to scare away evil and that had satisfied householders. The detectives had either not spotted the burns or had dismissed them as scorch marks from a candle. Jessica Sherwood had pins, thread, wine, all of which might be found in a witch bottle, items not dissimilar to those scattered around Tiffany Stoker. There was a pattern, Carla was sure of it. But the nagging question, and this was much harder to answer, was why the women had been targeted. Perez had been sure Madison's killing was down to location, but Carla could see no significance in a scrubby wasteland such as Silent Brook. The only way of discovering the connection was to revisit the sites once again.

Carla found the Franklin Mall on her car's GPS. The cubist nightmare at the river had given Carla a low opinion of James Franklin's design ethos, so she was surprised to see that the mall was a two-storey circular building with an organic feel to the design. She parked near an entrance and looked around. It was difficult to tell where exactly Stella had been found, but she could see nothing in the lot that echoed with Silent Brook. It was an ordinary suburban car park filled with cars and pickups. At night it presumably looked a little different but not a place to be feared.

She looked at her watch. It was too late to go back to the office and too early to retire home and listen to Patricia's updates on the church bake. And she certainly wanted to avoid another invitation for a glass of sherry. As she felt a trickle of rain down her back, she decided she might as well take the time to shop for a new coat. Not for fieldwork. Her waxed jacket would serve her well for years to come, but something she could wear around college. As the doors swung open, Carla was momentarily disoriented. Instead of a straight row of stores, the corridor opened out like a petal and in the distance narrowed again. It made for an odd design ethic. Surely the point of a mall was that you looked at shops on both sides of you as you walked along. It's what she did certainly, but anyway, she hated shopping and was always desperate to get it over with. Here, as shops curved away from each other, she was forced to choose a side and went to her left, looking for a women's clothing store that wasn't too expensive. When she got to the end of the corridor, she realised she was in the centre of the building. She looked up and saw that the level above was a food court while the ground floor space could be used for music events and fashion shows. A woman was singing into a microphone and a crowd huddled around her, clapping out of rhythm to the tune. Carla stopped for a moment to listen to the music, her eyes taking in the other 'petals' leading from the centre. Petals?

Two hours later, she was a hundred and fifty dollars lighter and had sunk two cups of coffee in quick succession, the caffeine struggling to keep up with her adrenaline. Erin lived in a tall townhouse that shrieked New England, but its interior was sparse in contrast to Patricia's homespun decor. As Carla had suspected, there was no sign of a husband, but she did encounter a six-foot-tall teenager who made himself a peanut butter sandwich while Carla gulped at the glass of wine Erin had proffered. Erin had looked surprised to see her but had opened the door wide and pulled her inside.

'So let me get this right. You have this idea that the items left around the Silent Brook victim were a sort of deconstructed witch bottle.'

'If there is a pattern, then it would make sense. These witch bottles were handmade. You would take bits and pieces from the home and stuff them into it. Stuff that had a significance – teeth, needles, wine, feathers but also glass and coins. As we saw around the victim.'

'And what does Viv say about all this?'

'I don't think she has a problem with me suggesting there's some kind of ritual protection around the death of Tiffany Stoker, but she's not much interested in connecting the cases. As far as she's concerned, I'm a rank amateur.'

Erin snorted into her glass. 'Well, you are.'

'The main point is that I'm pretty sure I can identify similar objects around the deaths of the other three women. There is a connection, I'm sure of it.'

Erin looked unconvinced. 'If, from what you tell me, everyday objects were given magical properties, then aren't you going to find these in a house anyway? Wine, coins, thread. You'll find it here. Does that mean I'm a target?'

'Of course not.'

'Isn't there a possibility that you're seeing patterns where there are none? Use your scientific brain. Suppose a student came to you at a dig and made these assumptions. Wouldn't you ask for more evidence?'

'Of course I would, which is precisely the reason I haven't gone to Viv yet. I don't want to be laughed out of the place.'

'And what about the Franklin Mall? You have to be careful. Franklin's a big cheese round here. What's his mall got to do with any of this?'

Carla took a breath, wondering if she was sounding insane. 'The design is a really strange pattern. From the outside it's round, so what you'd expect inside would be a centre and shops radiating out from the hub.'

'Makes sense.' Erin topped up Carla's glass.

'And that's what you have to a certain extent, but these rows aren't parallel. They're shaped like this.'

Carla retrieved her notepad and drew a flower shape. 'Can you see? There are six entrances to the mall, which I guess isn't particularly unusual. When you wander up and down though, the shops sort of bow away from you and then come back together in the middle. It makes for a daisy wheel pattern.'

'Okaaay.' Erin gave the drawing on the pad a glance. 'The architect liked daisies. What's this got to do with anything?'

'Daisy wheels are often inscribed on buildings. Above doors, in attics, in cupboards. They serve a similar purpose to the witches' bottles. They're known as hexafoils or apotropaic marks. They can be quite complex, wheels within wheels, but the essence is the same. You can draw it with a compass, and it consists of a single endless line to confuse spirits and trap them within the design.'

'Neat,' said Erin. 'I might draw one above my bed. It'll be handy for repelling the next loser I bring home from a date.'

Carla smirked. 'When I was a student, I drew one in the house I was living in. I met Dan, my husband, so it must have worked.'

'But what's the connection? You got a psychopath obsessed with symbols or something?'

Carla slumped, her enthusiasm dulled by the wine and Erin's scepticism. 'I don't know, to be honest. It's just more evidence of a pattern.'

'Look. I didn't do the autopsy on Stella King, but I remember the case. She ran away from home in Boston. No one knows how she wound up in Jericho, but hitched a ride would be my guess.'

'You can take another look at the file?'

'I can look at *our* files, but that's it. I've no access to anything outside the facility and, like you, I've a heavy teaching semester, so my ability to give headspace to this is limited. You want the investigation material, you'll need to go to the police.'

'There's another thing I wanted to ask you about.' Carla dug in her bag and pulled out Lauren's notebook. 'I found this amongst Lauren's things.'

Erin raised her eyebrows and looked at the page Carla was pointing at. 'Look, there's Detective Baros's name and three numbers. Recognise them?'

Erin shrugged. 'They mean nothing to me. Why your interest?'

'Don't you think it's strange that the police officer's name is in a notebook from this year? Lauren had attended Madison Knowles's crime scene, but that was the previous year. It sounds like she was having a rethink before she died. Those flame marks are like the ones I saw in Madison Knowles's house. And, incidentally, her notebook from the period covering Madison's death is gone.'

'Ask Baros. He's a dick, sure, but he's not incompetent. He'll tell you what Lauren's conclusions were even if he gives you the update with a sneer on his face.'

'Viv called him and Perez in to ask if they had Lauren's notebook. He didn't mention anything then.'

'That's Baros's modus operandi. Reveal the bare minimum. You'll have to show him the notes and ask if they mean anything. Sorry, but he's not the first cop to answer to rule.'

Carla glanced at her watch. 'It's too late to call now. They'll think I'm an obsessive.'

Erin laughed. 'Really?'

'Lauren didn't mention anything to you?'

'I barely knew the woman. Look, let's have a breather. Do you want some food?'

Carla shook her head. 'There'll be something waiting for me at home that I can heat up. Can you do me a favour? Could you make a list of the unsolved murder cases over the past three years? The ones everyone's alluding to but don't really talk about. I know about Stella King, the burnt woman, Madison Knowles and Jessica Sherwood.'

Erin winced. 'I'm about to get my ass kicked over that one.'

'What do you mean?'

Erin reached for a letter and pulled her glasses down from the top of her head. 'Letter from my boss. That's right: a letter. Who the fuck actually writes to you these days? Wants to talk to me about my handling of Ms Sherwood.'

'Think you're in trouble?'

'Probably not. Just got to be seen showing willing. It's a strange case. Look, let's sleep on it. You've admitted you're going to need a lot more on this before going to Viv. Let's reconvene in a few days.'

27

Erin heard Ethan creep down the stairs after Carla left, his sneakers squeaking against the wooden floor. He had a habit of making himself scarce when Erin had visitors, which was fine by her but, given how little they saw of each other, left her feeling she was letting him down in some way. Mom guilt.

'Who was that?' he asked, twisting the lid off another bottle of soda.

'Can you give the caffeine a miss tonight? You'll be buzzing on that stuff.'

He ignored her, pouring a stream of liquid into a tall glass.

'Her name's Carla James. She works at the college and I'm her mentor.'

Ethan did a mock choke into his glass.

'Very funny, wise guy. She's a Brit, so I guess it's all a little overwhelming for her at the moment.'

'I heard her talking about witches.'

'Did you, elephant ears? I thought the house rules were no earwigging when we're talking work. You know what I do for a living.'

'It wasn't you doing the talking, was it?'

True, thought Erin, but Carla had needed to let off steam and Erin had been happy to let her ramble on.

'You should send her to your friend Jenny.'

'Who?' Erin's circle of friends was small and she couldn't immediately think of any Jenny.

'You know. Goth, black hair, pierced tongue?'

'Jenny?! She's not my friend; she's a colleague. She assists me in the medical room. We're not pals.'

Erin recalled Jenny and Ethan meeting when she'd had to drag him along to a work Christmas party. Her ex-husband, who lived nearby, had been on a business trip and no one had wanted to babysit Christmastime. Jenny, she recalled, had chatted to Ethan for a while and Erin had been grateful that at least one of her colleagues was willing to spend some time with her son. She'd never asked Ethan what the conversation was about.

'Are you telling me that Jenny is a witch?'

'Mom.' Ethan scowled at her. 'Did I say that? She's a pagan.'

'Oh. I. See.' Erin made a mock emphasis on each word. 'So that's completely different from a witch.'

'It is. It's... actually I don't remember how it's different. It just is.'

Erin frowned. 'I'm not sure Jenny's the right person to ask and I don't want her to think I'm intruding in her personal life. Whatever she gets up to outside work is her own business.'

She remembered she'd fought against appointing Jenny to the position of Mortuary Assistant. She hadn't liked the girl's gothic make-up and distrusted her motives for wanting to work in the facility. She didn't want any members of staff with a morbid interest in death. She'd been overruled, which was nothing new, but Jenny had proved a model assistant with a calm matter-of-fact attitude towards the cases brought in for autopsy.

'How's your dad?' she asked Ethan to change the subject.

'Fine. He's going away next week on business, so I can't go over.'

'Nice of him to tell me.'

'Mom. I said I'd tell you and I'm doing that now. It doesn't make any difference, does it? I'm fifteen. I don't need a babysitter any more.'

'All right.' She raised her hands in submission.

'You were talking about murders in Jericho, weren't you?'

'Hey! That *is* work and I'm not answering any questions.'

He ignored her. 'You were talking about murdered women, and you missed someone out from your list.'

'What do you mean, missed someone?' Erin was feeling touchy after receiving that damn letter. Now who had she forgotten?

'You talked about women who had died recently, but you never mentioned Iris Chan.'

'Iris Cha—' Erin stopped. 'Shit. You're right, I'd completely forgotten about her.'

'It had you pacing up and down your bedroom at the time. How could you forget her?'

Erin sighed and folded her arms. 'Because I had other cases to give me sleepless nights since. Shit. How could I forget Iris Chan?'

—

Iris had graduated from Jericho College, majoring in veterinary medicine, and taken a job in a bookstore over the summer. The retail industry was not the usual destination of graduates of the illustrious college and detectives later wondered if there was a man behind Iris's decision to stay in Jericho. Her family were from Maine; they owned a chain of restaurants dotted up and down the coast, but there was no expectation Iris would work there. Instead, her mother had approached family friends who owned a practice and it had been agreed that Iris would join the business in October as a junior veterinarian. By September, Iris's mother had become concerned that she wasn't making any concrete plans to leave Jericho and an argument had ensued. Again, there had been the shadow of a man in the background, but that had been the extent of it.

Iris's body was found in Shining Cliff Wood on a September evening. She had entered the wood and used her belt to hang herself from a tree near to the path used by dog walkers and tourists. It was initially ruled a suicide. A bookstore colleague said Iris had confided in her that she definitely didn't want to return to Maine. She'd also confirmed that Iris had a boyfriend but was very coy about him. Married, she'd decided, and asked no more questions.

Erin had completed the autopsy and had initially agreed with the police assessment. Woods are a common choice of setting for suicides. From the Aokigahara of Japan to the conifers of New England, the desperate are drawn to the primaeval comfort given by forest landscapes. Then the witness came forward. Iris was striking. She had long dark hair that she plaited and wrapped around her head. Old fashioned but chic. The witness had seen a woman matching Iris's description entering the woods with a male dressed in black jeans and a dark coat with a beanie hat. The witness was sure it was a male, but his description had ended with that.

Footprints had been useless near the site – Iris's body had attracted wild animals who had scuffed up the area, but Viv Kantz had widened the search area and discovered the presence of two sets of prints. Suddenly, it was a murder investigation, although the working theory was that it was a joint suicide plan where the male had decided to bail. That, at least, was the assumption. Erin had done her bit. Iris's cadaver showed no sign of physical abuse and her colleagues said she seemed happy if reticent about her boyfriend. So, it was to all intents and purposes a consensual partnership. But, thought Erin, who knows really what goes on in people's relationships? The man had never come forward.

A year later, however, a local man had confessed to the crime. That's why she hadn't thought about Iris Chan. It was case solved.

28

Monday's classes were spent in a frenzy of teaching, debate and assignment setting. The students were by and large good-humoured, but Carla began to get a sense of underlying tension. Even this early in the term, her class members were competitive and determined to do well. If anyone was struggling, they weren't admitting it to Carla, who was always on the lookout for the anxious and stressed amongst her students. She kept an eye open between classes to see if she could grab Jack for a brief consultation. She needed help to decipher the significance of Stella's shoes, which she was sure were part of the same ritual protection being harnessed by the killer. The more evidence she could find to back up her witch bottle theory, the greater her chances of getting Viv to take her seriously. Jack, however, was proving elusive and books from the college library weren't helping her to get to the heart of the matter.

Her afternoon group, she remembered, had a class with Jack before hers and she tracked down the room number and hung around as the doors opened. Unsurprisingly there was a gaggle of female students hanging around to chat with him, including Julia, who she'd be teaching in a quarter of an hour. *His groupies*, thought Carla sourly. When he caught sight of her in the doorway, he extracted himself and came over to her, not before she'd spotted a flash of displeasure on Julia's face.

'You wanted me?'

'I do, but I don't think you'll be able to answer my question in ten minutes. It's work related. Are you around later?'

'Of course. Do you want to meet in my office?'

'I'm teaching until five. Are you OK to hang about until then?'

'Not a problem. Can you give me a clue what we're going to talk about? I'd hate to disgrace myself professionally.'

'Glittery shoes and witchcraft.'

'Ah. I see. My specialism. Am I allowed to suggest *The Wizard of Oz*?' He caught a glance at her expression. 'Well, I shall get my thinking cap on and hope you'll be sufficiently impressed.'

He didn't return to the seminar room but took the opportunity to slip away back to his office. Carla looked at her watch and saw she had a few more minutes before class and needed to check something with Perez. While she had Jack's full attention later, she'd run past anything that might help the argument she was constructing. It really wasn't much different to developing an academic argument. Make sure it's well developed, backed up with examples and have an answer for any counter-arguments. The receptionist at the precinct put her through without any hesitation and Carla explained her reason for the call to Perez.

'I looked at the photos of Jessica Sherwood,' said Carla, 'but I didn't make a note of the contents of the room. I was looking for a pattern, but I think I need to focus on how individual items might link to a much wider design.

Do you think you could read out what you found in the living room so I can make a list?'

'What, every item? What do you think this is, *Property Brothers*?'

The reference was lost on Carla. Must be some kind of TV house show. 'Not the furniture. Just maybe things that might not always be there. That could be moved between rooms, for example.'

Perez sighed. 'Fine, but lucky you got me and not Baros on this one.'

That's why I called you, thought Carla, hanging on while Perez called up the list on the screen.

'OK, here goes. There was an open bottle of wine and half a glass full on the table.'

'I noticed that in the photos. Did her bloods show she'd been drinking alcohol?'

There was a pause. 'No alcohol present in the blood.'

Carla jotted down 'wine'. 'Carry on.'

'The usual living room stuff. Lamps, cushions, a rug. You can carry them between rooms, but there was no evidence they belonged anywhere else. Miss Sherwood was a quiltmaker and there was her quilting stuff in the room.'

'Can you itemise them for me?'

Perez gave a longer sigh. Very soon she'd run out of breath to increase her puffs. 'Right. Fabric, a quilt in progress, thread, needles, scissors.'

'Can I just stop you. What colour thread?'

'Red cotton in the needle, which matched the quilt.'

'You mean she prepared the quilts by hand?'

'I... I don't know. Quilting isn't my thing.'

'Me neither, but I'd assume you'd use a machine.' Carla wrote 'red thread' on her list. 'Anything else?'

'I think that's it. Got any ideas, prof?' The detective's tone was hopeful.

Carla considered her answer. She really needed an ally inside the police other than Viv, but she had to be careful how much she revealed. Perez's ultimate loyalty would be to her colleagues, not Carla. 'I'm just wondering if I can connect Jessica Sherwood's death with Tiffany Stoker's. If I can, it'll be to do with the contents of the room or something found on her person. It's early stages, so keep it to yourself.'

'What about Madison Knowles?'

'I don't know. I found some burn marks on the windowsill which might fit in with what I'm thinking about. Did you see them?'

'Candle marks according to forensics. Students are always burning things. Patchouli in the Seventies; essential oils in the Nineties. These days, candles from Macy's.'

'But they were high up on the frame.'

'Yeah, we noticed that. We thought either a tall candlestick or she'd picked it up maybe while answering a call and had held it too close to the wood.'

And Erin thinks my theory is bonkers, thought Carla. 'Is there anything else in Madison's room that might not have been in the images I looked at, something that might not have been deemed important enough to photograph.'

'You saw it all except the contents of the wastepaper basket. Want me to read them out?' Perez sounded almost eager to help.

'Sure.' Carla looked at her watch. She had precious little time until her next class.

'OK, here goes: scrunched-up paper, very little on them except for doodles.'

'Doodles?' Carla's heart leapt. 'What design were the drawings?'

'Design?'

'You said there were jottings on the paper in the basket. What were they?'

Carla expected another sigh, but there was silence.

'Did you photograph them?' asked Carla.

'Of course they were photographed. Hold on.' Carla waited, anticipation making her jumpy.

'OK. Five sheets of paper in total. Writing in blue ink was consistent with course notes. Madison was studying English Literature, so there were references to texts she was studying. We had them checked out.'

'And the doodles?'

'A load of circles with a flower in them. They were written in black ink, so Madison must have changed pens.'

Hallelujah, thought Carla. 'Were they checked out?'

'Of course. Nothing doing apparently.'

'OK. Can you tell me exactly who looked at these designs?'

Perez sighed. 'If you think it's important. You'll have to give me time to find out the name of the expert, OK?'

After her class had finished, Carla presented herself at Jack's office. He might have only been tenured for a year, but he had made himself at home in the space. Unlike Albert's higgledy-piggledy mess, Jack's room was a study in restrained academia. The scant books lining an oak bookcase were key texts he was teaching on his course but not the battered editions she'd expect from someone opening and studying the works to prepare a syllabus. Jack noticed her glance.

'Every year, Anna buys me new hardcover copies of my coursebooks. I tell her to stop, but it's become a tradition. And remember, Jericho loves tradition.'

His honesty disarmed her. 'Do you have copies that you actually read?'

He opened a drawer and brought out a thick book missing its cover. 'There you go.'

Carla laughed. 'That's more like it.'

He put his fingers to his lips. 'Don't tell anyone. They think I'm more style than substance.'

'Who's they?'

Jack wouldn't be drawn. 'Take a seat. What's all this about the shoes? I'm assuming it's something to do with the woman at Silent Brook?'

'Connected to her. If I told you a woman was wearing a pair of high-heeled shoes two sizes too small covered in silver glitter, what would that say to you in terms of house protection?'

Jack leant back in his chair, his gaze on her. 'So that's what this is about. Well, shoes can be found in a house tucked in a cupboard or the usual places you might find a witch bottle, such as behind a fireplace. They're often singular; one is enough as it holds the imprint of a person's soul, which allows the shoe to entrap evil entities. Any cache of objects hidden around the home for this purpose, we call "spiritual middens". It's an academic term, but laypeople with an interest in the subject use it too.'

'What about two shoes? Can you think of any significance at all?'

'There have been examples of pairs found under floorboards and so on, but I have to tell you I don't think I know of a single case of silver glitter.'

Carla laughed again, the conversation cheering her up. She thrived on her ideas being challenged. 'I think I deserve that. Can I ask you about specific items found within witch bottles? I mentioned them briefly at dinner the other evening. I've looked up what I'd expect to find in the bottles, urine, wine, hair, but I'm looking for more oblique references. I'm trying to tease something out.'

'I'll do my best.'

'First up is wine.'

'Wine? There's certainly evidence of that substance being found in the bottles. There's a history of wine being used to ward off evil. One method involves infusing the liquid with St John's wort seeds, snapdragon and wintergreen. People believed snapdragons protected you against curses.'

'What about wine from a bottle?'

'The symbolism is the same. A witch bottle was found in England containing wine mixed with urine.'

'Right.' Carla looked at the next item on the list. 'What about red thread?'

'Was it attached to a needle?'

'Apparently, yes.'

'Was it knotted?'

'I think so.'

'You're dealing with two things there. Knotted thread is found on witches' ladders. Do you know them?'

'Not at all.'

'It's where threads and human hair are wound around a stick. It's perfectly possible they were put in witch bottles, but I don't recall any instances. The needle, however, serves a similar purpose to nails. Cold iron is traditionally considered to repel witches and other creatures. It partially accounts for the popularity of horseshoes.'

Carla was overcome with a wave of exhaustion and sat back. So many different references but a mishmash of imagery. It was as if the killer – if her pattern theory was correct – was a magpie, happy to pick and choose whatever suited their needs.

'Carla, what's this all about?' asked Jack.

'I think Jericho's got a serial killer who's an expert on witch bottles.'

Jack froze, his expression difficult to read. 'I see. Do you think I might know this person in the course of my work?'

'I don't know. There's the sense of a personality who knows enough to use the elements individually but not in their true form. They're happy to swap an iron horseshoe for a cheap trinket, for example. I don't think we're looking for an academic.'

'Then I'd be inclined to leave it to the professionals. You put a foot wrong and any defence lawyer for whoever they catch will have a field day with your involvement. Think about it. You don't want to be messing up an investigation.'

'Viv knows of my theory.'

'Then fine, but remember your training. You can find patterns anywhere if you look closely enough. Who's to say that the thread doesn't just belong to someone's quilt-making kit?'

Carla stood and shoved her notebook into her bag. 'I appreciate your help.'

Jack looked as if he wanted to say something else but smiled. 'Sure. Have a great evening.'

Only as she was driving home did she remember that at no point had she mentioned Jessica Sherwood or her quilt-making hobby.

29

'Got anything planned this evening?' Erin kept her voice casual as she removed her face mask.

Jenny was finishing the hose-down of an autopsy table, whistling a tune from *West Side Story*. A young driver, five double vodkas under his belt, had lost control of his pickup, hit a crash barrier and gone through the windshield into a tree. His nineteen-year-old pregnant girlfriend had died in the truck. Even a seatbelt won't protect you from an eighty-miles-per-hour crash. Two senseless deaths and Erin was dog-tired after telephoning the results through to the police department. She had a meeting with the dead girl's family scheduled for the next morning.

'Just going to chill.' Jenny kept her eyes on the water swooshing down the drain at the bottom of the metal table. She was wearing black jeans and a T-shirt printed with the words 'black is my happy colour'. Other than a row of rings down one ear, her piercings were invisible today. Jenny had recently begun to dial down the goth look at work. Perhaps some of Erin's reservations had got back to her.

'Fancy a quick drink?' Erin saw, out of the corner of her eye, Jenny lift her head in surprise.

'I... I guess so. Is anything the matter?' Jenny turned off the washer and stared at her. 'I haven't done anything wrong, have I?'

'Of course not. I just wanted to ask you something about one of our victims. It won't take long.'

'Which case?'

'Tiffany Stoker, found at Silent Brook. Ethan said you were a pagan and I have a couple of questions about your beliefs.' Erin could feel herself reddening. 'It's completely off the wall and I'm a little embarrassed to ask, so feel free to say no.'

'Off the wall is fine by me.'

Jenny took her to a basement bar, with the word 'Havoc' over the door. Despite its name, the music was muted inside and, except for a couple making out in the corner, they were the only patrons. Erin ordered two bottles of Grasshopper at the bar and took them over to a booth at the back of the room where Jenny was settling herself in.

'Cheers.' They clinked bottles and took a long swig. Jenny must also be tired, but perhaps curiosity as well as a sense of obligation had encouraged her to accept Erin's invitation. Their usual discussions in the autopsy room were about work first, occasionally Jericho gossip. It was telling that it was shy Ethan who'd got to know about Jenny's belief system, not her.

Erin took another swig of beer and got to the point. 'I've a new mentee at the university, a Professor Carla James. Have I mentioned her?'

Jenny shook her head.

'She's an interesting personality and I'm quite taken with her, probably because she doesn't really need mentoring at all. She's an archaeologist with an interest in people, which is a new one to me. Don't laugh, I mean she likes to know what makes people tick. She's made a name for herself by focusing on the emotions involved in the sites she's excavated. I get the impression she likes to do her own thing.'

'Cool. You like her?'

'I do, although I think she's a little lost. She was widowed a few years ago and I get the impression she's come to Jericho for a new start – or at least that's the idea. But like most drastic moves, I think she's probably realising losing your existing network of friends and colleagues comes at a price.'

'You know what my stepmom always says about Jericho,' said Jenny. 'People who move here either stay a few months or they never leave.'

Erin had heard the saying before and it applied to her. She'd come to the town as a student and twenty years later, she was still here. 'I've got a feeling Carla wouldn't know where to go even if she did decide to move on. Home in England has a lot of bittersweet memories for her. Anyway, the reason I mention her is that she was called by Viv Kantz to the killing of the woman found at Silent Brook. She's come up with this theory though about the objects found around the woman. Know what a witch bottle is?'

'Of course I do. They're pretty neat. Why'd you ask?'

'Carla thinks that some of the items distributed around the body could be a sort of deconstructed witch bottle. The coins, the hair and so on which are usually found inside the glass have been placed in the open air. I'd never even heard of these bottles until she explained them to me.'

Jenny considered. 'It's a possibility that someone might have updated the items to the twenty-first century.

Syringes instead of needles; it's kinda neat. Does it help find her killer though?'

'I don't know, but Carla thinks she might have found a pattern with at least one other victim.'

'You're kidding.' Jenny's eyes widened. 'One of our unsolved killings?'

'Yes, thank God. I guess you'll know what a daisy wheel is too?'

'Yup. The six-petalled flower enclosed in a circle. An apotropaic mark. I went looking for them with a couple of friends one summer. There are plenty of examples around here. We found them at the top of staircases, on attic beams, scratched into floorboards.'

Erin stared at her. 'People just let you into their homes?'

Jenny snorted. 'Homeowners are proud of them. They may go to church on a Sunday, but they're happy to have a hex sign protecting the family from evil spirits inside their home. Which victim are we talking about?'

'Do you remember the killing of Stella King?'

'I remember. I think she was strangled and her body found in a car park.'

'The Franklin Mall, yes. Ever been there?'

Jenny gave her a look. 'I'm not a mall kind of girl, Erin.'

'It's designed in the pattern of a daisy wheel.'

Jenny, who had been about to take another swig of beer, pulled the bottle from her lips. 'No way.'

'According to Carla, it's designed as a daisy wheel and she's wondering if there's any connection with the burnt woman.'

'The Franklin Mall is a hexafoil? You wait till my pals hear this. We'll take a look this weekend.'

Erin gripped the girl's arm. She was whippet thin but strong. 'Look, can you keep it quiet for the moment? Don't even mention it to your friends. Carla's got the bit between her teeth and, if she's right, we might be looking at someone who has killed more than once.'

'A serial?'

'It's possible, isn't it? They happen in other towns, so why not ours? I need a bit more info though to see if I can help Carla. Ethan tells me you're a pagan, not a witch. What's the difference?'

'Well...' Jenny paused. 'This is strictly out of work, right? Nothing I do impacts on what happens in the medical examiner's facility?'

'Of course.'

'Well, paganism is used by some as a catch-all phrase to basically mean non-Christian. They'd include witches, practitioners of Wicca, Norse pagans, devil worshipers, that sort of thing. For me, paganism is the worship of nature and the earth. I'm not interested in anything weird.'

'Do people still practise witchcraft now?'

Jenny shrugged. 'I guess so. In fact, I'm pretty sure they do, but if you're thinking about a killer, it's not the witch community you want to be looking at. You're seeking someone who fears them. That was the whole point of witch bottles and daisy wheels. They were to ward off misfortune they believed witches could put on a house and its occupants.'

'Fear of women's powers perhaps. I'm wondering if there's a link to Salem and the trials.'

'Could be. Don't forget though that there was no evidence of witchcraft practice. Those women – and men by the way – were transgressive in the eyes of the patriarchy and persecuted accordingly.'

'I appreciate the women were likely innocent, but I thought there was perhaps a practice or set of beliefs they were accused of.'

'The belief in sorcery and unnatural practices can be traced back to Greek culture – a curse tablet, for example, was placed near the dead, asking them to work magic for those still living. The idea of witches wasn't invented by the Christian church.'

'But we assume the persecutors believed the women were guilty?'

Jenny shrugged. 'Why not?'

'So why might a killer adopt these old symbols of witchcraft protection?'

'Interest in ancient beliefs, hatred of women, campaign against deviancy, religious extremism. That's just for starters.'

Erin sat back and let out a long puff. 'We're looking for a killer who hates women? I get misogynists' victims on my autopsy table with depressing regularity, domestic violence being a particular favourite in the private lives of our esteemed residents. Why the hell would our killer play around with these bloody symbols? I think Carla's got a nice theory, but she's going to have to come up with a lot more than this. I appreciate your help though.'

Jenny raised her bottle. 'My pleasure.'

30

By comparing Madison Knowles's mother to the wailing woman in the legend, Viv Kantz had done her a huge disservice. It took Carla five minutes on the internet to track down the woman's name. Tammy Knowles had refused to let her daughter's death slide from the news and had become Madison's advocate. By Carla's reckoning, she had mounted a campaign of press attention, political lobbying and street activism in an attempt to bring the killer to justice. Lucy Keyes's mother, if the accounts were accurate, had been a lost figure, calling her daughter's name in the woodland around her house. Tammy, in contrast, was a modern day activist and a thorn in the police's side.

On the 'Justice for Madison Knowles' Facebook page, there was an email address, but the text warned that any information should be directed to the police in the first instance. It also specifically asked mediums and psychics not to contact them, so that had clearly been an issue in the past. Carla sent an email explaining who she was and that she was Lauren Powers' replacement at Jericho College. She didn't add any detail – she was pretty sure Tammy would know who Lauren was. Sure enough, within ten minutes, Carla received a reply offering to meet her at a coffee shop in town, the same place Erin had taken her at the start of term. She wanted a meeting within the hour.

Tammy was already waiting for her by the time Carla got to the venue. The look of desperate hope she gave her as she clambered onto the high stool made Carla's heart ache and she was pretty sure she was about to disappoint the woman.

'What can I get you? This one's on me.' Tammy had a hand in the air to attract a server.

'I'll have an espresso, thanks. I've a long day to get through.' Carla pulled out Lauren's notebook.

Tammy gave the order, all the while looking at the scuffed jotter on the table. 'You been doing some research of your own?'

Carla shook her head. 'This belongs to Doctor Powers, who I mentioned in my email. She was a prolific notebook keeper.'

'Can I see?'

Carla handed her the book. 'This is from the period just before Lauren died. The notebook which covers the dates when she visited Wildmarsh Street in the aftermath of Madison's death is missing.'

Tammy kept the notebook in her hand but didn't open it. 'Missing? You mean you can't find it?'

'All the notebooks were kept in a cupboard in Lauren's office. There's one missing.'

'You think someone took it?'

'Not necessarily. Lauren might have had it on her or left it at home rather than keep it with the others in the office. She might also have given it to someone. I need to do a lot more digging. However, what I do have is that notebook from this year and I'd like you to look at this page.'

Carla took the spiral pad from Tammy and flipped to the page where Detective Baros's name was written next to the three numbers and the row of burn marks.

'Is this it?' Tammy couldn't keep the disappointment from her voice. 'Detective Baros was one of the investigators.'

'I'm aware of that, but I wanted to know whether you knew the significance of the numbers? They might be related to Madison's case. I know that your daughter's killing was the only investigation Lauren was asked to assist with.'

Tammy puffed out her cheeks. 'They mean nothing to me. Why don't you ask Baros?'

'I will when I can track him down.'

Tammy kept her eyes on the page. 'And what's your role in all this?'

Carla hesitated, wondering how much to tell her. She didn't want a summary of this conversation appearing in the Facebook group. 'I was asked if I'd assist as an expert consultant for the killing of Tiffany Stoker at Silent Brook. You may have read about the death in the paper.'

'She worked at the Lake House, right?'

'That's her. Did you know her?'

Tammy shrugged. 'I've dined there a few times. You think there might be a connection?'

'There might be and possibly with other crimes that have occurred.'

'Which others?'

Carla swallowed. She had to remember this woman was an advocate. Anything she told her was unlikely to remain private for long. She could just about get away with suggesting a connection between her daughter's death and that of Tiffany. Carla, after all, had a semi-official role in being called to Silent Brook. However, she wouldn't want to incur the wrath of Viv by making any other connections she couldn't prove.

'I'd rather not say at the moment.'

'Crimes in the past.'

'Yes.'

'Jesus.' Tammy put her head in her hands. 'Do you know what I've spent the last two years doing? Waiting for Madison's killer to strike again. I mean, he had to be some kind of psychopath, hadn't he? We never proved any connection between Madison and him and as far as I'm concerned, they never met before the night she died. I've done a lot of reading about how psychopaths stalk their victims. They deliberately choose strangers. You know he tried another girl's door, don't you?'

'I heard about it. It appears he was prepared to strike any girl in the building. So why squeeze past a more accessible sorority house?'

'I don't know. Given that we're assuming it was nothing personal against Madison, I've been waiting for him to strike again, but there's been nothing. And now you tell me there might be a connection to others. The girl at Silent Brook was burned alive, wasn't she?'

'She was.'

'God, I'm no expert, but that doesn't sound like Madison's killing at all. Do you know how many books I've read about Ted Bundy? I was sure the killer was focusing on college students, and I've been pushing for better security on campus before he attacked another girl. Now it looks like I've been focusing on the wrong thing.'

Carla could feel the outpouring of the woman's grief. She reached out and touched Tammy, holding her hand. 'I lost my husband a few years ago. I can't even try to compare heartaches, but I do know the despair you're feeling. I can't tell you what I suspect because it's so flimsy that the theory, if it's dismissed out of hand, could end any potential investigation. Do you understand that?'

'Of course.' Tammy withdrew her hand. 'What can I do to help?'

'You've become well known as Madison's advocate. Could you use your channels and see if you can discover what became of Lauren's notebook? The police may have it if Lauren was carrying it with her when she killed herself. Can you put in a formal request emphasising that it might contain key information relating to your daughter's death? They might tell you to get lost, but it's worth a try.'

'I'll do it as soon as I get home. Anything else?'

'Not that I can think of at the moment. I'm going to try my own approach with Baros, but I don't think he's my biggest fan.'

Tammy snorted. 'I know the feeling – the police think I'm a complete pain in the ass, but so what? You've given me a glimmer of hope though that there may be a way of solving my daughter's death and that'll do for today. You think this monster is still killing?'

Carla thought of the knotted thread next to Jessica Sherwood's body. 'I do.'

31

As Carla drove towards the police precinct, she was overwhelmed by the feeling that her progress was being followed. It must have been paranoia because, when she scrutinised her rear-view mirror, there was no one behind her, except the odd pedestrian out for a morning stroll. Perhaps her suspicion was due to the fact her office, cleared of Lauren's things, continued to omit a foreign smell that Carla couldn't find the origin of, but she'd resigned herself to the fact that the space was accessible by anyone in the department. As she neared her destination, Carla pulled over and, after a minute or so, let a few cars overtake her. None of the drivers paid her any attention and eventually she started the engine and turned into the precinct. The day was turning colder and she caught sight of Baros running across the parking lot, his jacket collar pulled up. The wind in his eyes probably shielded the sight of her loitering next to her car. As she stepped forward, his face fell.

'Come to pay us a visit?'

'Not exactly. I just wanted a quick word with you.'

'How quick?' He unlocked his car but leant against the door.

'Five minutes max?'

'Get in. It's too cold to wait outside.'

She waited as he leant across to open the passenger door and she slid into the seat. The car's elderly exterior hid the beauty of its inside. Carla, who'd never particularly liked cars, whistled. 'Wow. What a beauty.'

She could see from his expression he was pleased. 'Like it? I've spent a small fortune keeping it maintained. So, what can I do for you?'

As she'd done with Tammy Knowles, she showed Baros the notebook.

'That Doctor Powers's book? She came to the house on Wildmarsh Lane back at the start of the investigation. Didn't spot anything that we didn't, although she looked long and hard at those scorch marks. Perez says you were asking about them too.'

'You don't think their location was strange?'

He shrugged. 'Tell me how it moves on the investigation and I'll listen.'

'I'm not there yet, but I think Lauren had spotted something and had begun to tease out a theory. I'm trying to walk in her footsteps if that makes sense. Do you see these numbers that are next to your name? I'm wondering if she contacted you a while after Madison was killed to perhaps discuss them with you?'

Baros shook his head. 'Never saw her again after she came to Wildmarsh Lane.'

'You're sure?'

'Positive.'

'She never called or emailed saying she wanted to talk to you?'

'Nope.'

And yet Jack had been adamant that Lauren had picked up the trail once again near the time of her death. It was possible Lauren had been waiting until she had something more concrete to show Baros. 'And do you recognise the numbers?'

'They mean nothing to me. Do you know what they are?'

Carla shook her head. She saw he was waiting for her to leave the car. 'Well, I'll be going then.'

'Perez said you were asking about the contents of the bin in Miss Knowles' room. What's that got to do with anything?'

'I'm trying to work out a pattern.'

'Raised a bit of a hornet's nest, you know. Viv's pissed at you stirring things up.'

'I didn't get that impression at Albert's party. She arranged for me to see the photos.'

Baros turned on the ignition. 'Take it from me, she's pissed. Don't know what you've said or done, but I'd keep out of her way. Now Perez is looking again at the Stella King files.'

'She is?'

'What we really need is a hit with one of those old murders. Just one and we'll all relax a bit.'

'Maybe they're all connected. Maybe looking at one of the killings in isolation is missing the point.'

'Maybe you've been watching too many cop shows. I'd leave it if I were you.' He turned to her, his face blank. 'Never a good idea to upset people here.'

Carla opened the door and stepped out into the freeze. As he drove off, she wondered what exactly he'd been warning her about.

To ruin her day, Carla got home to an email from Sylvia once more complaining of being neglected by her children. Carla would have willingly ignored it, but the final line contained a message that chilled her to the bone. Her mother was threatening to fly out to Jericho to pay Carla a visit, possibly in early December. Carla was tempted to reply immediately, but any suggestion that it really wasn't a good idea would make her mother more determined to buy a plane ticket.

Carla sat on the bed and instead forwarded the email on to her brother Pete, telling him she really could do without Sylvia as she was helping police with a crime investigation. Could he help? Half an hour later, she received a brief reply: *Sounds intriguing. Leave mother to me.* Well, it might work. Pete was her mother's favourite and an invitation to visit his house in London might trump any plans she had for a stateside visit.

Carla climbed off the bed and crossed to the window, her thoughts on her difficult relationship with her mother that Dan had shielded her from while he was alive. Now he was gone, Sylvia had unsuccessfully tried to dominate Carla's life and only the heavy teaching load had allowed her to say truthfully she couldn't spare weekends back in her childhood home. Her reverie was interrupted by the sight of a figure in a workman's jacket walking along the pavement on the opposite side of the street. His shoulders were hunched up and he paid no attention to Patricia's home, but a few houses down, he came to a stop and wrote something in a small notebook. Carla frowned, leaning to get a better glimpse of the man, but he hurried on, his eyes on the road ahead. She wondered why she was so jittery – it might be the recent visit to Madison's crime scene that had made her fearful for her personal safety. Pulling the curtains to, she jotted down the man's description. She would be looking out for him again.

32

The pattern continued to gnaw away at her, but Carla was forced to focus on her students, who were demanding, needy and utterly wonderful. She was touched by the way in which they were prepared to embrace her own specialism of the archaeology of emotion. It was a sometimes difficult concept to grasp – partly focusing on the emotions of the archaeologists but also the emotions around death and bereavement. Not just grief but also fear, anger and, surprisingly, hope.

'But why archaeology?' asked Helena, one of Carla's more astringent students. She was at Jericho on a scholarship and keen to prove herself in every class. 'Why aren't you teaching social history or anthropology?'

'Because I'm a trained archaeologist,' said Carla, not for the first time in her career. 'It's what I love. Site work, the camaraderie of digs, the physicality of unearthing the past. But we can bring what we've learnt from other disciplines to complement and contextualise the conclusions we reach. Remember, societies are often dominated by patriarchal assumptions – take the burial of stillborn children who were often dumped in mass graves or unconsecrated ground.'

'Like in Ireland,' said a student.

'Exactly. The assumption made by the church hierarchy – childless males – was that these graves were unimportant, but there's plenty of evidence that they were visited by their mothers from the presence of lumps of white quartz on the ground. What can you conclude from that?'

'That they were grieving,' suggested Irene, a student who perpetually ran late but once she was settled was difficult to contain.

'It shows a resistance to hegemonic mortuary practices,' said Helena, her face blooming with excitement.

'Yes, it does,' said Carla.

'Do you think,' asked Irene, 'that you can apply what we've learnt to modern day burials? Take that woman who was burnt up by Silent Brook—'

'That's not a burial,' snapped Helena. 'It's a slaughter. The woman was alive when she died.'

Carla saw she had all the students' attention. The news that she had attended the crime scene was clearly common knowledge and they were waiting for her reaction.

'I think,' said Carla slowly, 'that some assumptions about dispossessed women are due closer scrutiny.'

'But why Silent Brook?' asked Helena. 'Why there?'

'That,' said Carla, 'is a very good question.'

Back in her office, Carla felt both invigorated and exhausted. She picked up the phone and dialled the number she'd been ringing the last two days but got through to the same deadpan secretary who told her Mr Franklin was currently unavailable. She leant back in her chair, frustrated. Occasionally, she wanted to pick up the phone to Dan and tell him about the new life she was making for herself. He'd loved the start of term gossip and had often been the one to soothe her frayed nerves after a difficult semester. This was what she missed most, although she occasionally thought she caught sight of Dan on the street as she went shopping for groceries. The flash of a balding head or the way someone stood, hands in pockets, while looking through store windows.

Patricia was occupied with a forthcoming grandchild. Her daughter-in-law was having a difficult third trimester and Patricia was often at their home, helping out with the other grandkids. Carla cooked quick meals in Hoyt Lane's homely kitchen. Soups and fish dishes with a salad. She wasn't thriving exactly, but neither did she feel at sea as she had done when she'd first arrived in Jericho. Only at night, as she listened to the ticking of Patricia's grandfather clock, was she able to admit that what she was doing was waiting. She had set various cats among the pigeons and was waiting for feathers to fly. She had no other strategy than to wait and see.

She missed Erin but had been reluctant to disturb her busy mentor. Erin, however, must have had Carla on her mind as she invited her over to supper by text. As Carla closed her office, she heard Albert's laugh coming from the office at the bottom of the corridor. She watched as the door opened and he emerged with a colleague, a tall man whose profile was in shadow. Albert turned his head briefly towards her but snapped his gaze away again, ushering his colleague away from Carla towards the back staircase. Only when his companion turned briefly towards her did she wonder if it was the elusive James Franklin. It was hard to tell from this distance, but neither man was inclined to loiter.

'Been thinking about you a lot. Going to tell me what you've been doing with yourself?' Erin kept an eye on Ethan, who was sitting with them, slurping as he devoured his mac and cheese. Carla had barely eaten the dish back in England. It hadn't been Dan's favourite and she was happy to give that carb- and fat-rich dish a miss. Ethan, however, had his plate filled and was ignoring Carla and Erin as they chatted.

'No need to worry about me. I've been busy with classes.'

'Well, that I can sympathise with. It's a juggle trying to combine both jobs, especially when Baros is giving me a hard time. Talking of him, is that all you been doing?'

Carla shrugged and put a forkful of pasta in her mouth.

Erin glanced at Ethan. 'I had a chat with my assistant Jenny about daisy wheels. Can you believe she went on a sightseeing tour of them a few years back?'

Carla put down her fork and picked up the goblet of red wine. 'Did she have any helpful observations?'

'Not really, although I did manage to surprise her about the design of the Franklin Mall. My guess is that half the pagans in this county have been over to visit the place since Jenny heard it was built as a hexafoil. I told her to be discreet, but I don't think she paid me any attention.'

'I don't think it really matters, although I do think the design is important even if I can't yet work out why.'

Erin glanced at Ethan's bent head. 'You're not listening to this, are you?'

'No.' He pulled his ear buds out of his pocket and continued to eat.

'There are two possibilities,' said Carla. 'One is that the architect who designed Franklin Mall, whoever that might be, thought a hexafoil pattern would make an innovative shape but didn't feel the need to emphasise the pattern. It was certainly never included in the publicity. I've looked on the internet.'

'Which is odd as it's such an unusual design.'

'Well, that was certainly commented on, but no mention was made of hexafoils.'

'OK. And what's the other possibility?'

'That James Franklin himself commissioned the design from the architect. I'm erring towards this as Franklin seems to be a dominant personality in this town based on people's reactions when his name is mentioned. My view is that he'd have a strong view on the architecture of a shopping mall bearing his name.'

'Why don't you ask him?'

'I would if I could get hold of him. I've rung his office three times but can't get beyond his secretary.'

'You could try accosting him in the parking lot outside his HQ. He has to go home at some point.'

Carla watched Ethan snort into his food. 'You're trying to get Carla arrested, Mom.'

Erin pulled a face at her son. 'You're supposed to be listening to music. You know,' she poured Carla another glass of wine, 'he's the town's biggest benefactor and that must include the college. Why not speak to someone there? They might have some more details and you might be able to charm out an email for him.'

'I don't know anyone—' Carla thought of Anna Caron. At Albert's cheese and wine party, much had been made of her society connections and she had said she knew Franklin. 'Do you know Jack and Anna Caron?'

'Know of them, certainly. He's in your department, isn't he?' Erin picked up the dish and proffered it to Carla. 'More?'

'I'm struggling to get through this lot.'

'I'll take it.' Ethan slid the rest of the mac and cheese onto his dish and put his head down.

'Did you get any further with those numbers in Lauren's notebooks?'

'Dead end. I did, however, manage to show them to Charlie Baros.'

'Lucky you. How was he?'

'Barely polite and said the numbers didn't mean anything to him. I did believe him though.'

'What numbers?' asked Ethan, his head still over his food.

'These.' Carla pulled out her notebook. 'They could be some kind of code or cipher. Definitely not telephone numbers.'

'They're map coordinates,' said Ethan, after finally lifting his head and pulling out an ear bud.

Carla and Erin stared at him. 'Are you sure?' asked Carla.

'Wouldn't you recognise them if that was the case?' asked Erin.

Carla shook her head. 'Of course. There would be two numbers, a longitude and latitude reference. Where they intersect would be the coordinate.'

Ethan was shaking his head. 'It's not considered as accurate as the Universal Transverse Mercator. It's an aviation system also used by the military. It'll pinpoint a smaller point than the GPS system.'

She looked at Erin, who shrugged. 'Never underestimate what random things teenagers pick up.'

Ethan crossed his arms. 'Thanks, Mom. I won't say anything else.'

'No.' Carla jumped up. 'You might have something. Let me get my phone.'

Erin shook her head. 'Don't use your phone; use my laptop. We all want to see this.'

Erin had cleared away the food despite Ethan's grumblings. She called up a mapping software app that used the system and they were huddled around the screen. The app had a zoom function which would allow them to look with a degree of accuracy at each coordinate.

'We'll do them in order,' said Carla. 'Lauren was a scientist and unlikely to place the numbers randomly.'

'What's the first number?'

Ethan read it out as Carla typed. She saw immediately it was Wildmarsh Street, the house where Madison Knowles Taylor was killed. Erin had noted the address too. 'It looks like she's making a note of the coordinates of the killings. What's next?'

Ethan read out the number. The map zoomed into the Franklin Mall car park. 'Stella King.' Carla let out a long sigh. Here, once more, she was walking in Lauren's footsteps.

'What's the third number?'

Carla typed in the coordinate, and it came up on the map as a sea of green. 'It's just woodland.' She leaned forward. 'Shining Cliff Wood. Mean anything to you?'

'Mom!' Ethan gripped Erin's arm.

'What is it?' asked Carla.

'It's where Iris Chan was found killed.'

'Iris Chan? Who's she?' asked Carla.

Erin sighed. 'A graduate of Jericho who was murdered a few years ago.'

Carla felt a surge of anger. 'Why has no one mentioned her to me?'

'Because it's not an open inquiry. There's a lifer in jail serving his sentence for the killing.'

Carla felt her stomach fall in disappointment. 'Is there a possibility that he might be responsible for the other two killings?'

'No chance. Madison Knowles came after Iris Chan. When I attended the scene at Wildmarsh Street, I remember thinking it was just as well we already had a killer for Iris with a confession.'

'He confessed?' said Ethan. 'You never told me that.'

'I don't discuss my cases with you, remember?'

'You talked about Iris Chan a lot, Mom.'

Erin sighed. 'This is making my head ache. What about some more wine?'

Carla looked at her watch. 'Not for me.'

'So, what are we saying by these doodles, that Lauren was trying to link the cases? It's interesting, but you say one of her notebooks is missing. We're never going to be able to get into her head as to why she thought Iris Chan's murder was connected to the other two deaths.'

'But why write down the map coordinates? That's what I don't understand. Surely the most obvious thing to do would have been to write a list of names. Madison, Stella and Iris. She was working through a list of cases. Why write down the coordinates?'

Erin, she saw, got the point. 'I don't know. We think the locations are significant, don't we? The house on Wildmarsh Street, the Franklin Mall. They're both random and also unusual.'

'And the woods?'

'Spooky but not particularly strange. There's a lot of mythology connected to the place, but don't let that affect you. This is New England, remember.'

'OK.' Carla made a screenshot and called up the image. 'What about if I draw a line between the three spots? Does that help? Where's the drawing tool?'

Ethan took the laptop away from her and expertly joined the three places. 'You know, they're pretty evenly spaced.'

'They are. Well spotted,' said Erin. 'But the pattern doesn't mean anything to me.'

'Me neither, but that doesn't mean there isn't one.' Carla rubbed her eyes, focusing once more on the screen. 'But Lauren was an archaeologist, which meant land and location were important to her, surely.'

'Exactly.' Carla's voice was loud in the kitchen and both Erin and Ethan lifted their heads. 'She was in the middle of trying to work things out when she died. I need the file on Iris Chan.'

Erin made a face. 'Good luck with that. I wouldn't bother trying to tap up our not-so-friendly detectives. You'll get nowhere with Baros and Perez. You need to go straight to the top.'

199

33

'No way.' Viv Kantz looked like she wanted to throw the pile of reports on her desk straight at Carla.

Carla hadn't gone through Albert but had turned up at the station unannounced. Baros's warning that the lieutenant was unhappy with her had stuck and she'd not wanted to give Albert the chance to head off the meeting. Viv kept her waiting for over an hour, finally coming to the lobby herself to collect Carla. Viv was only mildly interested in Lauren's notebook and the map coordinates. When she heard the name Iris Chan, she slammed down onto the desk Lauren's notebook that Carla had handed to her.

'You know, you remind me a little of Lauren. She had the bit between her teeth on this too. I have a sound conviction for the Iris Chan murder and we're proud of the investigation here. Iris's killer, Michael Lines, is safely in jail and that's where he's staying.'

Carla had anticipated this argument. 'Which means he can't have been responsible for Madison's death. What about Stella?'

'He had an alibi. Believe me, nothing would have made me happier to pin that one on him. I'd really like to clear up the murder rate in this county, but his alibi was sound. He was in hospital getting stitched up after a fight. The medical records gave us the time of admission and discharge. It wasn't really his MO anyhow. Lines was an obsessive, but he didn't use sex workers.'

'Do you think it's possible he had an accomplice? It seems that Lauren might have found a connection between the killings.'

Viv nudged the notebook towards Carla, the gesture dismissive. 'The only thing that piece of paper shows is that Lauren was looking for a connection. Do you know who Michael Lines' defence attorney was? Actually, don't answer that. The name Larry Foster will mean nothing to you. The point is, once he hears that I'm investigating other killings that might be connected to Iris's killer, he'll be on it like a terrier. He's another obsessive like you and Lauren.'

'Thank you very much.'

'Don't get me wrong. I probably have that particular gene too, but I don't want this conviction brought into doubt without any evidence.'

'Did Michael Lines have a connection to Iris Chan?'

'Former boyfriend. They met at Jericho, but Michael dropped out due to mental health issues. As I'd expect, the relationship didn't last the change in status of the two. Life at the college is intense, I don't need to tell you that. Iris was a hard worker training to be a vet. Michael got a job in a bar. Nothing wrong with that. Zoe's doing something similar, although she'll be getting a kick up the butt from me if she doesn't find a vocation sooner rather than later.'

'How did Michael take the break-up?'

'Badly. It started with social media posts – you know, borderline stalking – then Iris found small deposits made into her bank accounts with threatening references. "You'll die" or "slut". He didn't even bother trying to hide it. I mean we could trace the bank account back to him no problem.'

'Were you involved in investigating the stalking behaviour?'

'It only came to light after the killing. Iris was a cool figure. She told her friends she could deal with it and they believed her.'

'You initially thought she killed herself though, didn't you?' Erin had given Carla the bare bones of the case and, once more, Carla had been shocked how quickly the investigation team had been happy to jump to conclusions in relation to the death.

Viv sighed and looked towards the window as if the sight of Carla was giving her hives. 'We did. She was hanging from an ash tree and it looked like suicide until we did a bit more digging and found the threats. The problem was Michael Lines had an alibi as he'd been working in the bar all evening. But then a customer remembered they hadn't seen him for half an hour. We reinterviewed other patrons and it was the same. Between nine and nine thirty, no one saw him and that was about the time we had a witness to Iris and an unknown male entering the woods.'

'And he confessed.'

'Not straight away, but he was interviewed for around twenty-four hours and he eventually admitted to the killing.'

'Who interviewed him?'

Viv scowled. 'Now, hold on. Those interviews were by the book and they held up in court too despite the defence's best efforts. Don't go down that route.'

'Could I go and see him, maybe? There might be a connection to the other killings.'

'I'm asking you not to.' Viv's expression was flinty. 'In fact, I'd rather you left the rest of this to me.'

But you can't actually stop me, thought Carla, admittedly unaware of the protocol of visiting prisoners. Perhaps his attorney Larry Foster would be a better bet. 'Thank you for your time.' Carla rose to go, but Viv waved her back into her seat.

'I want to ask you something else. Are you behind Tammy Knowles putting in an official request to see if we have Lauren's notebook?'

'I don't know what you mean.'

'I thought so. Can you please leave Tammy alone. She has made various accusations against my department and everything needs to be done by the book. Her grief has turned her into an obsessive. Another one.'

'She didn't come across like that with me.'

'Didn't she? Well, she's turned up at my house on more than one occasion and threatened my kids. Did she tell you that?'

Carla grimaced. 'Nothing of the sort. I found her very rational and focused.'

'I'm not having my family put at risk and I'm asking you not to contact her again.'

Stunned, Carla nodded.

Viv stood without meeting Carla's eye. 'Take a break from all this, Carla. I understand you know what it's like to lose someone close, but my sympathy has its limits. Remember that.'

34

Jenny happily handed Erin a list of the places she'd visited on her daisy wheel jaunt. In contrast to her gothic look, Jenny's handwriting was full of loops and swirls, a style she probably adopted as a teenager and never lost. The list was impressive, around twenty places in total, and Jenny assured her she'd visited every site on the list. What a way to spend a summer vacation, although Erin couldn't help feeling a little jealous of her colleague's passion. If she was given the opportunity to spend a summer on one of her own enthusiasms, she'd struggle to identify anything to occupy her time. Not for the first time, she envied Generation Z and their determination to do things their own way.

'And every one of these marks has been in the building for centuries?' asked Erin.

Jenny, who was transferring images from her camera onto a laptop, laughed. 'Oh no. There's been intermittent revival of interest in ritual house protection since it first began.'

'You mean someone could buy a house and the first thing they do is score a hexafoil in a doorway.'

'Exactly. It's a little niche, but it does happen. What we were interested in though were the older markings. The earliest we found goes back to the seventeenth century.'

Erin glanced at the list again, but it failed to reveal any secrets. There was even a cemetery on the list, which wouldn't have been difficult for Jenny and her friends to access. Lawrence Hill was the oldest graveyard in the town, although it had closed for burials a few years earlier. It was a vast tract of land surrounded by an iron railing fashioned into a series of interlocking arches. Very gothic and useless for keeping out kids at Halloween. Nevertheless, it was an easily accessible public space as opposed to the private houses where Jenny had pestered householders for admittance. She must mention the spot to Carla.

Erin tucked the list away in her desk drawer, wondering how Carla was getting on with Viv Kantz over the Iris Chan killing. That had been one of Viv's big successes and she'd gained a promotion because of it. Erin wouldn't want to be in Carla's shoes that morning as she was pretty sure the lieutenant wouldn't take kindly to someone interfering in a closed case. More than once, Erin had been on the receiving end of Viv's acidity. She had an unerring sense of bullshit and wasn't afraid to call it out. Also, unlike with most cops, there was no scandal to her name except for that car accident all those years ago. Even then, she'd come out unscathed – the dirt had refused to stick.

Erin spent the rest of the morning on the autopsy of a morbidly obese man whose weight came in just short of three hundred pounds. As he'd died in hospital under the care of a physician, a post-mortem wasn't strictly necessary. His weight had contributed to a raft of medical conditions, but the family had still wanted to know which one had killed him. It would be a time-consuming job to extract the organs from the layers of fat covering them. Eighteen years earlier, when Erin had first stepped foot in a pathology lab, the overweight had been the exception. Now she was no longer sure what a normal weight was, but it was a damn sight heavier than the average when she'd started her career.

As the autopsy progressed, it was clear her patient had died from myocardial infarction due to coronary artery insufficiency. In other words, his blocked arteries had caused a fatal heart attack, although he was also showing signs of fatty liver disease. She would need to tread carefully when she phoned the relatives. The deceased's wife matched him almost for size and Erin would need to ensure her report suggested no fault on the man's part. Obesity, after all, was a more complex phenomenon than simply eating too much.

In the shower, Erin leant against the wall as the water rained on her scalp. She was dog-tired and not sleeping well. Carla had stoked a hornet's nest with her questions and she was no nearer making any sense of what was going on. She had warned Carla that Jericho didn't give up its secrets easily. For her, if the deaths were linked, Erin's money was on a local killer. It had the hallmark of obsession and subterfuge and where better to hide your deviancy than in a town like this. For all she knew, she might know the person responsible.

As she towel-dried her hair, she could contain her curiosity no longer. She picked up the phone and called Carla.

'How did it go?'

Carla groaned. 'I'm in the doghouse. Viv didn't want to even discuss Iris Chan. She was steaming, so I didn't dare ask her about Lauren's death.'

'What do you mean?'

'I was thinking it all over last night. Don't you think it's funny that Lauren died shortly after doing a spot of investigating? Not a million miles from where I am now and she winds up dead.'

'Now hold on.' Erin felt a surge of anger. 'I did that autopsy. Lauren died from drowning and there were absolutely no defensive wounds. She'd weighted her pockets down with quartz stones.'

Erin heard Carla suck in her breath. 'Quartz? You never told me that.'

'You never asked. So what?'

'But quartz isn't something you pick up from the ground around here, is it?'

'Of course not. These were polished stones. She must have brought them from a dig.'

'From a dig? You don't pick up polished stones from a dig.'

'All right, she bought them in a shop. The fact she carried them to the site shows intent. What's your problem?'

'It doesn't matter.' Carla sounded desperate to cut the call.

Erin sighed. Carla was upset and had probably done her career some damage by going up against Viv. Albert wouldn't like his wife's authority challenged, which could make things tricky for Erin. She was going to need an ally and Erin liked someone prepared to go against the established order.

'Look, let's not argue about Lauren and focus on Iris Chan. The coordinates are on Lauren's list, which would suggest the site's important.'

'I'm sure of it.'

'Then why don't I take you there? We can have a look round and see what you think. You showed your cards too soon to Viv, who won't open the Iris Chan file unless a judge tells her to. So, now you're on the back foot.'

Carla groaned. 'I've made a mess of things, haven't I?'

'Probably, but you've got me. That is, until you start questioning my professional competence. Lauren drowned. I'm positive of it.'

—

Carla had a class which finished at three. Erin would have preferred to leave the trip to the following morning when the light was at its best, but Carla wouldn't wait. They drove to Shining Cliff Wood as the sun was sinking over the horizon. They probably had an hour of daylight left max and that wasn't enough wiggle room if they got lost or distracted by something. If Silent Brook was scrubby and down at heel, Shining Cliff was dank and unwelcoming.

They parked up on the road near to its entrance. It was a popular tourist stop and Erin pointed out to Carla a spot across the highway where a witness had provided the statement which had led to the arrest of Michael Lines.

'There were two vehicles that parked that evening so the occupants could take a walk in the woods. They had dogs with them and initially no one remembered seeing Iris either enter the woods or on one of the footpaths.'

'And police initially had the death down as a suicide.'

'Correct. Hanging is the most common form of suicide among what we call completers. In other words, those who were successful. However, when the case gained a bit of traction publicity-wise, a witness came forward from out of state. She and her husband had passed through

Jericho and had decided to exercise their pooch before leaving town. However, the wife began to feel ill – an off bowl of clam chowder – and told her husband to go on ahead while she had a rest in the car. She remembers seeing a person of Iris's description – she had a distinctive appearance, remember – going into the woods with a man wearing a dark coat and black beanie.'

'Hardly a heart-stopping description.'

'Tell me about it, but, nevertheless, it suggested that Miss Chan wasn't on her own. The witness couldn't remember much else. Iris's companion was taller than her – she was around five six in height – but she couldn't tell us by how much. But she was reliable, and it made all the difference to the course of the investigation.'

'OK. Can we see how far they went into the woods?'

They stopped for a moment as a pickup slowed down as it passed by, its driver openly staring at the two women.

'Recognise him?' asked Carla.

'No. I think he's getting off on scaring us a little.' She gave him the middle finger. 'Do you still want to go in given he's clocked us?'

As they were considering, a car pulled up behind them and a family of four along with two Alsatians spilled out.

'Reinforcements,' said Erin. 'Let's get in.'

As they left the road, the noise quietened and the air grew damp and thick. 'Iris was found off the path. I'm going to do my best to find the spot, but I'm not promising the exact tree or anything. I don't have that good a memory.'

'It's better than nothing. There's no way I'm going to get a look at this police file.'

They peeled away from the family as the path forked, Erin looking for the bench where she remembered she had placed her belongings before ducking under the police tape to inspect the body. They came across it under a huge oak tree, although it was a different design to the one Erin remembered. The simple wooden seat had been replaced by a grey stone bench, probably paid for by Iris Chan's family. The backrest bore an inscription of Iris's name and the years of her birth and death.

'It's simple but beautiful,' said Carla, running her fingers along the inscription. 'Did you meet the family?'

'I'm afraid not. I really hope the location of the bench hasn't changed because it's the only reference point I've got. Iris was found a hundred feet from here.' They pushed on under a canopy of greens and brown until Erin sighed.

'It's around here. I don't know which tree. They all look alike. Is the place saying anything to you?'

'No. It's got a weird atmosphere, hasn't it? If you were to hazard a guess, which tree do you think is most likely?'

'Carla, I don't know. All I'm seeing is trees and then some. Iris died, what, two years ago. There'd be no marks left from the investigation.'

Carla was looking around the space, her eyes drawn to the branches forming a canopy above them. She frowned and walked towards a tree dominating its neighbours, its huge trunk gnarled with age. 'Do you know what variety this is?'

'Um, ash, I think.'

'It's definitely ash. It's the only one I've spotted here.'

'Why've you picked it out?'

'For a start, it's the largest around here and Iris's killer would have wanted to make sure any branch was sturdy enough to carry her weight. Ash trees are also connected to witchcraft. Ash berries were sometimes left in children's cradles to protect them from disease and malignant spirits.

In some druid traditions, the staffs of holy people are made from ash.'

'You believe in all that druid stuff?'

Carla smiled. 'Not really, but it's not what I believe, is it?' She was inspecting the trunk, her face close to the striped bark.

'Don't take too long. It's getting dark and I've got better things to be doing than tree hugging out here.'

'I can come back now I know where—' She stopped. 'Erin!'

Erin stumbled towards Carla, panicking at the tone of her voice. 'What is it?'

Carla had used the light from her mobile phone to illuminate a patch of the trunk. 'Can you see?'

'There's a circle and some petals like the ones you were talking about, but maybe that's just because we were talking about hexafoils the other day.'

'They're not random markings. You have to trust me on this. Someone's scored this in a hurry, which is why it's a bit rough and ready.'

'Are you sure?'

'They're ritual markings I'd expect to find in a building. Why weren't they spotted at the time?'

'I don't know. Do you think it's possible the killer came back sometime afterwards to make the mark?'

Carla continued to run her hands over the grooves. 'I'm not sure.'

On the drive back into town, Carla was distracted, fiddling with her phone as she tried to get a better view of the image. Erin wanted to tell her to give it up and concentrate on the prestigious job she'd been recruited for. There were plenty of academics who would happily step into Carla's shoes and Erin suspected reputations were hard to shrug off in Carla's world. One word from Albert, and her mentee would be sent back to England with a note on her personnel file that she was difficult to work with.

'What next?' she asked.

'I'm thinking I need to try James Franklin again.'

'You back on Franklin? What's he got to do with Shining Cliff Wood?'

'Well, I don't know, but there's got to be a connection to him. The shopping mall was designed by him, Lauren went into the water by Suncook, which he owns, and his name's in Lauren's notebook next to Baros's.'

'There's no connection between him and Shining Cliff.'

'I'd still like to try.'

'You've got no chance. Think Elon Musk of Jericho. This man has influence. You don't just pick up the phone and ask to speak to him.'

'I must be able to somehow. If he's a public figure, then what about if I turn up to one of his events?'

'He has a security guard for public appearances, I think. It's not a permanent thing, I suspect. I see Franklin driving around town occasionally. He has a black Range Rover, so he's easy to spot and he's often driving by himself. He had security with him when Franklin Mall was opened though and the same with Suncook.'

Carla turned in her seat towards Erin. 'When was this?'

Erin felt herself colour. 'I don't know. The mall's been open a few years. The gardens just before that. Why do you ask?'

'I don't know. If the locations are important, then perhaps the killer was at the openings.'

'Them and a couple of hundred other Jericho residents.'

'I'll give his office a call again anyhow.' Carla had taken a mulish tone. 'I can only try.'

God, she's infuriating, thought Erin, thinking of the email she'd deleted the previous evening. 'Look, there's this fundraiser taking place soon. It's run by the town's guild every year. I'm a member because I was strongarmed into joining one year and never got round to cancelling my subscription.'

'Don't tell me Franklin will be there.'

'Guest of honour. There's an auction and they want his money for the bids. I've never been to the dinner, but I'm invited every year.'

'You can get me an invitation too?'

'Yes, according to the email I had, but it'll cost you two hundred bucks. You got the money to pay for mine too?' Out of the corner of her eye, Erin saw Carla wince. 'Forget it.'

'No, you're on. We're going.'

35

His design was going awry and it was impossible to tell why. Until now, he'd been confident of the unbroken line. The girls had died according to his plan and he had smoothed over the traces without any difficulty. The bottles, even without the glass to encase the objects inside, held true. The meaning remained obscure and the combined forces of local law enforcement along with visits from the FBI and profilers had failed to spot the link. Even as he had scrawled the mark near his final victim, he had been sure of the potency of its power directed towards the one person who might spot its relevance. Now, the line was breaking and he wasn't certain if it was an error on his part.

The mark had been hardest to place in the wood, which was ironic. The soft bark should have been perfect to score in the design. However, as his knife dug into the pulpy wood, a dog had run up to him. He'd dispatched it with a kick, and it had returned yelping to its owners, leaving him to close the pattern freehand.

Iris Chan. She had been trouble from the start and he should have known it was her death that might return to haunt him. There was someone asking questions, burrowing beneath the deaths, who might mess it up for him as he neared the end. It was time to speed things up and push forward his plans. To echo the slogan of a T-shirt Iris had owned, he hadn't come this far to come this far.

36

The Lake House had gone the extra mile for the fundraiser, or perhaps it was trying to save its reputation after a news article had appeared naming Tiffany Stoker as one of its employees. Either way, rather than the dimly lit lamps to guide cars down the drive, rows of glimmering lanterns had been suspended from the overhanging branches. The effect of the lights against the swaying trees and moonless night made for a disorientating approach in the taxi. Carla had offered to drive; it was her fault, after all, that she'd dragged Erin along this evening, but her friend had suggested a cab so they could both have a drink. Even the driver looked a little overawed by the setting. As they approached the hotel, Carla reflected it wouldn't be out of place in a Du Maurier novel. It shouted gothic and, once again, Carla wondered why Tiffany had been lured to Silent Brook. Her killer could have got eerie energy in the grounds of the hotel without the trouble of transporting his victim to a patch of land next to a busy highway.

There was a line of cars waiting to drop guests at the entrance and get their vehicles parked. Carla and Erin stepped into the sharp night air.

'November is my favourite month,' said Erin. 'I love deep autumn.'

'It's funny how much the landscape changes even over a small geographic area. Take Shining Cliff, which has an odd feeling to it. I didn't feel comfortable from the moment we entered the woodland and yet I've used the nearby rest stop to fill my car without noticing a thing.'

Erin smiled at her as she patted her auburn hair which she'd styled into a French pleat. 'Concentrate on James Franklin tonight. That's what we're here for. Remember you're four hundred bucks poorer for it.'

The drinks reception was held in a small ballroom tucked behind the central staircase with around two hundred guests squeezed into the small space. Carla spotted Viv and Albert in the centre of the room, talking to another couple. Albert was unrecognisable in his deep blue dinner suit which matched Viv's long dress. Erin had spotted them too.

'Let's play it cool given we haven't come over here to talk to Viv and Albert. We need to find Franklin and effect an introduction.'

'I don't know what he looks like.' This wasn't completely true. Carla had spent the previous evening trawling the internet for photos of the town's entrepreneur. His white-blonde hair hinted at Nordic ancestry, and he should be easy to recognise.

Erin had spotted someone she knew. 'Over there is a colleague who taught me while I was at med school. Let me introduce him.'

Carla spent ten minutes talking to an obstetrician who clearly had little in the way of a social life except for work and fundraisers. His politics were also a little conservative for her, and probably Erin, who'd waltzed off to look for someone more interesting to talk to. Carla wondered if she'd end up stuck with the tedious doctor all evening when she felt a tap on her shoulder. She turned to see Jack and Anna Caron hovering, Anna's smile a little fixed as she pulled the medic away from Carla.

'Has doc been talking babies with you?' asked Jack.

'I don't think he has any other topic of conversation. I suspect he was a little disappointed when he discovered that I was childless.'

'Anna will give him her ear for ten minutes or so. He brought her into the world and he does love to keep in touch with his deliveries.'

They moved towards the window where tiny blue panes of glass dulled the lamplight on the sills. Carla put down her glass of champagne.

'I hope I didn't touch a nerve when I asked you about children at Albert's party. It's an unusual question for me to ask and I was sorry as soon as I opened my mouth. As someone who was constantly questioned about baby plans when I was married, it's not something I usually do myself. I could have kicked myself afterwards.'

Jack made a face. 'From Anna's reaction, you could probably tell it's not happening for us. We've been trying for three years now and Anna is discovering that money can buy you most things but not everything.'

But it might give her the opportunity for surrogacy or other means denied to the poor. Carla kept her thoughts to herself. Infertility brings its own grief, and she should allow this couple a little breathing space.

'Why didn't you have any?' asked Jack.

Carla picked up her glass and took a sip. 'We decided to wait until we were both tenured so we could have parental benefits. Then Dan became ill, and it was off the table. I had no intention of bringing a child into the world who would never know its father.'

'You're young enough to marry again. Would you like children?'

Carla looked at her feet, uncomfortable at the question. 'I wanted children with Dan; now I'm not bothered. I guess it's down to your situation, isn't it? At this moment in time, I can't imagine myself with kids.'

Jack smiled. 'Seems a perfectly reasonable attitude. Sorry for my curiosity, which as you know is the bane of academics. Would you like me to introduce you to anyone? I promise you no more tedious obstetricians.'

'Well, given you're offering, I wouldn't mind an introduction to James Franklin. I was talking to one of his staff down by the river recently. He gave me a potted history of his life and he sounded fascinating.'

'Of course.' Jack frowned. 'We'll have to fight our way through the adoring throng around him, but we should be able to elbow our way past.'

'You know him well?'

'Anna's been friends with him since he was a boy.' He led her by the arm across the room. Viv briefly glanced at the pair, her expression giving nothing away as Jack, clearly an expert in these situations, slid in between other partygoers.

'Franklin, can I introduce you to a colleague, Professor Carla James. She's recently joined the faculty at Jericho.'

Franklin turned to greet them, his tall frame towering over her. 'Jack! I wondered if I'd have the pleasure of seeing you and Anna here.' His gaze settled on Carla. 'An archaeologist? We appear to have a good complement from the university tonight. How are you finding our town?'

Carla had to struggle to meet his eyes. He radiated an overbearing confidence that she'd encountered before only in the very rich. She'd met financial donors at Oxford, attending receptions at the request of the Master hoping to gain valuable sponsorship for their college. Carla had usually stayed for around an hour and slunk off, uncomfortable in the world of privilege and power.

'I'm beginning to settle in. I'm very impressed so far by the motivation of my students.'

'And Jack is helping you get your bearings, I hope.' James clutched Jack's shoulder, making him flinch.

'I'm doing my best, but Carla seems to have grasped the soul of Jericho already.'

The two men's eyes locked and Carla wondered what the history was between them.

'I met one of your workers down by the river the other week. At Suncook Park next to the church.'

'I hope it was looking good. A lot of thought went into the design.' Franklin stopped, possibly trying to guess if she'd been informed of Lauren's suicide. Carla doubted he was unaware of what had happened on his land. 'Have you seen any more of my developments? You'll notice my architecture has progressed since I first started building here.'

'I've been to the mall. I certainly like the design of that.'

'Good.' Franklin was interrupted by the clanging of a glass bell and the announcement that dinner would be served. Terrible timing and Carla found herself moved away from Franklin as the huddle made for the double doors into the dining room.

'I've looked on the board. I can tell you what table we're on,' hissed Erin. 'Did you manage to speak to Franklin?'

'Yes, but not long enough to get any information out of him.'

'Hard luck. Maybe you can try after dinner. We're not on his table obviously. We're in the cheap seats in the far corner of the room.'

As Carla and Erin took their places, it was obvious the organisers had decided to seat guests by occupation. Their table was made up of college employees, all looking uncomfortable in their evening suits. Carla looked for Jack and Anna and saw they were on Franklin's table along with Viv and Albert. She picked up the menu as a familiar figure took the chair next to her.

'I fear we're on the flotsam and jetsam table,' said Max, offering her some wine. 'I hadn't realised you were coming to the dinner.'

'It was a last-minute invitation from Erin. You know her, don't you?'

'Of course, our paths have crossed over the years.' He smiled across at Erin. 'I gave a guest lecture to one of her classes last year. I even met her son Ethan when I dropped her home once.'

'You're here alone?' she asked and wondered about the flash of what looked like displeasure that crossed his face.

'My wife was a member of the townswomen's guild. I feel I'm honouring her in some way by keeping up the tradition of attending these dinners.'

Surprised, Carla turned to him. 'I hadn't realised you'd been married.'

'Yes, but I've been a widower for ten years. It does get easier. I've wanted to tell you that since we first met, but it's never felt like the right time.'

'I'm sorry. Was your wife ill for long?'

Max poured her a glass of white wine. 'She died suddenly, but I'd rather not talk about it if you don't mind. It was a long time ago and all water under the bridge.'

Carla wondered if she'd misread the signals. Perhaps Max had been upset over Lauren's effects because it brought back memories of his wife.

'I noticed you were upset that Lauren's room wasn't clear. Her death must have been upsetting for you.'

'It was a tragedy for the faculty and all of us who knew Lauren. Her emotions were often up and down, but we never thought she was suicidal. You never really know the extent of people's emotions, do you?'

'No, but I've made a career out of trying.'

'Right, of course.' He made an effort to smile as he turned to the guest on his right. Carla caught Erin's gaze across the table and rolled her eyes. The evening, she suspected, was going to be a complete waste of money.

37

The day after the party, Carla was gripped by a fatigue she couldn't shift. Patricia, sensing her mood, sent her back to bed after a breakfast of tea and toast as even the thought of coffee made Carla's stomach turn. It was a relief to have her choices taken away from her. If she'd felt fitter, she'd have forced herself to go for a walk even though the cold was of the type to seep into her bones. Patricia came into the room with a hot water bottle and an ancient electric fire. As the bars heated, the smell of burning dust infused the room, bringing back memories of staying in her grandfather's house in the winter.

Carla reached for her laptop and began a search for the killing of Iris Chan. She should be resting her brain as well as her body, but it was impossible to relax. Shining Cliff Wood was an evocative name, but, for Iris, it was where she had met her end. As she read the account of first the discovery of Iris's body, the subsequent police hunt and the arrest of Michael Lines, she had to admit the case against him was strong. So, what was it that had attracted Lauren's attention? Carla pulled out the map Ethan had printed from the computer with the three coordinates mapped out. Joining a line between the dots had created a constellation pattern which wasn't helpful at all, but Ethan had been correct in saying that the markers were evenly spaced. Carla got a ruler out of her pencil case and checked. They were equidistant.

Carla leant back in her pillow as Patricia knocked on the door. 'You know, I've been thinking and one remedy for fatigue is turmeric milk. Ever tried it?'

Carla shook her head. 'I don't usually drink hot milk.'

'Well, try this. I've added some cardamom in it too.' Patricia placed a hot mug in Carla's hands and looked down at the map. 'Is that Jericho?'

'It is. What made you recognise it?'

'I think it was the river. See this bend here.' Patricia placed a finger on the map. 'When I was young, I went swimming with friends. We were fearless, but when my father heard about it, he gave me the strap. The only time he ever hit me. He'd lost a childhood friend from the same spot and we'd been warned not to go into the river.'

'When my colleague Lauren was looking for somewhere to enter the river, it seems she too knew how dangerous the currents were.'

'Where did she go in?' Patricia sat on the bed.

'Here, next to St Luke's church.' Carla put her finger on the map, covering the little park with the round flower beds. As Patricia leant in, Carla was aware of a shift. Her finger was more or less the same distance from the spot where Iris Chan had died as Iris's death site was from Madison's house.

'What's the matter? You've gone white as a sheet.'

'I think I've just spotted something.' Carla lifted the covers, her exhaustion forgotten as she placed the map on a table and measured the distance between the two locations exactly. As the map had been printed from a website, there was no scale, but Carla guessed there was around three to four miles between all four spots. Once more she was struck that the points connected looked like a system. Carla began scrabbling around for a pen.

'Can you help me, Patricia? Silent Brook is around here, isn't it?' Carla found the highway out of Jericho and guessed at the underpass. Patricia bent over the map and nodded.

'Okay, and the body was found about here.' Carla drew an X on the map. 'Now, can you point out where Penn Street is where Jessica Sherwood was killed?'

It was the only crime site she hadn't visited. Patricia took her time, finding first her house and then moving her finger along the streets until she stopped. 'This is Penn Street. I can't be 100 per cent sure where Jessica's house is.'

'I can make an educated guess.' Carla put down her ruler and drew a curved line between each point. 'The ruler was a mistake. I need to think organic.'

'You're drawing a circle.'

'I am, and this point here is where I think Jessica's house is on Penn Street. But it's not just a circle.' What Carla really needed was a compass, but the map was only approximate, so she would need to draw it freestyle.

'What in the Lord's name is that?'

'It's a hexafoil.' She looked expectantly at Patricia, her heart pounding in her chest. 'It doesn't mean anything to you, does it?'

'No, but I can see a pattern. It has a flower in the middle of a circle.'

'That's exactly what it is. It's an unbroken line. It shows me two things straight away: why the killing at Franklin Mall had to be first. Because it's a static building with the daisy wheel design. All the other points will have been chosen because they will have allowed the daisy wheel design to form. It also answers the question why Tiffany was moved to Silent Brook. It was the place to fit the pattern.'

'Are you telling me that these women were chosen because of the place and nothing about themselves?'

'More or less, but I believe the killer knew Tiffany Stoker and Iris Chan, even if in completely different contexts. Iris Chan had a boyfriend she didn't want to talk about.'

'And what's the second thing it tells you?'

'That Lauren Powers must have been killed. She hadn't completed the circle. How could she when Jessica and Tiffany weren't dead yet. The killer might have been planning to lure another to the river, but Lauren would do because she was asking the wrong questions. Wrong for the killer. Right for her.'

'You're saying someone has calculated the design and killed around it. It sounds a little far-fetched. They start with Franklin Mall and move on from there.' Patricia sat on the bed, her eyes on the map.

'No, they start with the centre. Shit, of course, they start with the centre. See where these petals intersect, where in Jericho is it? I've done my best to make the petals accurate, but I could be a little off.'

Patricia lifted up the map. 'It's just a graveyard. It's called Lawrence Hill cemetery, the oldest in Jericho. Some of my own family are buried there.'

'A cemetery?' Burial places were Carla's passion. She'd dragged Dan around crumbling churchyards with graves so precarious Carla had thought they'd sink to join her ancestors below. Together, they'd also visited Victorian municipal cemeteries usually in no better condition but presided over by towering angels, their fingers pointing to heavens. Never, however, had she been so desperate before to visit a graveyard.

'I'm going there now.'

Patricia laughed. 'You just lie there and drink your milk.'

Carla was already out of bed and pulling on her jeans. 'I'll be fine. You enjoy your Sunday with your new grandson.'

'Hell, it's my policy to leave new parents on their own for the first few days unless they specifically want me. I'm not one of those hovering grandmas. I'll take you to Lawrence Hill. It's been years since I visited.'

38

Carla wondered if the midpoint had a special significance for the daisy wheel. It was the part of the hexafoil where the curved lines intersected and must surely hold some particular significance. She really needed to talk to Jack about it but, for the moment, she wanted to get a feel for the graveyard. Lawrence Hill was one of the few inclines in town and Carla was intrigued by the location. Hills were popular burial sites – they protected graves from flooding, precious farmland was left for cultivation, and, during more religious times, there was the theory that graves were closer to the divine, 'Nearer, My God, to Thee'. Once, she suspected, the cemetery would have been a few graves on the hillside marked by a simple cross. Now, it had been enclosed with iron railings and an ornate gate featuring an image of a skull that wouldn't have been out of place in a Dickens novel. Carla shivered. The conversation with her students about the reputation of places had heightened her senses. It was unlike her to be fearful of a cemetery, so it must be something else, a sense of things askew and out of the natural order.

'Is it ever locked?' she asked Patricia as she swung open the gate.

'I can see a padlock, so I guess they shut it at night.'

Any killer would have easy access to the ground though over the shoulder-height fence. They stepped through the gate onto the gravelled path leading up the hill. This side was around an acre in size and, from the looks of it, had received no recent burials, although it was hard to tell where the oldest part of it was located. As with English cemeteries, the graves ranged from the simple to the ornate. One she passed had a statue of a small dog resting against its owner's legs.

'What are we looking for?' asked Patricia, looking around her in dismay. 'I don't think I ever realised how big this place is.'

'I don't know. It has to have some significance as the centre of the wheel, but it might be simply a connection to the early origins of Jericho as a town. Why don't you let me have a look around? Do you know where your relatives are buried?'

'Vaguely. I remember visiting this place as a child with my mother. I'll head up the path and take a look.'

Patricia set off towards a mini mausoleum erected by one of the town's more respected citizens. If Carla had been here just for pleasure, she'd have roamed around the graves, taking images of the markers and mentally plotting the space's development. But she needed to empty her brain and try to think. The cold wind bit into her face as she walked along the path, eventually following Patricia up the hill where the graves became small rectangle tablets dated from the mid-nineteenth century before things got a little out of hand gravestone-wise. She was looking for anything that might signify ritual protection or spiritual middens as Jack had called them – daisy wheels, glass bottles, animals, dolls – but the graves gave nothing up to her.

There was a small municipal building at the top of the mound, but when Carla pulled at the door, it was locked and probably derelict judging by the layers of ivy and moss on the stonework. Carla looked around for someone who might be a regular visitor to the cemetery, one of the legions of people who cared for a place in the absence of official interest. There were a few hardy visitors wrapped up in coats and mufflers, but they looked as if they were using the area as a cut-through on the way to the other side of town. Only one figure looked promising, a woman in the distance wearing a brown fur coat which reached to her ankles. She was tending flowers on a grave, making sure each stem was around the same height as the others.

She straightened at Carla's approach, a pair of scissors in her hand. She was older than Carla had first thought, probably into her nineties. Her face was covered in wrinkles with the exception of her cheeks, which were baby smooth.

'What do you want?' she asked in a husky voice. Carla's presence was unwelcome, she saw, and she took a step back.

'I'm sorry. I don't mean to startle you. I'm looking for a grave and I wondered if you could help as I can't see anyone else to ask.'

The woman peered at her. 'English?'

'Yes, I am. I've only been in Jericho for a couple of months.'

The woman pointed at the grave inscribed Arthur Ramsbottom, 1921–2003. 'My husband was from Lancashire. Came out here for university and never left.'

The woman was offering her an opening, but Carla had never set foot in Lancashire. She cast around for a reply.

'Jericho College seems to have attracted the best talent for decades. Was he ever homesick?'

'Ever?' The woman laughed. 'He never stopped going on about the place. We have a fine house down by the river, but he used to go on about his two-up two-down with its outside toilet like it was Buckingham Palace.'

Amused, Carla looked around her. 'Do you come here every week?'

The woman looked affronted. 'Every other day. I have since 2003.'

'Do you look at the other graves?'

Carla's spirits sank as the woman shook her head. 'I don't have time. I live with my son now and he's had children late in life. I'm on babysitting duty. Who are you looking for?'

'Not anyone in particular. I'm looking for a grave with an unusual marking or feature. Could be a bottle or maybe a circle with a flower inside.'

'You mean the Miller graves?'

Carla's heart leapt. 'What are they?'

'Graves with a pattern just as you describe. Pretty they are, too.'

'Where would I find them?'

The woman pointed up the hill to her right. 'There's an enclosure. Four, maybe five, graves with a little iron fence around them. All of them have got circles with flowers in them.'

'Thank you.' Carla hugged the woman in her elation. 'You know, if I ever get to Lancashire, I'm going to remember you.'

The woman's eyes filled with tears. 'Don't think of me – I couldn't stand the place when I visited. Think of Arthur.'

Now she knew what she was looking for, Carla was on more comfortable ground. She saw the plot in the distance. Unlike the grave of Arthur Ramsbottom, it had a forlorn look. Grass between the gravestones had been allowed to grow a metre or so – perhaps it was too much bother to trim regularly. Up close, she saw there were five graves in total, all with the surname Miller. Three were from the late nineteenth century and two from the 1920s. All five graves had the hexafoil at the top, nestling under the point.

Carla glanced up and saw Patricia walking down the hill. She waved her over. 'Take a look at this.'

'This what you've been searching for?'

'I don't know. Do you know anyone called Miller?'

Patricia gave her an 'are you joking' look. 'It's a common name here. Probably as common as it is in the UK, although no one specific comes to mind.'

'But there must be some significance to why this graveyard is the centre of the hexafoil. Perhaps we're looking for a killer related to the Miller family.'

Patricia shrugged. 'I don't know.'

Carla turned to her. 'Did you find your ancestors?'

'I did indeed.' She hugged Carla. 'You've done me a big favour. Lots of lovely memories raised. I'll be coming back more regularly. What's your next plan?'

Carla gave the little set of graves a final look. 'Find someone prepared to take my theory seriously, which means a visit to another crime scene.'

39

As a child, Carla had once stolen a Mars bar from her local shop. It had been both thrilling and terrifying, but it hadn't taken long for the guilt to kick in. After a few sleepless nights, she'd confessed to her mother, who'd frogmarched her down to the store to pay for the stolen chocolate. Carla was feeling that same excitement and terror at breaking into Jessica Sherwood's house. It was the only site she hadn't visited and she wanted to check for the presence of a daisy wheel or another apotropaic mark. She was now convinced the pattern would be there but hidden away like the scrunched-up doodles in Madison's trash. The killer was toying with them – happy to put the witch bottle material in a prominent position but much more restrained when it came to the hexafoils. This contradiction was bugging Carla, but she couldn't yet guess a reason for it.

She'd been tempted to wait until nightfall. She welcomed the anonymity of the dark but, once in the house, she'd be forced to use a torch, which would draw attention to her presence. In the end, she set her alarm for six a.m. and was out of the house before Patricia was awake. She took her car, intending to head on to campus after she'd checked over the location.

At Penn Street, she walked past Jessica's house, checking how easy it would be to enter the garden unnoticed. She was relieved to see an easy route round to the back of the house, leading, hopefully, to a window she could jemmy open. She had in her bag her archaeology trowel and was about to use it for a criminal act. Happy that the coast was clear, she doubled back on herself and slipped through the entrance. Following the path to the back of the house, she passed through a gate with a broken lock, wondering if this was how the killer had entered the house and why no one had thought to repair it.

At the back of the house, she looked at the property's layout and decided the basement was the best bet. The first door she tried was locked and the catch held. After rattling it a few times, she moved to the window, sliding the trowel's blade under near the catch and pulling. The metal snapped off, hitting Carla in the face, and she swore as she felt the sting of the cold metal.

In frustration she tried all the other windows on the ground floor, each of them holding firm. The winter sun, low on the horizon, bounced off the final window to the right of the house, reflecting her image back to her. The glass was hazy, at odds with the well-maintained exterior of the rest of the building. Carla squinted. Was she seeing patterns where there were none? She ran her hands over the smooth glass. Whatever was on the glass was disfiguring it from the inside. Cupping her hands to shield out the light made no difference. She needed to get into the house.

Stepping back, she screamed as she felt a body close behind her. She turned as a hand gripped her arm.

'Would you like to explain what you're up to?'

Baros pulled her away from the glass and pointed at the window of a neighbouring house. 'That's the home of a concerned citizen worried about a prowler at the property of a woman who was murdered.'

'I can explain.'

'Please do.' Perez came around the corner, her hands on her holster. Baros smirked at her. 'No need for the weapon; Albert would never forgive you.'

'What she doing here?'

'Just wondering the same thing.'

Sick of the double act, Carla took a breath. 'Look, do either of you have a key to the house?'

'Nope,' said Baros. 'Why?'

'There's something etched on the glass, only it's been executed from the inside. I'd like to get in the house to see it.'

Baros made a show of considering the proposal. 'What mark?'

'Look.' Carla led them to the window and showed them the scratching. 'I'd like to make a tracing of it. It'll be clearer what it is then.'

Baros looked at Perez. 'What d'ya think?'

Perez bent over the glass. 'There's a fingerprint.'

'I touched the glass, I'm sorry,' said Carla.

'Inside. Look.'

While Carla had been looking for patterns, Perez was all cop. It seemed Baros was prepared to listen to his partner. He looked at the smudge. 'We won't lift a print off that.'

'Could you try?' Carla looked from one to the other.

Baros shrugged. 'Maybe. The neighbour has a key. I'll get it.'

The house looked as if it was waiting for its owner to return. Jessica's coats were hanging on a peg ready for a winter she'd never see and a fan of mail littered the carpet. Perez bent down, picking up the envelopes and placing them on the hall table. Inside, Carla could see the pane of glass was in the room where Jessica had died. She crossed to the window, Baros close behind. 'Don't touch anything,' he warned.

Closer up, Carla saw the daisy wheel scratched into the glass and held her breath. 'See it?' she asked the pair.

'What is it?' asked Perez.

'It's this.' She found a pen in her bag but no paper. Instead, she drew on the back of her hand the image.

'It's called a daisy wheel.' She showed them the drawing. 'Recognise it?'

Perez got the connection straight away. 'Similar to the drawings found in Madison's wastepaper basket.'

'What?' Baros leant forward. 'It looks like a bunch of lines to me.'

Carla ignored him, focusing on keeping Perez's attention. 'Can you see the similarity?'

Perez looked from the image on Carla's hand to the window and back again. 'Maybe. What's its significance?' asked Perez.

'It's a protective mark to ward off evil spirits. When there's a house involved, it's placed where I'd expect it. Entry points where evil could enter, such as a window. In the open ground, they're harder to place. I found one on the tree where Iris Chan was killed.'

Baros took a step back. 'The lieutenant's told you to lay off that case. She told us not to discuss Ms Chan with you. We worked long hours to get that one solved and we're not having you mess things up.'

Carla, furious, shouted at the pair of them. 'Look at it. You're telling me a retired teacher carved out a protective mark against witches on a window? I'm finding a pattern and all you do is argue.'

'I'm not listening to this.' Baros stormed out, banging the door to the room behind him. Perez looked thoughtfully after him, frowning.

'Let me talk to him. We need to have a meeting with the lieutenant given what we've just found. She know about any of this?'

'I promised her I wouldn't be looking into the deaths any longer.'

'Why are you here then?'

'I think I've found a pattern linking all of the recent killings of Jericho women. I just needed to visit this scene to confirm everything. I'm going to ask for a meeting as soon as possible to let Viv know. I only gave her a loose theory before. I now have something concrete.'

'Did you mention the daisy wheel to her?' Perez's voice sounded odd.

'Not really, but I did talk about anti-witchcraft symbolism. She wasn't very happy.' She saw Perez had lost her colour. 'What's the matter?'

'I'm not sure. I need to go back to base and look something up. I can see why the boss was pissed at you. Catching Michael Lines was one of our big successes.'

'You're happy with the way everything went?'

Perez scuffed her feet. 'I interviewed Michael Lines. It was me and Baros. Then my shift finished and I left Baros to carry on with another detective. I couldn't believe it when he told me he'd confessed. He'd shown no sign of it when I was sitting in.'

'You think the confession was extracted under duress?'

Perez shrugged. 'I don't know.' She paused. 'You know, I've been reading through the Stella King files. It was my first homicide and I feel we never did the girl justice. Is there anything I should be looking for?'

'There's a daisy wheel there already in the shape of the mall. I also think the horseshoe trinket has a significance. I don't know if there's anything else to find. What about relooking at the police work in relation to suspects?'

Perez turned away. 'Stella was Hispanic. Did you know that? Do you know what the murder clean-up rate for us is compared to victims of white ethnicity?'

'I don't know. I guess it's a lot less.'

'Significantly less. We did our best on that case, but there's only so much you can do as a lowly detective.'

'Are you suggesting that there were people above you less interested in solving the case?'

Perez took a step back. 'I'm not saying anything. Just watch your step.'

40

After her Tuesday morning tutorial, Carla was surprised to find a voicemail from James Franklin asking her to call him. Not only was she convinced she hadn't made much of an impression on him at the fundraiser, but she was pretty sure the only people who had her new mobile number were Patricia and Erin. She'd made do with her English phone at the start of term until she'd seen the dent September's bill had made on her bank balance. She called the number back and got the secretary who had stonewalled Carla's attempts to reach Franklin earlier.

'I'm Professor Carla James from Jericho College. Mr Franklin left a message for me to ring him.'

'Mr Franklin is in a meeting right now. Can I get him to call you back?'

Carla made a face. Franklin wasn't the only one with a busy schedule. 'I'm teaching all afternoon. Tell him I'm free from five thirty.'

'Hold on a minute.' The phone went silent until she heard the baritone of Franklin's voice.

'Carla. Thank you for calling back. How are you?'

'Well, I'm fine, thanks.'

'Look, I'm tied up at the moment, but I wondered if you fancied having dinner sometime. There are a couple of things I wanted to chat to you about.'

His manner was brisk and impersonal. Whatever the reason behind the call, he wasn't asking her on a date. She relaxed, pulling her diary out of her bag. 'Can I ask where you got my number from? I was surprised to get a call on this phone.'

Franklin paused, unused to explaining himself. 'My secretary found it for me.'

His tone was evasive, but Carla was pretty sure that if she pushed it, his secretary would cover for him.

'That's fine.' She wondered what he wanted from her. 'When did you have in mind?' Far better he choose a date than admit that she was free most evenings.

'How about this Friday?'

Let me check my social calendar, thought Carla. 'That would be fine.'

'I'll get my secretary to book a restaurant and let you know the venue. I can pick you up from your house.' Franklin rang off before Carla could give him Patricia's address. He probably knew it already. She wondered how a man of his status found out personal details of private citizens. One possibility was he had a private detective on call who could furnish any information quickly. Another, more disturbing, possibility was that he had a contact at the police department.

Carla looked at her watch. She had half an hour spare, which was probably enough time to drive to a deli and grab a sandwich. She'd still not got used to the concept of getting into your car to pick up something as inconsequential as a bagel. She was beginning to put on weight from the lack of exercise; the yoga she did in her room hardly counted. She'd need to be careful as her five-foot-two frame wouldn't tolerate more than an extra couple of pounds. She grabbed her keys and headed to the parking lot. In the distance, she saw the uniformed figure of Viv Kantz leaning against a Mercedes parked next to her own car. She had her arms folded as Carla approached.

'What part of stay away from my investigations don't you understand?'

Carla frowned. 'What have I done to upset you?' She pressed her car fob to open the car door and flinched as Viv grasped her arm.

'I thought we had an agreement.'

'Things have moved on since our last chat. I've found—'

Viv's grip on her arm tightened as she pulled Carla away from her car. The lieutenant was slight but muscular and her strength made Carla's legs wobble. 'I don't want to hear what you've found. You're jeopardising months of hard work with your unfounded accusations and wild theories.'

It took all of Carla's strength to shake her off. 'What the hell's wrong with you?' Carla's voice carried across the campus car park. Two female students made towards her but stopped when they saw Viv's uniform. 'You've asked me for a pattern and I'm offering you one. Why ask for expert help if you've no intention of paying any attention to my conclusions?'

The girls might not be coming any closer, but their presence had Viv in check. 'It's a half-cocked tale of superstition. Now I hear you've been trespassing on murder scenes. The killing of Jessica Sherwood is high priority. I have the Mayor's office on my back and I don't need you messing things up.'

'Did Baros tell you about the daisy wheel I found etched into the window? None of your team noticed it. Call yourself professionals.'

Viv stepped forward, her face red with fury. 'Now you listen to me. There's no evidence Miss Sherwood's killer scraped that pattern. Forensics have taken a look – anyone could have placed it there. The house is over fifty years old.'

'But the daisy wheel is important. I want to show you a map with the crime scene of the six killings.'

'Six? What the hell are you talking about?'

'I'm adding Lauren Powers to the deaths—'

Viv took a step towards her in fury. 'Listen here, I'm not having my professional competence questioned by someone who knows nothing about how things work. We have due process here and I follow it to the letter. Doctor Powers's death was a suicide and you'll be very sorry if you continue along this line of inquiry.'

Carla saw how Viv had got her reputation. In her rage, she was terrifying, but behind the anger, Carla glimpsed an implacability that would blind her to anything which did not fit in with her view of the world.

'I want you to hand over all your notes right from the beginning when I called you out to Silent Brook. I'll send Baros around this afternoon to pick them up and I want everything. Maps, drawings, notes. I'm calling an end to this as of today.'

'And if I say no?'

'I'm not someone to be messed around with. That will become clear to you if you persist.'

'So that's how things work in Jericho, is it?'

Viv held her gaze. Her deep brown eyes were flecked with green. 'Don't underestimate me. My priority is to keep residents safe.'

Carla opened her car door. 'And you're doing a terrific job of it.'

41

Viv drove off without a backwards glance as Carla sat at the wheel, her stomach turned to ash. There was no way she was going to be able to force down a sandwich. Her diet started with a tongue-lashing from Jericho's senior law enforcer. Nice work. Returning to the building, she passed Max's office and saw him through the open door, crouching on the floor, looking for a book at the bottom of a large oak bookshelf.

'Got time for a chat?'

He swivelled around, pleased to see her. 'Sure. Come on in, Carla.'

His office was a mirror image to hers, but he was a man who liked things just so. The books were arranged alphabetically and his desk was clear except for his computer and an empty mug.

'Is everything OK?' he asked her, getting to his feet. He rubbed his knees, wincing. 'I think this year's dig has taken a toll on my joints.'

Carla watched him walk stiffly to his chair. 'I've just been warned off by Viv. It was horrible given I've only been trying to help with an investigation where I was asked for my opinion.' To her dismay, Carla felt her eyes fill with tears. Max stared at her for a moment and pulled open a drawer of his desk. He brandished a small bottle of bourbon and two tumblers.

'Emergency rations.' He poured a glug in each of the glasses and handed one to Carla. 'Congratulations, you've seen the tough side of Viv Kantz. Don't feel bad. We've all had a dressing down from her at one time or another.'

'I think this was a little more than that. I felt threatened.' Carla sipped her drink, feeling the alcohol hit her empty stomach.

Max frowned. 'Do you think it's possible you've become obsessed by the death of the woman whose crime scene you visited? I'm not surprised, you know. I don't think we've really come to terms with what happened to Lauren here. Death casts a long shadow.'

Carla groaned. 'It's much more complicated than that, Max. I have a hunch that might link the deaths of Tiffany Stoker and Lauren to other women who have died.'

He paled and tipped another slug of whiskey in his glass. 'The deaths are connected? How?'

'It's a long story, Max. I don't even know where to start.'

'You don't need to tell me details that you want to keep to yourself but, if you'll excuse me saying, it sounds like you need some support.'

Carla looked across at him. Beneath his dour exterior, he was an essentially kind man. 'All I can say is that I think I've found a connection with daisy wheels. You know, the marks you find in old buildings. You must have heard of them.'

'Apotropaic marks? I know of them, of course, but it's not my specialism. Doctor Caron is the person you want to speak to.'

'I have asked him, but I get the impression he's an outsider looking in when it comes to Jericho. Does that make sense to you?'

If Carla had expected him to be pleased that she was questioning Jack's competence, she was to be disappointed. Max frowned, considering her question. 'You know, I don't ascribe to the theory that people need to be born in a place to study its archaeology. I'm not just talking about the colonial attitude where the white western academics travel to developing countries to tell them about their past.'

'Sure.' Carla had met some wonderful colleagues in Egypt, sick of their treasures being plundered by European treasure hunters.

'But I do think that you can develop an area of study when you've no experience of that culture. Take my specialism of Roman archaeology. I wasn't born in Europe, but I spent my twenties in England unearthing first-century settlements there. I've never felt at a disadvantage.'

'I don't know why I mention it. I was asking Jack about ritual house protection and his answers seemed a little superficial. I wondered why.'

Max lifted his glass and regarded the contents, probably wondering whether to have a third shot. 'House protection?'

'That's right. My interest began with witch bottles, but now I'm trying to dig further into the use of the hexafoil pattern as a means of counter magic. I'm wondering if the pattern has any resonance that you know of that I'm missing.'

Max considered the question. 'In Roman houses there was a shrine, a lararium that honours the Lares spirits who may protect your home.'

'And these house protections are used down through history. But what would it say to you if they were used outside the home?'

'You mean barns and so on.'

'More like shopping malls and woodland.'

Max frowned. 'The thinking is a little skewed. I mean, evil is considered to enter a house where there are draughts. Doorways, chimneys, windows. How's that going to work in a wood?'

'I don't know,' said Carla, remembering the scored marks on the ash tree in Shining Cliff Wood. 'It sounds like the work of someone who knows the basic theory but not the thinking behind it. The first day we met, you said you'd been called to help in some of Viv Kantz's investigations. Were any of them murders?'

'There was a former student of Jericho, Iris Chan. I'm not sure if you know about her.'

'She was found in Shining Cliff Wood.'

'Yes, exactly. I wasn't exactly called in for my expertise. I'm no expert in woodland or hangings come to that. There was a reputational issue for the college and I was asked to go down, the same day the body was found, to see if there was anything that might relate back to us here.'

'Asked by whom?'

'Albert. To be honest, Viv thought I was being called in to give some answers in relation to the landscape, but that wasn't my understanding with Albert. It was a case of the department keeping its reputation.'

'And was there anything that might impact the college?'

'I couldn't see anything. Miss Chan had left the previous year and, for whatever reason, had decided to stay here. You know, her former boyfriend was convicted of her killing.'

'So I believe.'

'That's the only murder case I've been involved in. I've been called in to help with suspected cases of trading in illegal antiquities but nothing involving homicide.'

'You think Iris Chan's murderer definitely did it?'

'I've no idea. He was given a fair trial, I assume. Why do you ask?'

'I think Iris's death might be connected to Tiffany Stoker's and those of other women.'

'Really? You know, if you've any concerns, you can always come to me. What's the connection to daisy wheels?'

Carla thought of Viv's response. 'I'm not sure I'm ready to share my theory yet. Can I ask you something else? It's about Doctor Powers.'

'Go on.'

'I've heard that before she died there was a love affair that went wrong. Do you know anything about that?'

Max shrugged. 'Lauren was a private person. She kept herself to herself. Sometimes she was happy, other times less so.'

'You were friendly?'

Max paused and she saw he was struggling to contain his emotions. 'Lauren and I dated briefly, but that was a while ago. It was a few years after my wife died and I wasn't really ready to start seeing anybody. I still cared about Lauren though and we remained friends.'

'You don't know who her current lover was.'

Max raised his eyes to her, his face pale. 'She dated James Franklin. Do you know him?'

Shocked, Carla swallowed. 'I wasn't aware of that.' She remembered Franklin's name in Lauren's notebook. 'Of course I've heard of Franklin. It would be hard to avoid him in this town. I met him at the fundraiser we attended the other evening.' She didn't mention that she'd be having dinner with him on Friday.

'Of course. He's easily the richest man in Jericho, possibly in the county. I know he and Lauren were dating.'

'And you think he's the lover who supposedly drove her to suicide?'

'I don't know about anyone driving Lauren to the act. It's a choice, isn't it?'

Carla nodded. 'Yes, it's a choice. If you have one.'

42

Carla had discovered that Michael Lines was in his third year of incarceration at a jail in New York state but he'd retained a local county-supplied defence lawyer. Larry Foster was as hard to get hold of as Franklin had been before their meeting, but Carla, after discovering an online news report of a current trial, eventually tracked him down to the courthouse. She found a seat in the room and sat through the final stages of a domestic abuse trial. In dismay, she watched the defence attorney argue that the victim had provoked her boyfriend by flirting with his friend. It put Carla in a foul mood as she left the room, hanging around the watercooler as she waited for the session to adjourn. Larry Foster eventually exited the courtroom, his expression neutral.

'Did you win or lose?' Carla asked.

He cast a brief glance in her direction. 'Win. They're low-life. I'll be seeing both of them back here before the year's out.'

He was in his sixties, probably near retirement, and his crumpled suit hadn't seen the inside of a cleaners for a long time. Carla revised her assessment of the Iris Chan case. Michael Lines didn't have a hotshot lawyer arguing for his release, which was the impression Viv Kantz had given. Instead, he was represented by this world-weary attorney who felt passionate enough about his client's case that he was pushing for a mistrial. The thought gave Carla hope. If this man was willing to call his clients low-life, why wasn't he letting Michael rot in jail?

'I'm here about Michael Lines.'

Larry stopped in his tracks and turned to her. 'Who are you? Press? I can spare you half an hour for an interview, but I get to see the copy before you run it.'

'I'm not a journalist. I'm an academic working at Jericho College and I think your client is innocent.'

He ran his eyes over her corduroy dress and flat shoes. 'You do, do you? Well, like I said, I got half an hour for you.'

Larry took her to a van parked on the roadside selling coffees through a side window. 'I know it's chilly outside, but I want to smoke. I'm interested enough in what you have to say to buy the drinks.'

Coffee in hand, she followed him to a nearby picnic bench and took a seat, wiping raindrops from the slats. Even with her coat on, she was freezing.

'So, what's a professor at the college doing getting involved in the Michael Lines case?'

She told him about Tiffany Stoker and the other women before her. The 'unsolveds' as Viv had called them. Then she moved onto Iris Chan.

'I went to Shining Cliff Wood. It's quite a place.'

Larry nodded. 'I used to play there as a child. We loved the name but were always sure to come home before dark.'

'There were stories about the forest?'

He shrugged, drawing deep on his smoke. 'Maybe, but I didn't hear them. The place was enough to give me the chills and my friends must have felt the same because, when the sun set, off we went. There was a witness who saw Iris go into the woods with a man. The first thing I want to tell you is that I believe her. She impressed the jury with her account and I consider her essentially truthful. What I argued was that the man wasn't Michael.'

'Was she able to identify him?'

'Not at all. He was wearing a black coat. Probably a worker's jacket and black jeans, plus a hat pulled down over his head. When they arrested Michael, they found items matching the description in his wardrobe, but I've got them in mine, so has my son. The clothes tell you nothing.'

'He was working in a bar, I believe.'

'Was there all night. The problem is that there was half an hour they couldn't account for, which tallied with the time the witness saw the pair enter the woods.'

'It was still light at nine-thirty?'

'It sure was in June. The problem was that he was Iris's ex. The consensus was that he was punching above his weight anyhow and nobody was surprised when she dumped him. The break-up hit him hard and he was a little, let's say, intense.'

'Could you clarify intense?'

'OK, well, he wouldn't leave Iris alone online even though she blocked him and made her accounts private. When she failed to respond, he'd deposit money into her accounts with threatening messages. It's a classic stalker tactic, I'm afraid.'

Carla sighed, her heart going out to women such as Iris Chan who were victims of men who didn't appreciate that their girlfriends were entitled to call an end to things when they wanted. She still needed to push how dangerous Michael might have been to his former girlfriend.

'You know stalkers do kill their victims,' said Carla.

'I'm aware of that, but I consider Michael to be a lost soul rather than a physical threat.'

'So how come people thought Iris would have walked into a wood with him if she was so desperate to finish things?'

'Her friends were telling her to have it out with him. Emphasise that she'd found someone else.'

'Had she?'

'We think so, but I was never able to identify him, which was a setback for our defence. Prosecutors argued she'd agreed to go for a walk with Michael that evening while he was taking some time off his shift. It's bullshit, of course, but hard to disprove.'

'How did he come across during his defence?'

'I never put him on the stand. The prosecutor would have decimated him. He's not the brightest bulb in the box.'

'According to police, he confessed.'

'After being questioned on and off for twenty-four hours. He'd changed his mind by the trial, pleaded not guilty. Told me straight away he hadn't done it.'

'And you believed him.'

'Not sure if I did at first. It makes no difference to me. Everyone deserves a fair trial whether they're guilty or not. Tensions were high. The college sent along a legal representative and I'm pretty sure there was stuff going on behind the scenes too. Then students were picketing outside the courthouse. "Leave our women alone." Finally, there was Michael, who changed his story about half a dozen times during the legal process. But apart from the confession, which I'm telling you was extracted under duress, he never again admitted to the killing.'

'And you believe there has been a mistrial.'

'The thing is, I do have a possible witness that Michael was at the bar in the missing half hour. He stood in the garden and saw a man smoking a joint. The smell of cannabis wafted over to him. That's unmistakeable, isn't it? Michael admitted to liking the odd joint and in one of his statements he said that he was probably standing in the trees near the bar smoking. I couldn't make the account stick though.'

'What makes you so sure he's innocent?'

Larry stamped on his cigarette. 'Gut feeling, the sense something isn't right. You know the police were desperate for a conviction. So, come on. You've had your pound of flesh from me. Why are you here? You think you can link Iris's death to the other girls who died?'

'I do, but I don't think I can tell you why. This isn't something your legal knowledge will help you with.'

'You're going to need to give me more than that. I've bought your coffee, remember?'

Carla made a face. 'All right. I think Jericho has a serial killer and there are other deaths, not all of them recorded as murder, which I think are relevant.'

He stared at her, a man who had seen and heard everything. 'You are kidding me.'

'I really don't think so.' As she said it, her gaze drifted towards a lump of trees opposite the courthouse where a retreating man hurried away. She stood, trying to catch sight of the figure, but he was gone in a flash.

'Did you see that man across the road?' she asked Larry, who was taking another deep draw on his second cigarette.

'What man?' he asked.

43

Larry had ended their chat by pushing for more detail in respect of Carla's serial killer theory. He was a lawyer after all and wanted to put the wheels in motion of a process that might end up with his client going free. Carla, however, was now convinced her colleague Lauren had been murdered and she was going to be very careful who she explained her theory to, especially given the uneasy feeling she could not shake off. She wondered if it was Franklin's private detective she was seeing out of the corner of her eye and decided she would ask him when they met. If it was not him, then she might be in trouble, as it suggested danger closer to home. If Lauren's notebook had been taken from her office, someone in the faculty must have a hand in its disappearance. Jack was a relative newcomer, although he would have been the first expert for Lauren to go to with her tentative conclusions. Max was another possibility. He had once been close to Lauren, but his interest in the daisy wheels when Carla had explained her theory was little more than academic interest. More likely was that Lauren had brought the notebook to her rendezvous with her killer.

Carla was convinced that Lauren hadn't sensed danger, which suggested the person behind the killings was known to her and someone she considered essentially benign. Carla was confused by the quartz stones that had weighted

Lauren in the river. Quartz, a glittery shiny mineral, had been used in house protection for centuries as some said the devil couldn't bear to see its own reflection. She was also pretty sure the glittery ill-fitting shoes worn by Stella King had also been chosen by the killer for that reason. What Carla couldn't understand was why a murderer would use these symbols unless he believed himself to be on the side of the angels. If he didn't think *he* was the devil, who did he think was?

Carla agreed to see Larry again and at this meeting she would provide more information that could be used for the basis of an appeal. Michael Lines, in the meantime, would remain unaware that back in Jericho, two people were convinced of his innocence.

When Carla returned to college, a security guard waved her over and pointed to a woman sitting on a bench under a plaque listing distinguished patrons of the institution. To Carla's eyes, she didn't look like a Jericho student. She'd made an effort with her appearance, but her dress was cheap and ill-fitting. Students spent a fortune looking grungy.

'Lady over there would like a word with you. I said you had a class at two, but she wanted to wait.'

Carla walked towards the girl. 'I'm Professor James. Did you want to speak to me?'

The girl stood up and smoothed down her dress. 'I'm Mandy. You came to the Lake House when Tiffany went missing.'

'You work there?' Carla shifted her bag and put out her hand.

'Not any more. I'm moving on this week, but I wanted to see you before I leave town.'

'You knew Tiffany?'

'We shared a room when she first arrived as they were short of space. When a unit became available, she moved across the hallway, but we were close.'

Carla looked round, conscious of the lack of privacy. 'Do you want to come to my office?'

Security let them into the building, giving her companion a visitor pass, and she hurried the girl along the corridor. The door to Jack's office was open and he looked up at them briefly as they walked by.

'Have a seat.'

Mandy appeared overawed by the setting. Carla would have preferred to take her to a coffee shop but, conscious of danger, was worried it was too conspicuous.

'How did you find me?'

'I asked Clyde, the manager. He was furious after your visit and wanted to know why you were involved. He looked you up on the internet and saw you were at the college. That made him even more mad.'

'I really am Miss Popularity this week.' Carla cast a look at the door, wondering how secure their conversation would be. She'd heard Jack shouting that time on the phone, but his words had been indistinct. 'What did you want to tell me?'

'Clyde was really upset about the fact that Tiffany's killer was probably at the hotel sometime. He cornered me again, asking if I knew who Tiffany had been dating.'

'And did you?' Carla kept her voice casual. The girl looked ready to take flight at any moment and she wouldn't be opening up to Baros anytime soon. This was the only chance she had to get any important information from her.

'No, but I know she didn't like him. That's why she wanted to get away for a few days. He was creeping her out.'

'Did she say how?'

'She didn't give any details, but I know it came after a visit to his house. I got the impression that something really scared her.'

'She went to his house?' Carla shifted in her seat, trying to calm her eagerness. 'Did she give any clue where this was?'

Mandy shrugged. 'In Jericho. He was definitely local.'

Carla groaned. 'Can't you be any more specific?'

'I can't. Sorry.'

Carla thought of her dinner date that evening. 'Was he wealthy?'

'I think so. He had a car but never wanted to pick her up from the Lake House. She used to hitch a lift downtown.'

'But her purse and phone were still in her room. He must have picked her up the night she died.'

'Maybe, but I don't think anyone saw him.'

So Tiffany did have a secret life. Again, that closed-minded view that rootless people drift from one job to another. They still had emotions and passions and it took time to discover them – time that the detectives had refused to give the case. 'How do you think they originally met?'

'Plenty of people coming and going in the hotel. She could have met anyone.'

'Do you have a lot of functions like the fundraiser I went to last week?'

'All the time.'

Franklin took Carla to an upmarket Italian restaurant by the river. Carla's spirits sank when she saw the subdued lighting and minimalist decor. She was sick of European restaurant food. She couldn't understand why any of her dates couldn't just take her for some clam chowder or fresh crab. She would have to ask Erin to drive her to the coast so she could indulge in her love of seafood. Men, she decided, were just too keen to impress her with their European credentials. Franklin had insisted on picking her up from Patricia's house, although Carla would rather have driven herself. Patricia was out, so she left a detailed note of where she was going on the kitchen table, photographing it and sending the image on to Erin, who replied with a thumbs up.

If Franklin was the killer, she would be at risk. The daisy wheel had been closed but, until the motive behind the killings could be identified, there was always the possibility that a new hexafoil could be started. The danger was real and she would need to downplay her role in the investigation into Tiffany's death and any other views she might have on the other deaths.

Franklin turned out to be a relaxed companion. He had none of Max's high-handedness or Jack's intensity. Despite his vigour, he looked tired and his complexion had the colour of grey clay. As she'd anticipated, he ordered for both of them, although at least he did ask if she liked fish before consulting the waiter on their daily catch.

'Have you been to Italy?' he asked her.

'Of course. I went there on my honeymoon.'

Franklin frowned, concentrating on tasting the wine. 'Bittersweet memories for you then.'

'Not really. Italy has only happy associations for me. What about you?' Carla was in no mood to be quizzed all evening. Franklin was a man who liked to control the flow of conversation, but his questions, although casually put, were scrutiny all the same.

'Vacations only for me, too. It's one of my favourite places.'

Carla looked at her overly fussy starter and thought of the trattoria by the sea where she and Dan had eaten squid ink risotto and quaffed cheap wine.

'Have you ever been married?'

Franklin looked surprised at the question. 'Briefly when I was in my early twenties. It only lasted a year. I don't think my ex-wife had bargained for a workaholic husband. We're still friends and she remarried shortly after our divorce.'

'I believe you dated my colleague, Lauren.'

'Lauren? We certainly dated, but it wasn't serious. You heard what happened to her?'

Carla nodded. 'Her things were still in the office when I moved in.'

'You're in her office? I guess it figures. The college has a reputation of moving on from trauma swiftly. It was a shock when I heard she'd died. She gave no indication of any mental anguish while we were together.'

'She went in the river by Suncook Park, I believe.'

'So I heard.' Franklin leant back in his chair, putting down his fork. 'Let's change the subject, shall we? I was fond of Lauren.'

They paused while the waiter took away their plates. 'Did you go to college here?' she asked him.

He laughed. 'Good guess, but I went to NYU. I was desperate to get away from this town and experience the city. I wanted to go west coast, I had my eye on UCLA, but there was no way my folks were going to agree to that. New York was the compromise.'

So, for all his status in Jericho society, he had at least experienced another world. 'You studied architecture?'

He laughed. 'Film studies. I know, but I had a blast. Then my father died and I returned to Jericho to look after the family construction business. Let's just say I'm putting my creative flair into my designs.'

He'd given her the opening she'd been waiting for. 'I went to one of your constructions a few weeks back. The mall named after you.'

'Not my choice of name, I hasten to add.' He shrugged as if he had no say in the matter. 'It went to a poll in the local press and that one got the most votes.'

He hadn't asked them to choose another entry though, thought Carla. She smiled. 'It's got an unusual pattern. Did you decide on it?'

'Ultimately, although it went through various committees before landing on my desk. Do you like it?'

'It feels very organic.'

'Organic. That's the right word. I liked the swirling feel to the pattern.'

It's a hexafoil, she wanted to tell him, but the thought of Lauren's body laden with the quartz stones in the river held her tongue.

'What are your interests, Carla? I know that you're an archaeologist, but that's it. What's your specialism?'

'I'm interested in the dead, which probably sounds a bit self-evident for someone who digs up the past, but I'm interested in the archaeology of emotion. There's a tendency for rationalism in my job, which I'm all in favour of, but I like to dig into people's feelings – fear, love, anger – behind some of the decisions they made and how that might upend any orthodoxy that's been adopted in academic studies.'

'Can you give me an example?'

Carla picked up her glass of wine. 'Sure. Take my colleague Jack Caron's interest in ritual house protection, you know, dead cats in fireplaces, dolls stuffed into rafters.' She kept her voice light. 'For an archaeologist, the discovery of these artefacts are fascinating in themselves. It allows you to plot patterns of distribution, changes over time, the continuing importance of ancient metals such as iron as protection. What I'm interested in though is the emotion behind them. In New England, for example, an unfamiliar country might have contributed to feelings of alienage and loss among settlers. But other emotions might have been present. Religious extremism – the Pilgrim Fathers, after all, were fleeing persecution – might have encouraged these ritual practices, preachers reinforcing the sense of magic from the pulpit. Religion and folklore practice were closely entwined and constantly shifting.'

Franklin was staring at her. He had unusual mid-blue coloured eyes which he fixed on you as you were speaking. Women probably found it attractive, but the intensity of his gaze was difficult to meet and it had nothing to do with magnetism. Something she had said had struck a chord and the memory wasn't welcome.

'I don't know much about religion,' he said, finally. 'I suppose you're right.'

'You don't use them in your own buildings?' She kept her tone light.

This amused him. Whatever she had said that he hadn't liked, it wasn't this. 'No need for protective charms in my houses. I build them well enough.'

44

Lauren had been the hardest to kill. He considered her to be intellectually on a par with himself; not a chance woman unlucky enough to be in the right place at the wrong time nor a casual acquaintance sucked into his scheme. He'd first met her at a garden party hosted by Anna just before Lauren had taken up her position at the college. She was new to Jericho and had the imprint of the Arizonan sun on her skin. The attraction had been immediate, but there had been plenty of reasons for keeping their relationship quiet and Lauren had gone along with the silence. Enjoyed it, even. She'd not been your typical archaeologist. She liked to switch off after work and talk about a new movie or an art exhibition in Boston she intended to visit when she could grab some time off. He had, however, seriously underestimated her talent for spotting what was off. Lauren had noticed what all the algorithms of visiting experts had not. A pattern, or at least the beginnings of one.

With further deaths, the shape would have been easier to identify, which meant Lauren had to become part of the design. It had taken a while to tease out what she had discovered, but once she had confided in him, the revelations poured from her. She had been easy to lure to the river. A romantic spot, Suncook was well-lit in the evening. The lights of the church had been on and into the air came the odd note of music. Organ or choir practice, he wasn't sure, but Lauren hadn't been on her guard.

Once overpowered, he dragged her into the water and held her by her coat until she drowned. The stones came later. The glittering pebbles had their own meaning and, he suspected, it wouldn't take Carla long until she spotted what others hadn't. Time was no longer on his side and plans needed to be put into action.

45

'Carla, can I have a word with you in my office?'

Albert was waiting for Carla in the corridor near her office. He hadn't sent his secretary to find her or emailed a message saying he wanted to talk to her. It suggested this meeting was off the cuff and unofficial. His usually genial face was set and she had a pretty good idea what was coming.

'Of course.'

Viv had been furious with her and there was no way she'd have kept it to herself. Carla was beginning to realise that the professional and personal were blurred in Jericho. People went to kindergarten together, attended birthday parties, graduations and, if they were bright enough, Jericho College. Gossip was rife and yet secrets well kept. She wondered what exactly Viv had told Albert.

Carla took the seat in front of Albert's desk. It looked like he was marking some mid-semester papers and she could see his red scrawl correcting the writing of some hapless undergraduate. To his credit, he didn't beat about the bush.

'I know I made a mistake taking you out to Silent Brook the first day of your job here.'

Carla stayed silent. Right or wrong, at least Albert was putting himself first at fault.

'However, Viv tells me the death has become a bit of an obsession for you. I blame myself. You only lost your husband a few years ago and of course you were going to be affected by what you saw. From what Viv says, the investigation into the death of Tiffany Stoker is progressing well.'

'That's not true. The detectives involved haven't a clue what they're doing and her death is going the same way as the others. The case will be allowed to go cold because no one is looking for the pattern.'

Albert made an effort to control his temper. 'Viv also accepts she made a mistake granting you access to the files of Jessica Sherwood, Stella King and Madison Knowles. She was desperate to find a possible link between the deaths and was willing to grasp at anything.'

'There is a pattern, if you'll let me—'

'I don't want to hear it. Viv tells me that you've been asking questions about the death of Iris Chan. That case is nothing to do with you. It was a very painful case for this college. Iris had only recently graduated and it came not long before the killing of Madison Knowles. Two students' deaths could ruin this place's reputation.'

'They're connected. If you'd just—'

'They are not!' Albert shouted at her, his frustration spilling over. 'After an extensive trial, Michael Lines was convicted of Iris's murder. You are interfering in something you know nothing about.'

Trembling, Carla took a deep breath. 'I was simply pointing out to Viv the extension of the pattern. It all fits if she'd listen to me.'

'This so-called pattern, according to you, extends to the death of Lauren, is that true?'

'Yes, it does.'

'So not only are you questioning my wife's professional competence but also that of your mentor too. The medical examiner was very clear that Lauren's death was suicide.'

'Which is why I'm so positive it's someone very clever behind the killings. I've tried to explain the pattern to Viv, but she's not seeing the design.'

'You also say there's a connection to the sex worker who died outside Franklin Mall. Are you telling me that he's in some way involved? Franklin is a significant benefactor to this college. We are doubly blessed as he didn't even attend this institution. What role does he play in this?'

'I don't know.'

Albert lowered his voice, his calm more intimidating than his temper. 'You need to leave this to the professionals. Viv is very upset about you raking up Iris Chan's death and I will not have the reputation of a valued colleague, as Lauren was, trashed because of some random theory. I've already had questions about your professional competence.'

'What? Who's questioned my work?'

'That's none of your business. I'm giving you an informal warning that I don't want to hear you've been undertaking a private investigation in college hours. I can't stop you doing what you want in your spare time, but under no circumstances are you to harass people like James Franklin.'

'Was it him who complained about me?'

'This conversation is over.'

Furious, Carla stormed back into her office, resisting the temptation to slam the door, now beginning to see what

Erin had warned her about at the beginning of her tenure. Men, especially those with long family links to the town, held the balance of power in this institution. There was no one Carla could complain to. While she could argue she had been brought into Tiffany Stoker's murder investigation as an unofficial consultant, she had no defence when it came to the other women.

The conversation had been revealing, but what had struck Carla was it wasn't her questioning the conviction of Iris Chan that had brought about her reprimand; it was her insistence that Lauren had not died by her own hand. She had struck a nerve, and she was at a loss why it had made first Viv and then Albert so angry.

She heard a knock on the door. 'Come in,' she shouted. It was unlikely to be Albert coming to make amends.

Jack opened the door, his expression wary. 'I heard about the row.'

Carla put her head in her hands. 'Who from?'

'Albert was steaming this morning looking for you. I guessed you'd be in for a dressing down when you went into his office. What did he say?'

Carla lifted her head, her face set. 'That I'm not doing my job. That I'm obsessed with seeing patterns where there are none. That someone has questioned my professional competence.'

'Who's questioned your competency?'

'I don't know. Do you?'

'Me? I've heard nothing but good reports about you and I certainly don't have any complaints.'

'Maybe it's not a colleague but someone external who doesn't like what I'm doing. I wondered if Franklin had said anything.'

'Franklin? But he doesn't know you at all, does he? You only met recently at the fundraiser.'

'We had dinner together the other evening.'

'*Did* you.' Jack's face had an odd expression.

'We talked about Lauren, but I didn't actually say anything to him about her death. I also asked him about the architecture of his developments. Again, he didn't seem particularly perturbed, but I think it's a big coincidence Franklin asks me out the same day Viv finds me to give me a talking to.'

'Still convinced about your witch bottle theory?'

Carla frowned and waved her hand. 'I don't want to talk about it. I've some thinking to do.'

'Try me. We could go get a drink if you like.'

Carla looked up at the clock on her wall. 'It's only three p.m.'

'Got any more classes today?'

'No, but I've been warned that during office hours I'm to be doing my job, not meddling in affairs that I have nothing to do with.'

'I don't think Morrell's counts as meddling. Come on. You might as well be hanged for a sheep as a lamb. As a reward, I'll tell you a few things about Albert and Viv.'

Morrell's was quiet. The lunch crowd had disappeared and the few stragglers left appeared to be conducting business meetings over a glass of wine. While Max had placed them at a table in the middle of the room, Jack chose a booth.

'What shall we have? Gin and tonic?' he asked.

'Why not. I'm just looking to see if Zoe is about. Did you know she worked here?'

'Albert probably mentioned it. Anna doesn't like it here, so we don't come often.'

'How is she?'

'She's fine. We're having a bit of a break from things. I thought I'd better say it first before you heard the news from someone else. We only decided yesterday, but she's already gone back to her folks, so her mother will have already told all her friends.'

'God, I'm sorry. Are you OK?'

Jack shrugged, his mouth turning down at the corners. 'It was a mutual decision. Things have got a little tense recently and neither of us was happy. We're hoping the break will put things in perspective.'

'You mean in relation to children?'

'In relation to everything.' He took a deep breath. 'So, tell me about your dinner with Franklin.'

'There's nothing to say. He rang me out of the blue and asked me to dinner. He took me to a French restaurant, nothing like the one we visited, and I had a very expensive meal, I assume. There weren't any prices on the menu.'

'You didn't tell him about the work you'd been doing into the deaths?'

'No, but I wouldn't be surprised if he already knows. You know, I keep getting this feeling that I'm being watched. I wanted to ask Franklin if he employed a private detective. I mean, he knew my phone number and where I lived without asking me.'

Jack frowned. 'You know, a half-decent detective could find out any of that information without leaving their office, so why would they need to follow you? I've heard, for example, some of the cops down at the precinct aren't averse to a backhander from Franklin. He likes to know what's going on in the town.'

'What about Baros and Perez?'

'Don't know them, I'm afraid.'

'Viv?'

Jack paused a moment too long. 'I'm not sure.'

'I bet it was Franklin who called Viv. He sounds like he's got the whole place in his pocket.'

'What's going on, Carla?'

Carla pulled out a pen and drew the daisy wheel on a napkin. 'Mean anything to you?'

'Of course.'

She was watching his face intently, conscious more than ever that he knew more about the subject than her. The murderer was prepared to play with symbols of counter magic, which suggested a confidence in their knowledge.

'I think the killer has killed six women, including Lauren, to match each point exactly on a daisy wheel pattern and I can't get anyone to believe me.'

'You mean he's taken an apotropaic mark as a larger pattern.'

Carla sank half her G and T in her excitement. 'Exactly.'

'Why?'

She grimaced. 'I don't know.'

Jack laughed. 'Sorry, I don't mean to be rude, but isn't motive a key element of any investigation?'

'All right, rub it in.'

'Sorry. Who've you told this theory to?'

'Anyone who will listen. Viv, two of her detectives – Baros and Perez – Erin, and now you. I tried to tell Albert, but he wouldn't give me the time of day.'

'And you can't get anyone to believe you?'

'No one. I mean, Viv has called in all these experts and I'm the one who found the pattern and she doesn't want to know. What does that say to you?'

'That perhaps she has a vested interest in keeping things quiet. You know, Viv relies on her reputation to run things. It's not an easy position to hold. There have, however, been whispers that not everything is rosy.'

'What do you mean?'

'I don't know. No one will actually come out and say anything against Viv, but I do hear the odd whisper. I tell you who will know: Anna.'

'Will you ask her?'

Jack sighed. 'You know, we've just separated. It's not something I can casually drop into the conversation.'

'Will you though?'

Jack took a long sip of his drink. 'For you, Carla, anything.'

46

'I'm so close and so far.'

Erin could see Carla's rage and upset threatening to spill over after a couple of drinks with Jack Caron. Erin wasn't sure that she approved of that friendship, but Carla, she suspected, wasn't a woman to take advice on relationships. In professional matters, she was a little more relaxed and Erin liked to think she'd been open enough to admit that initial conclusions might have erred. Erin didn't like where things were at all. She was beginning to view the killer as a shapeshifter, hiding in plain sight. Carla had done a pretty good job of convincing her that there was a lone person at work in Jericho, even if Viv and her team of detectives remained hostile.

They were sitting in one of the booths at Morrell's but were sticking to coffee. Carla was a bit tipsy and needed to let off steam after her conversation with Jack. Erin's opinion of Viv had taken a dip and it wasn't just because she was making life difficult for Carla. She had invited the archaeologist in to advise on the case, expecting miracles, and Carla had initially brought nothing to her. So, Viv had ploughed on, listening to the half-baked theories of Baros and Perez. Carla had been expected to get back in her box and continue with her job as if she hadn't seen the body of a woman burnt alive. If that had been it, Carla would have plenty to grumble about, but she hadn't complained.

Instead, that curious mind had picked over the items and found a pattern of sorts that she'd been able to apply to other victims. For that, she deserved a medal, not Viv's disgust.

'You know, and I'm talking as your mentor here, there are processes in place to protect you from harassment. Albert has no right reprimanding you based on Viv's attitude. If a student or member of faculty has complained, then there are due processes to work through. Albert can't hide behind the Kantz name forever.'

Carla took a gulp of her coffee. She was trying to sober up and the lipstick she'd put on made her look younger than her years.

'Don't rock the boat, Erin. Albert is keeping it informal because, first of all, I'm new, and secondly, I don't think going down to Silent Brook was exactly part of my job description. As you say, there are plenty of complaints I could make too.'

'And you're pretty sure that there's a fingerprint next to the hexafoil carved into the window.'

'It's smudged and, even if I could get Baros and Perez down to take an imprint of it, I doubt it would identify the killer. What's infuriating is I don't even think they've been asked to do that. I'm completely discredited and I don't like the feeling at all.'

'Why don't you just get your head down until the end of term. You've just arrived and no one would think any less of you if you concentrated on your job for the next six weeks. Then have a think about how much Jericho suits your career plans. I'm talking to you as your mentor here, Carla.'

Carla shook her head. 'I can't. The fingerprint shows the killer is not infallible and it's that weakness that I intend to exploit.'

'Not giving up then?'

'Not a chance.'

Morrell's was heaving as usual. Erin kept an eye open for any cops she might know, although really she was just anxious about Baros and Perez putting in an appearance. Carla was looking well. She was wearing a dress Erin hadn't seen before and she'd put on weight, which suited her. There was a flush to her cheeks and Erin wondered if it was simply down to the excitement of her discovery.

'The thing is,' said Erin. 'When you're in a bind, you need to look for your allies. They're not always who you might think of immediately. Who have you clicked with at college? You sat next to Max at the fundraiser. Could you count on his support?'

'I suppose so. He plays his cards close to his chest, but I think he's a fundamentally decent man.'

'What does he think of your theory? Have you talked about it at all?'

'A little. It's not his specialism. Most of his research has been on Roman Britain, so he's not able to add much to what I've discovered.'

'They didn't believe in all that then? That's gratifying. You know, I've always approved of the Romans.'

Erin caught Carla's eye and grinned, but Carla didn't return the smile.

'I also get on OK with Jack Caron,' she said. 'Do you know him at all?'

'The Byronic Jack. I wonder how his looks go down with the students.'

'Too well. They don't stop talking about him when they get to my class.'

Erin wondered if she'd imagined the flash of jealousy. It must be galling to an attractive and engaging woman like Carla to have to seize the impetus as students reeled from Jack's class.

'You know, he and Anna have recently separated.' Carla lifted her cup, assuming an air of nonchalance.

'You are kidding me.' Erin leant across the table, shocked. 'I hadn't heard that. What happened?'

'He didn't really say. They were trying for a baby and it wasn't happening. I get the impression that they need a break from each other.'

Erin leant back. 'Well, I can sympathise. Kids are a nightmare when you can't have them and even worse when they come along. Well, well. Jack Caron single. That will make things *very* interesting.'

'What do you mean?'

'Well, it's Anna with the money and I bet there's an iron-clad prenup in place. Jack will have to curb some of his more exuberant behaviour if they do end up getting divorced.'

'Exuberant in what way?'

Erin shot her a glance. Carla had plenty of strengths, but playing it cool wasn't one of them. *Keep away from Jack Caron*, she wanted to tell her. Even the devil is good-looking when they're thirty.

'There's a college society called the Norsemen. Ever heard of it?'

Carla shook her head. 'Should I?'

'You will eventually. It was started by those with Nordic genes, but it's come a long way since the 1930s. Jack was admitted and looking at him, I doubt his ancestors ever set foot in Scandinavia. There was a scandal in the middle of last year. A student was assaulted on campus.'

'Not by Jack?' Carla looked aghast.

'No, but by a friend who he alibied when the police came knocking. Very convenient it was too.' Erin reached out and clasped her friend's arm. 'Be careful. This town looks after its own. You're still grieving and it's a minefield out there. Watch your step. No one likes their competence challenged. That's why you've made so many enemies.'

Erin suddenly felt weary, the exertions of the day catching up with her. She should, of course, be fuming with Carla, who was suggesting she'd missed a clear case of homicide when it came to the death of Lauren Powers. However, Erin couldn't summon up the same outrage she'd directed towards Baros when he'd questioned the competence of her autopsy of Jessica Sherwood.

The problem was drowning was one of the hardest murders to prove. Erin often joked that if she was planning to kill, say, a spouse, she'd wait until they were in the bathtub and grab their ankles to pull them underwater. If they'd had a drink or taken a few painkillers before the act, so much the better. A sedated victim was easier to manage than an alert one. Drownings in a river were a forensic nightmare. Evidence would be washed away, bodies eaten away by water-based critters and full of contusions from slapping up against rocks and other debris.

Erin had done her job and concluded, based on the medical evidence, that Lauren had drowned. Officially, it had then been up to the police to decide on who was responsible for her death. If you're going to assume suicide, then you're going to look for circumstantial evidence, such as a broken relationship or financial disarray.

Lauren, it seemed, was suffering from a love affair gone wrong. Erin didn't think she'd be getting an official letter over this one. It was the police department who'd investigated the killing as suicide, not her.

Carla shrugged, her expression defiant. Erin had a fair idea the plane she'd be taking home at the end of the semester would involve a one-way ticket. She'd never known anyone to create so much upset as Carla had over the last two months.

'The thing is, you've kinda gone off the whole witch bottle thing, if you don't mind me saying. I mean it was pretty off the wall when you first mentioned it, but Viv was at least willing to give you a hearing. Now you've dropped it and you're focused on these daisy wheels. It'd help your case if you at least followed an idea through.'

Carla raised her eyes, colour coming back to her face at the realisation her intellectual abilities were being challenged.

'One of the features of ritual house protection is that there can be circles within circles. Symbols overlap, intersect. That's what we've got here. The witch bottle items are a little in your face. It didn't take me long to find them and Lauren was there before me too. It suggests that the killer was happy to play a little loose with this imagery. He's having a bit of fun.'

'Like "let's just throw some things in the mix".'

'Exactly, and the thing is that's actually reminiscent of anti-witchcraft symbolism around the world. It's a sort of free for all. The same with the scorch marks. However,' Carla paused to take a slug of her drink, 'when it comes to the hexafoils, they're hidden behind a curtain or in flower beds. Here, the killer is being much more circumspect about what he reveals or who he reveals it to.'

'A pattern within a pattern.'

'Exactly.' Carla's voice was too loud, which earned them a frown from a passing waiter. She lowered her voice. 'They were in a wastepaper basket, behind a curtain. One theory is that they weren't meant to be found, another is that the meaning is a lot more oblique.'

'That leaves the case wide open. What are you going to do next?'

Carla dipped her finger in her drink and drew a hexafoil on the table top.

'Concentrate on the daisy wheels.'

47

He was used to reconnaissance trips, but he was having to be very careful. His prey was sharp, more astute than all his previous victims combined. But he was cleverer still. He now needed to make sure he had everything in place for this next killing. For the first time, he felt the pinch of being watched. It hadn't taken him that long to realise that Professor Carla James had become invested in the mystery. Carla was close to discovering what was happening in Jericho, but it would be too late by the time she made the final connection.

When this was all finished, and that would be very soon, he was sure those left behind would pick over the case, searching for what they had overlooked. Of course, the funny thing was they hadn't missed much. What they'd failed to do was listen to someone who had spotted the pattern. He knew there was tension between the Mayor's office and the college. He didn't think any subsequent inquiry would do much to resolve the mutual suspicion. He doubted Carla's career would be much hurt by the role she played in events, but neither would she be getting a pat on the back anytime soon. This was a case earmarked for burial and Jericho would carry on as usual.

He watched as his target left her house, uncaring about her safety. Her absolute arrogance was a source of fury. In the trials of Salem, prosecutors had made sure that women knew they disapproved of the way society was changing. 'And now the world is altered: young gentlewomen learn to be bold,' quoting the famous jurist Sir Matthew Hale in their accusations. He was pretty sure he'd be called a misogynist, sociopath, deviant. But Jericho needed to turn in on itself and look for answers there. He was pretty sure that his final victim knew she was next, and the question was, what was she going to do about it?

48

Carla was fascinated by the preparations for Halloween. Growing up in England, the celebration had been a muted affair. Her mother would fill a washing-up tub with water and apples and she and her brother would take turns catching them with their mouths. Over the years, Halloween had become more of an occasion and she'd kept a box of sweets in her ground-floor flat to give to anyone who might ring her doorbell. In the US, it was something else. She overheard her students deciding on their costumes and film themes were clearly a thing. Most of the references went over her head, but the ghostly twins from *The Shining* had been chosen by a pair of fair-haired friends who could have passed for sisters.

She let her late afternoon class out early. They were itching to get going and their enthusiasm rubbed off on her. She was going to spend the evening trying to gather her thoughts on the dead women and come up with a plan on how to convince both Viv Kantz and Larry Foster that her hunch was correct. She'd not heard from the lieutenant since the confrontation in the car park and Albert was keeping out of her way. However, she'd detected a thawing in Perez's attitude towards her and the young detective was going to be her way into the police department once she'd gathered as much evidence as possible. Erin, however, had other plans and invited her for dinner.

'Ethan's got his friends over and they'll be going up and down the street dressed – wait for it – as characters from *Scooby Doo*. I swear they're regressing to childhood. Where's all this put away childish things?'

'Sounds pretty harmless. Where do I come in? I'm really not in the mood for dressing up.'

'God forbid. They don't need a chaperone. Just come over and bring a bottle of wine. You can keep me company. I won't get any peace until I know he's safely home.'

Given alcohol was on the menu, Carla decided to walk to Erin's. Although cold, the night was full of anticipation as excited kindergarten children began knocking on doors before the dark had even settled. Patricia was ready for them with shop-bought sweets and small cupcakes and Carla helped answer the door until it was time to leave. As she stepped out into the street, she saw that the excitement of the younger children had given way to a more boisterous atmosphere as cute costumes made way for the glitter and gore. There was smoke in the air from fires burning in hearths and Carla's way was lit with lights shining in doorways. She'd planned a route that would keep her to the main streets, and she joined a group of ten-year-olds covered in masses of fake blood. Two boys at the back were counting their haul and fighting over who would get the giant Hershey's bar. Her phone rang in her bag and Erin's voice came down the line.

'I've been thinking. You won't get a cab easily this evening. How about I come by and pick you up. It's no trouble.'

'No need. I'm walking.'

Erin sucked in her breath. 'You are kidding me. It's about four miles. Stay where you are; I'm coming to get you.'

'Erin, I'm doing fine. The walk will do me good. I'm following kids down the street. Everyone is out and I'm perfectly safe.'

'Well, keep to the main roads for God's sake.'

Carla carried on, taking a left turn down a road leading to a stretch of the river she hadn't seen before. The water was faster here. If Lauren had decided to end her life, her body, even with the stones, would have been carried downstream and out of Jericho. It was the place someone determined to end their life would choose rather than Suncook. Despite Viv's anger, the police had not done their jobs properly that night. Carla suspected once suicide was seen as a most likely explanation, perceptions of motivation, location and choice of method allowed a narrative to be constructed far from the truth. It had nearly happened with Iris Chan too until a witness had come forward. More incompetence.

Carla carried on upstream, glad that the path was busy. The wealthy homes next to the river were being made for by the trick or treaters – richer pickings for the revellers. She passed the spot in the river that Lauren had entered and Suncook Park where the worker's bottle had rolled onto the grass. The space was illuminated in the dark and showed the rose beds pathetic in their autumn sparseness with just the stems and the iron stakes used to support the plans during the summer showing. Now that foliage had been dropped, Carla could see the pattern made by the circular beds formed five daisy wheels. Shit.

She stopped, trying to recall her conversation with the gardener. He'd mentioned Franklin but not whether his boss had ever paid the park a visit, let alone overseen the design of the rose beds. However, the pattern was in front of her eyes. She wobbled up the incline and took a photo of one of the rose beds. Franklin had shown little interest in the park when Carla had mentioned it. She would call him again, if she could get past his damn secretary, and ask him outright who had designed the beds. If he began hedging with her, she would know he himself had something to hide.

Carla crossed the bridge and walked down the steps to the path on the other side of the river. Erin lived a couple of streets behind the waterfront row of restaurants, a prime real estate plot. Downtown had a busier air but fewer revellers. Parents were probably escaping from the excitement, taking the opportunity to have a bite to eat. As Carla turned down a passageway, the air stilled and the sound of traffic and people chatting dialled down to nothing. She was minutes from Erin's house and she sped up, conscious of the deserted passage lined by a high wooden fence. *Calm down*, she told herself. Jericho was safe and it was locations that were important to the killer. She stepped with relief into the street-lit road, blinking as a car sped past, its headlights dazzling her.

As she was congratulating herself on making it up the passage, a hand grasped her head, pulling her back into the dark. She twisted, grabbing her attacker's shirt, which tore away from her grip. She saw he was wearing a mask, a grotesque crone's face made up of wrinkles and warts. A cheap party trick designed to instil fear. She tried to tear it off, kicking at the man while pushing her hand against his neck. She dimly recognised his scent and struggled to articulate a name that she could use to fight back. As his grip shifted, she managed to get her mouth around his bare hands and she sank her teeth into flesh. He yelped in pain and let go for an instant. It was enough leverage to free herself; she stumbled away into the path of a car, landing with a thud on its bonnet.

—

'Who did you tell you were coming to Halloween at mine?' Erin placed a damp face cloth on the swelling emerging on Carla's forehead.

'No one. I haven't seen anyone to speak to since you invited me. Only Patricia knew I was going out, but I didn't tell her where.'

'Then he must have followed you from Hoyt Street. Did you notice anyone behind you?'

'The streets are packed. I walked behind a few groups who would peel off when they came to a house. On the path by the river, it was quieter, but there were still people.'

'You say he was wearing a costume.'

'He was all in black with a warty mask with the image of a witch or scary old woman, the type you might meet in the woods. The thing is, when I entered the passage, I'm sure no one was behind me.'

'Then they must have sped up when they realised the alley was clear. Nice that he now has an imprint of your teeth. If I were you, I'd try to have a little chat with Franklin tomorrow and take a look at his hand.'

'I'll be doing that along with a few other suspects.' Now her terror had subsided, Carla wanted to pay a visit to each of the men who knew about her daisy wheel theory and see who was hiding their hands. What the assault had left her with was the conviction she knew her attacker, although she still couldn't identify the smell.

'How do you feel?' asked Erin.

'Terrible.'

'I've called the cops. Someone will take a statement, although I guess your attacker isn't walking the streets with his mask on any longer.'

'Oh, God. I hope it's not Baros.'

'Don't worry. It'll be common patrol who deals with this kind of thing.'

Erin was wrong. When the doorbell rang, Baros and Perez stood on the doorstep looking grim. Baros stepped over the threshold before his partner.

'We heard the call over the radio and thought we'd pick it up. When we heard the address, we thought it was you, doc.'

He didn't look overly sorry that the victim was, in fact, Carla. She'd already turned away an ambulance. Her new post gave her medical insurance, but she wasn't sure of the procedures around hospital admission and how much she'd have to pay herself. Other than a banging head and an attack of the shivers, she was more or less unharmed.

'So, what happened?' asked Baros, settling himself on Erin's sofa. His eyes were on the bottle of red Carla had been carrying in her shoulder bag. Perhaps he'd ask her to whip out her ID so she could prove she was over twenty-one.

'I was grabbed outside the passageway that leads onto this road. The thing is, I'm sure I know my attacker,' she said.

Baros flicked a glance at Perez. 'Go on.'

'When he grabbed me, I recognised his smell. I know it sounds ridiculous, but there was a scent around him I recognised.'

'Aftershave.'

'I'm not sure it's that. Maybe deodorant or soap. I can't say for sure. He was sweating, probably with adrenaline, and I could smell that too, but there was a familiarity to his scent that I'm trying to place. I think I might have smelt it in my office too.'

'If it's deodorant or soap, it's probably shared by many men.' Perez jotted something into her notepad. 'What about his height or build? These are harder to hide.'

'He was bigger than me.'

Baros cast a dismissive glance at Carla. 'I'm going for opportunist. Woman walking down a dark alley, a reveller takes a chance. Could be a teenager.'

'Come on.' Erin had heard enough. 'Halloween revelries are usually safe enough. Someone has targeted Carla, possibly because of her looking into the deaths of those women.'

Baros was dismissive. 'Doesn't sound very likely.'

'I think you should listen to her.' Perez's voice was unnaturally calm and Baros shot her a look.

'What's the matter with you? You got yourself a new pal, Perez?'

'The prof has got a theory about daisy wheels and I think you should listen.'

'You want to be back in vice or, worse, in uniform marshalling traffic? Didn't you hear the lieutenant? No witch bottles, no daisy wheels – we play this by the book. This lady here is persona non grata.'

Perez folded her arms. 'You saw the pattern on the glass at Miss Sherwood's property. There was a similar mark on the paving slabs near the generator. The place is full of graffiti, but this flower was different because it was made with red chalk.'

'Is this what you meant when we met at Jessica's house?' Carla held her aching head. 'More daisy wheels.'

'It was graffiti,' snorted Baros. 'Anyway, I didn't see it.'

'There was a photo. It's been wiped from the file.'

Carla stared at Perez. 'Wiped? Who by?'

Perez looked at Baros. 'I don't know.'

Baros stood. 'The boss says there's no connection and I'm with her.'

'If the mark was made of chalk, it can't have been there very long. Chalk would have been washed away in the rains. It must have been scored onto the paving around the time of Tiffany's death.' Carla pointed to her aching head. 'I've made enough ripples over the last few days and your killer has got wind of my theory.'

'I don't think—' Baros's radio crackled to life. 'We've got to go. Can you come down to the station tomorrow to make a statement? We'll put out a description of your attacker, but don't hold your breath.'

Perez put her notebook away, her eyes on Carla. 'You take care, prof. Maybe stay the night with your friend.'

'Oh.' Baros stopped. 'And I need to pay you a visit and pick up all your notes. Order from the lieutenant. I'll be there in the morning.'

'Well,' said Erin after they'd gone. 'You've got him riled. You know, I think I'm going to call Ethan and ask him to come home. I don't feel happy about him out there with a killer loose.'

49

Erin told Carla she was going to look for Ethan, who wasn't answering his phone. She gave Carla strict instructions not to answer the door to anyone, even if she knew them. *Especially* if she recognised the caller. Carla rested on the living room sofa, sketching hexafoils on a piece of paper as the killer had drawn or appropriated at each killing. The final image had been a rough chalk mark hidden amongst the other graffiti at Tiffany Stoker's death scene, according to Perez. Carla was pretty sure the colour wasn't accidental. Red ochre or oxblood was a popular colour in ritual protection, signifying blood and sacrifice. In Wales, where Carla had completed her undergraduate degree, some rural houses had been painted with red-coloured limewash, which had served the same protective function as a witch bottle.

Carla was still no clearer in shaping in her head the identity of the killer. Here was the biggest gap between her knowledge as an archaeologist and her unofficial role as an amateur investigator. She had no experience of perpetrators of crime and the killer would not come into focus for her. With the sixth point of the hexafoil, the deaths must surely be complete. She still couldn't guess at a reason for the pattern and, in this, she suspected the police were right. There was no connection between the women chosen. The pattern was in the setting, and it had taken two archaeologists – first Lauren who had got part of the way there and then herself – to discern, however faint, an ancient design.

Despite this, she was sure she was close to the truth. The attack this evening had felt personal and, despite Baros's assurances, Carla was pretty sure she'd met the person responsible. The three male colleagues she'd talked about the witch bottles and daisy wheels with were Albert, Jack and Max. All in their own way were highly unlikely to attack her outside Erin's. She often worked late on campus. The walk back to the car park was brightly lit but often deserted. It would be easy for them to strike there. The problem was, she supposed, that an attack on campus would result in questions and staff and students under the spotlight. Far better to try to halt her progress elsewhere. No, she would not rule out her three colleagues. Then there was Franklin. When he'd reached in to kiss her cheek, she'd inhaled his scent. Was this the same as that of her attacker, who had also smelled of fear, the chemical pheromone released in their sweat? Franklin, after all, owned the land that housed the mall and the flower beds. He had also dated Lauren.

Carla looked down at the doodles she'd completed. The problem with drawing the daisy wheels freehand was her circles were wonky and the petals misshapen. Original marks would have been made with a mason's compass or even a stick with a piece of string and pencil attached. Something to keep the lines steady. Carla's lines often missed the centre, making the shape lopsided.

The centre was the graveyard at Lawrence Hill. She'd gone there and found the Miller graves but had not had a chance to look into this further. On her phone, she typed in the surname and Jericho. As Patricia had predicted, it was a common last name. The graves had been unkempt, which suggested a living descendant might be excited enough to use the design in their killings but had no real connection to their ancestors. It would also account for the fact that there was no cohesion to the objects and markings placed at the murder scenes. Someone was playing with the imagery and nothing else.

Carla continued to flick through the images when she paused, scrolling back to an image where she had recognised a figure. A press photo showed the Miller graves; standing next to them were Albert and Viv Kantz. Carla opened up the news report. The article reported unusual stops on the tourist trail and the Miller graves had been singled out as a site to visit if you fancied something a little more unusual. What were the Kantzs doing there? Carla was in such a hurry to get to the bottom of the piece that she missed the important sentence twice. 'Standing next to the grave of her ancestors is Lieutenant Vivian Kantz.'

Shit. Viv clearly knew about the Miller graves and here was photographic proof. When Carla had mentioned witch bottles, Viv had barely reacted, simply mentioning a German grandmother. It was Carla's daisy wheel theory that had seriously upset the lieutenant. Carla rubbed her aching head, trying to make sense of it. Surely Viv wasn't the killer. A trained cop might be able to overpower a sleeping Madison but surely not Lauren with her muscled limbs. Plus, the person walking into the woods with Iris had been a male, taller than Viv's tiny stature. Either she had got everything wrong or Viv had an accomplice. Unless—

She needed to speak to Albert and Viv as soon as possible. Carla tried Albert's phone, but it was engaged. There was no point ringing the station as Viv would have made sure she was uncontactable for Carla. She would need to head out to talk to the pair in person, but Albert hadn't said where in Jericho he lived. She rang Erin, her hands still shaking as she tapped the phone.

'Where are you?'

'Still looking for Ethan. Everything OK?'

'I need to speak to Viv and Albert as soon as possible.'

There were whoops of excitement in the background. 'What? I can't hear you. Who do you want to talk to?'

'Viv Kantz,' shouted Carla.

'I thought you two weren't friends.'

'Can you just give me their address? This is important.'

'They live on Thaxted Street on the edge of town. Don't ask me for the number because I can't remember it. It's a square brick house, newly built by your friend Franklin. What's going on?'

'I'll tell you later.'

Carla left the house and jumped into a cab, which she managed to hail amongst the throng of people. She needed to get home to pick up her car. Tonight, more than ever with an aching head and shredded nerves, she needed to be mobile and safe. The younger children had left the street and the noise had grown more raucous. Somewhere amongst that noise, Erin was trying to track down Ethan. She didn't much fancy his chances once his mother had got hold of him.

Patricia had left the light on, illuminating the doorway. Carla already had the keys in her hand before the taxi drew up outside the garden. She thrust twenty dollars into the driver's hand and rushed up the steps. Making sure the door was secured, she ran up to her room, pulling out the map Ethan had printed for her and the rest of her notes. This was the moment to insist Viv and Albert listened to her. It was All Hallow's Eve, a night with its origins in the Celtic festival of Samhain when the souls of the dead were considered to return to their homes. It was a day too full of meaning to pass unrecorded and there was the terrible possibility that the killer would be making their way this evening to the centre of the circle. To Viv Kantz.

50

Carla typed Thaxted Street into her GPS and saw it was a short dead-end street carved into an otherwise barren landscape. Franklin was clearly extending the town's limits, changing the shape of Jericho as he pushed into surrounding tracts of land. She'd left a note for Patricia on the kitchen table and a voice message for Erin. It was the only back-up she could think of. The people she also wanted to contact – Jack, Max, Albert, Franklin – she was now unsure of their trustworthiness. If she got it wrong, the outcome could be devastating for her. As she turned into the development, she saw an advertising board jutting out from the hillside. Franklin Enterprises. All roads led to Franklin.

She parked up at the top of the road. A square brick house Erin had said, a description which was no use at all. There were ten of them, five on each side built in a mock colonial style. She tried to remember what car Albert had driven when he took her over to Silent Brook, but the day had become a blur. She'd have to improvise but wasn't sure it was a good idea to go knocking up and down the street. She'd watched too many Halloween films and would likely be met with suspicion as a lone woman. The Kantz family, however, would surely be known by their neighbours. She put on her old dig jacket, its earthy smell a source of reassurance and comfort, and set off.

The first two houses were empty. Neither of them had made any attempt to disguise the fact they were in total darkness, which suggested the area didn't have much of a crime problem. The resident of the third house took an age to come to the door. In the distance there was the sound of two little dogs yapping and eventually a burly man with tattoos on his arms answered.

'I'm sorry, I'm looking for Viv and Albert Kantz's house.'

'What d'ya want with them?'

'Albert is my boss at the college. I need to speak to him urgently. I can show you my pass if that helps.'

The man shook his head. 'You don't want to be knocking on random doors at night. Not everyone wants to answer the door after dark even if it is Halloween.'

'Point taken. I'll try another couple of houses.'

'They live across the way there.' The man nodded over the road and shut the door.

The house opposite had a light burning above the door and three glowing pumpkins with grotesque faces on the doorstep. The carvings were inexpertly done, executed with more enthusiasm than skill. The door opened immediately to Carla's knock. Albert stood on the threshold, his gaze focused on the empty driveway behind her.

'Carla, is there a problem?'

'I... I don't know.' Carla felt her knees buckle and Albert reached out to catch her. She got the scent of cigarettes. She never knew he was a smoker, hadn't got up close enough to notice and she realised with relief he wasn't her attacker. 'I'm sorry, I had an accident this evening. Can I come in for a moment?'

He took her into the kitchen and the expectant faces of Zoe and Liam turned to greet her. They were dressed as Princess Leia and Luke Skywalker and already had their buckets ready.

'We thought you were Mom,' said Zoe. 'She was going to take Liam trick or treating and she's not come home.'

'Do you know where she is?'

Zoe looked at her father. 'We're not sure. I've put on her costume and am taking Liam myself.'

'Okay, kids, off you go,' said Albert. 'Start at the top of the drive and work downwards. Remember to ask politely and, if there's a loud dog, keep your hands in your pockets.'

'Sure, Dad.' Albert took them to the door and let them out into the night.

He came back into the kitchen. His eyes were tired and he sat down at the counter, rubbing his face. 'Viv isn't home yet, which is strange. She never misses a Halloween. When the kids were younger, it was for the fun of it. Then more recently after all the deaths she's had to deal with, she didn't want Liam out by himself. I told her this is a safe area and the kids will stick to this road but still.'

'Perhaps she's caught in traffic. Have you tried her mobile?'

'Every ten minutes or so. It's switched off. Why are you here, Carla? I know things have been a little fraught recently with us and I'm sorry about that.'

Carla steadied her voice. What she needed, more than anything, was for him to believe what she was about to tell him. 'I'm worried Viv might be in danger. I think it's due to the killings that have taken place here.'

'Oh God, Carla. Go home. I'm trying to track down my wife. I don't have time for any madcap theories.'

The injustice of it made Carla smart, but she kept her cool. 'I'm asking you to ring the station and say you need to get in touch with Viv urgently. Pretend one of the children is ill if you have to but get hold of her.'

Albert studied her face for a moment.

'You're serious, aren't you?'

'Very. I was attacked earlier tonight. Whatever the killer is planning, I think it's going to be executed tonight.'

Albert paled and slid off the stool. 'Give me a chance to call Charlie Baros. It means if I make a prize ass of myself, I'm doing it in front of a detective I know.'

He took himself out of the kitchen to make the call and Carla used the opportunity to check her phone. There was a message from Erin asking if she was OK. *Fine. I think*, she typed as a reply. *I'm at the Kantzs's. I'll be in touch.*

Albert returned looking unhappy. 'Baros has been trying to get hold of Viv himself. Apparently, a group of kids has caused damage to a garden down by the river. Fallen statues, plants trampled on. Nothing spectacular but, as it's the Mayor's family, ruffled feathers need to be smoothed. A job for Viv, but no one can find her. Baros is coming over here. Says it's the second time he's seen you this evening.'

'He might want to listen to me this time. Shall we wait for him to arrive?'

'I'd rather you told me what this is all about now.'

'OK.' Carla pulled out her map. 'Could you listen to me until the end? I need your brain on this too, Albert.'

'Go on.' Albert had his eyes on the map.

'Here's the daisy wheel that I've overlaid with the locations of the crime scenes of six women who died in the last few years. One of which was your colleague, Lauren Powers. I'm sorry, I know it's painful, but there is a pattern. Look at the six points of the flower. One Stella King; two Madison Knowles; three Iris Chan; four

Lauren Powers; five Jessica Sherwood; six Tiffany Stoker. All dead.'

Albert bent his head over the map and looked at each of the sites. 'I can see that. What's in the centre?'

Carla experienced a surge of triumph. He'd asked the important question straight away. 'It's Lawrence Hill cemetery and, I think, specifically the Miller graves.'

'Jesus. What the hell is going on? What's my wife's family got to do with this?'

'I don't know. All I can assume is that the elaborate killings are a message to Viv. I did wonder if Viv was responsible for the pattern.' Carla saw Albert's face colour. 'I know, I'm sorry, but Viv was furious at the thought of the daisy wheels and it might have been because I was getting closer to their meaning. But the killer of those girls is male and I don't believe Viv is a killer.' Carla paused. 'Please at least reassure me on that point.'

Albert took a deep breath. 'I promise you she had nothing to do with those women's deaths. They've kept her awake at night with worry.'

'Then we need to look for someone else. I know my idea sounds off the wall, but I don't understand why it's been dismissed out of hand. I can only suppose that, at some point when she discovered I was arguing that the daisy wheels were significant, she realised there might be a connection with her family.'

'You think one of her relatives might be responsible for this?'

'I'm not sure. I don't understand why she's tried to close me down. It doesn't make sense after all the experts she brought in found nothing. It was she who invited me to Silent Brook on my first day.'

He stared at the map, trying to make sense of the pattern. 'If the very first mark you make is at the place where you place the compass, then shouldn't the first death have occurred at the centre?'

'Possibly, but when you've drawn the daisy wheel, you lift off your compass and, if you're correct, all the lines intersect. It's the end as well as the beginning. That's the whole point of the design; it never ends. The design is supposed to capture devilish forces and keep them suspended in perpetuity.'

Albert lifted his head, his expression anguished. 'Do you think my children are in danger?'

'I don't know.'

They both jumped as the doorbell rang, which Albert hurried to answer. Baros came in alone, his face tense. 'I've dropped Perez at the Mayor's house. She's taking statements. We've asked at the station and the lieutenant definitely left about forty-five minutes ago. She left no message where she was headed, but she was in a hurry. So, what's going on?' Baros shot a concerned glance at Albert. For the first time, Carla saw him off kilter.

'Carla has a theory about the daisy wheel and I think you should listen to her.'

This time, Baros didn't roll his eyes. 'Go on.'

Carla explained her theory once more as Baros stood close to her. Another male smell, this time soap and water, not the aftershave she might have expected to go with his sharp clothes. When she'd finished speaking, he chewed his lip, thinking.

'Can I report her as officially missing?' asked Albert. 'There's no way her mobile should be off.'

Baros nodded. 'Dial 911 and say it's a priority. I'll take the rap if it's a fool's errand.' He turned to Carla. 'You think she'll be at Lawrence Hill?'

'I think that's where she'll be killed. Locations have been important all the way with these killings, but I can't guarantee she's there right now.'

'It's the only place we have. I'll go there now.'

'I need to come with you,' said Albert, grabbing his jacket.

'Albert, please. Go and find your kids and wait with them away from here.' Baros looked at Carla. 'The prof can show me the graves.'

'I—' Albert looked between them.

'I think Viv would want you to look after the kids,' said Carla finally. 'We'll find her.'

51

Ethan was furious with Erin.

'Have you any idea how embarrassing that was, Mom? I've been dragged away in front of all my friends. Why are you acting all weird?'

Erin was in a foul mood and had no intention of rising to the bait. 'Carla was assaulted tonight. There's someone walking around out there who has killed before and I'm not having you wandering the streets while he's loose.'

'Carla? She's completely mental. No wonder she was attacked.'

Erin jammed her foot on the brake, earning her the horn from the car behind. She turned to her son. 'Excuse me?'

He had the grace to blush, fidgeting with the strap on his rucksack. 'I didn't mean it like that; it's just she comes out with this mad stuff and it affects us all. Nothing's been the same since she arrived.'

'Carla's seen what we were all wilfully ignoring. The killer knows it too. It's out in the open and I'm glad about that.' Erin pulled out into the road without looking behind her, which earned her another toot of the horn.

What she couldn't understand was why Carla wanted the address of Viv and Albert Kantz unless she thought one of them was the next target. They were looking for a killer of women, so it must be Viv who was in danger.

Viv, Erin thought, could look after herself, but what about Carla? What about Ethan? Erin could feel danger. The dead didn't scare her at all. The diseased, the deformed, the dismembered. Not one of them gave her nightmares, but now Erin sensed something much worse. She had to remember she was a mother and Ethan was the number one priority for her.

'Ethan. I'm taking you to your dad's.'

'What?' He turned to her. 'You can't do that. He's got his new girlfriend over.'

'Tough. I'm going to find Carla and I need to know you're safe. Pack an overnight bag.'

'I've got things in the closet of my room at Dad's.'

'Good. We'll go straight there.' Erin put her foot on the accelerator. There was a smell of sulphur in the air. Someone had got hold of fireworks and let them off on a neighbour's lawn. Erin decided the following year she and Ethan would be on vacation for the festival. She was sick to the teeth of witches, spirits and all things supernatural, whether real or imagined.

The roads became more congested as they reached the river.

Ethan said, 'Uh-oh, something's going on.'

In the distance she could see squad cars outside one of the big houses on the river. 'Looks like trouble.'

'At least no one's throwing themselves from the bridge,' said Ethan.

'Yet.' Erin leaned out of the window to harangue crowds who refused to move from the highway. 'I think all of Jericho is out tonight.'

'Except me.' Ethan crossed his arms, although he appeared more relaxed with being grounded. 'I saw your friend when I was out. I shouted hello, but he just ignored me. Funny, what's the point of having a costume if you're not going to wear it? He had the mask in his hand.'

Erin went cold. 'Friend? Which friend?'

52

Baros turned up the heater in his car as Carla shivered beside him. 'Delayed shock,' he said to her. 'Tell you what, I'll send you to the infirmary to get you checked over. I can get an ambulance to meet us at the cemetery gates.'

'No chance.' Carla dug into the pocket of her dig jacket and found a strip of Tylenol. She popped two in her mouth as Baros handed her his lukewarm cup of coffee to wash them down.

He frowned. 'I'll say this for you; you're tough. I hope this isn't a wild goose chase. The boss is missing and I'm following one of your hunches.'

'Albert's calling in Viv's disappearance now. View this as a parallel investigation.'

He gave a snort. 'Parallel investigation? I like that. OK, let's say your theory is correct. Who we expecting to find by the Miller graves?'

'It's so frustrating, but I don't actually know.'

'Come on. You have this theory about witch bottles and daisy rings—'

'Wheels,' she corrected. 'Daisy wheels.'

'Apologies. Daisy *wheels*. I was brought up in this county and I've never heard of them. We're not talking about your average piece of graffiti. You know what, I think we're looking for one of your lot.'

'My lot? You mean an academic?'

'Why not? We investigated all the wackadoos when you came out with your witch bottle theory. Nothing doing, so now I'm thinking who we couldn't get to, which leads me to Jericho College.' Baros glanced at her. 'You're quiet for a change. Don't like my theory.'

'I've got another one. Someone who is also hard to reach. How about James Franklin?'

Baros leant on his horn, startling an elderly driver who was dithering at a junction. 'You're kidding me. What makes you think that?'

'There are too many hexafoils connected to him. His mall, Suncook Park. Plus, he was Lauren Powers' lover at one time and his name was in Lauren's notebook alongside yours, remember. It's got to be someone she was prepared to meet at night.'

'Franklin? Christ. No wonder the lieutenant was trying to keep a lid on things. I'm not so sure you're right, though. You're talking about a psychopath and that doesn't sound like Franklin. I mean, I barely know the guy, but we'd be looking at someone with a history of violence against women. I've never heard a peep in relation to Franklin.'

'We're not dealing with someone with a personality disorder. I think this is about something else. The killer has targeted these women in a specific pattern to show off to Viv. The Miller graves connect the hexafoil to her.'

'What's Franklin got against her?'

'I don't know, but why didn't she say anything about her family graves when the hexafoil was mentioned to her? That was the point where she should have informed me of her connection to the design. She's covered up her connection for a reason.'

'I don't like what you're implying. And, for what it's worth, I don't think it sounds like Franklin.'

Carla grimaced. The problem was she now agreed with Baros. Her explanation was off, and she'd have realised it earlier if she'd had the courage to articulate her concerns to a detective. Baros, for all his sneers and arrogance, had a sound view of people.

They had arrived at the gates of the cemetery, which had been locked for the evening. It hadn't stopped adventurous revellers from getting in and lights could be seen dotted around the path leading up the hill.

Baros swore. 'It's a regular party here. Happens every year. If they're not trashing the gardens of the politicians, they're communing with the dead.'

'It works in our favour though, doesn't it? He's not going to assault a trained police lieutenant in front of a crowd of people.'

'You don't think? There were people in the woods when Iris Chan died. He's got no problem taking a chance. What I don't understand is how he got the lieutenant out here.'

'Perhaps he sent a message asking her to come. She'll want to know what he wants, if she doesn't already.'

Baros rattled the gate. 'One thing's for sure, we're not going through this.'

'I don't suppose you've any bolt cutters in the car?'

' 'Fraid not. We go the way of the others. Let me radio Perez first.'

He turned his back on her as he spoke into the handset. She heard him tell his partner about the Miller graves and, for once, he didn't sound his usual cocky self. When he'd finished, she saw him check his gun.

'You think I'm right about this?'

'I don't know, but I'm not taking any chances. Ready?'

Thank God she was wearing trousers. She stepped into his clasped hands and he lifted her above the railings. She grabbed the arched stakes to steady herself, Baros holding on to her until she found her footing the other side. He then lifted himself effortlessly over the fence.

He switched on his torch and led the way up the path. Whoops and shouts could be heard around them as shrouded and masked figures flitted by. Halfway up the hill, two boys jumped out from behind a stone grave, shrieking with their hands in the air. A glance at Baros's face and their cries subsided as they slunk off into the shadows.

'I often have that effect,' he said grimly.

Near the top of the hill, Carla led him across undulating grass covering bodies of Jericho's dead. Even in the darkness, Carla could see the Miller graves were deserted.

'Give me your torch.' She waved it over the small patch. 'These are the graves, but there's no one here. Shit.'

Baros's phone pinged. 'Perez is at the bottom. I think she should come up. Just because we've not found the boss here, doesn't mean your theory was wrong. We spread out.'

Carla felt her eyes sting. 'I was sure I'd find them at the Miller graves. It made sense. The killer started there at the centre and drew the circle incorporating the first location, Franklin Mall. All the other locations were chosen to fit the pattern.'

'You sure the centre is somewhere around here?'

'Positive.'

'Then we keep looking. No one else has got any other ideas where Viv might be. Listen, let's say you're nearly right, that the Miller graves are important. But who the heck knows about them? People who come regularly to the graveyard.'

'You mean the killer might have relatives at Lawrence Hill. Are any of Franklin's relatives buried here?'

'How the hell should I know? I'll put in a call to county hall, but unless someone's working late it won't be picked up until tomorrow.'

'Hold on.' Carla pulled out her phone and opened up the BillionGraves app. It claimed every marked grave had been recorded in the cemetery, but when she typed Franklin into the surname search, there were no results. 'Nothing.'

'Damn. He's probably got a private plot somewhere. That would figure.'

But Franklin wasn't fitting any more. There must be some link to his constructions, but she was now wondering if the scent she'd inhaled from her attacker was the same as the lingering aftershave she'd sniffed in her office. Her office space had been invaded by someone who left a trace of their presence, which meant it must be an academic as Baros had suggested. She typed Caron into the last name search, but this Quebecois name came up blank. Finally, she typed Hazen and got a single hit.

'I've got something. I have a colleague, Max Hazen. It's a long shot, but there's a grave here belonging to Linda Hazen.'

'Max Hazen's wife. Fuuuck.'

'Where is it?'

Baros snatched the torch out of her hand and started up the hill. 'We need to get to the newer part of the cemetery. It's the other side of the hill.'

He sped off, leaving Carla in the darkness. 'Hey,' she hollered after him. 'I can't see a thing.'

She fumbled for her phone and switched on its flashlight, giving her only enough light to put one step in front of the other. 'Baros, wait for me.'

As she was stumbling after him, Albert rang her mobile. 'Have you found her?'

She could hear a male voice talking in the background. 'No, but—'

'I'm coming to you. The kids are with a neighbour and he's guarding them with his rifle. I never even knew he had a gun licence. I've picked up Jack, who's coming to help. He knows about apotropaic marks and—'

'She's not at the Miller graves,' Carla interrupted, 'but we think she's here somewhere. Is there any connection between Viv and Max Hazen's wife?'

'Max? You don't think—'

'Please. This is urgent.'

'When Max first came to the faculty, he had a wife, Linda. She died in tragic circumstances.'

'She was killed?'

'I suppose he would say that. She was in an automobile accident. Only... my God. Is that what this is all about?'

'What happened?'

'Linda was in a collision with a police car which was speeding to a crime scene. The driver was exonerated. Linda was, by her own admission, nervous on the roads and she pulled out onto the street. Didn't even see it coming down the road despite its lights and sirens.'

'What's Viv's connection to it? Was she the driver?' Albert was silent. 'Please, Albert. Was she driving?'

'A much older colleague, Jerry Tate, was driving. Viv was his partner.'

'So why would Max have a grudge against her?'

'I don't know.'

He was lying. His wife was possibly with a man who had killed six times and still he protected his wife. She turned at a noise behind her.

'I think you need to go back to the car, prof.' It was Perez, who had her gun out.

'Baros has gone to the grave of Max Hazen's wife.'

'Prof Hazen?' Perez didn't sound surprised.

'What is it?'

'I've been running through the system the cars who were sent a letter for kerb crawling around the time Stella King was murdered. My guess was that the perp would have made a few trial runs before striking. I was going through the files and guess whose name came up.'

'Max. Shit, you weren't far behind me. Why's he doing this?'

'I don't know, but I'm new to this precinct. Ask Baros.'

They stopped as Perez's beam picked up a shape on the ground. Baros was on the floor, bleeding.

'Baros. You OK?' Perez dropped down next to her partner and spoke into her radio.

'Is he all right?'

'I don't know. Why the hell did he go charging up on his own? He knows the procedure.'

Baros rolled over, groaning. 'Bastard hit me with something. Wouldn't be surprised if it was a gravestone.'

'If he'd wanted to kill you, he would have,' said Carla, moving away from them. 'He just wanted to slow you down.'

'Hey, wait,' shouted Perez.

Carla pushed on. She had no idea what was going on, but the death of Max's wife had played a crucial role in the killings. She would head towards the newer part of the cemetery over the brow of the hill and try to find the right grave. She would try at least to reason with him. Carla plunged on, scrabbling around for footing over the uneven ground until, for the second time that evening, she smelled the fear of Professor Max Hazen up close.

53

'I have no argument with you, Carla,' said Max, his hand over her mouth.

Carla's legs buckled as he dragged her into the darkness. She couldn't put up the same fight as earlier and she felt the energy seep away from her. She was tired and hurting, and now on the back foot. She could smell his skin as he pulled her across a row of graves, fear and excitement mingling with an expensive, soapy scent. In her terror, she still needed to correct him.

'You... you attacked me earlier.'

'I just needed enough time to get to Viv and incapacitating you would have helped that. You've been asking the right questions, but it doesn't matter because it's nearly all over. I don't want to hurt you, Carla, but don't fight me.'

She didn't believe him. The misogynism was ingrained deep inside his psyche. It must explain the way he'd treated the women he'd killed, starting with Stella King, taken to the mall that he'd had a hand in designing. He'd played down his role in its design to Carla and had also told her he had little interest in ritual protection. Completely untrue. Carla, despite herself, tried to fight him. Those who said that people near death received images of old memories were wrong. It was the dead who came to greet Carla, urging her to hold on, but it was too much for her. A fresh start on a new continent would end in this graveyard and the irony was too much to bear. She struggled, but he held her fast.

'You don't have anything to fear. I'm just putting you somewhere safe while I finish things here.'

'Where is Viv?'

'Close by, alive. I'm not done talking with her yet.'

'I don't understand any of this.'

His grip tightened on her. 'I just want her to tell me, in her own words, what happened that night ten years ago.'

'Is that when your wife Linda died?'

'Exactly. It's nearly ten years to the day that Linda was killed by the squad car. If you'd left things alone, I think I'd have waited until the anniversary of her death to complete the hexafoil, but I don't suppose it really matters.'

'I don't understand why you're doing this. Why witch bottles? Why daisy wheels?'

'Viv Kantz has an unassailable reputation which I've watched flourish over the long years since my wife died. It's been a bitter pill to swallow.'

'But why?' gasped Carla as she felt his fingers dig into her arm. 'Albert told me Viv wasn't even driving.'

'Did he? That's the official account, certainly, but I now know different. When she hit the car, there were no witnesses, so her dumb partner, so near retirement, switched seats to take the heat off the cop who everyone said was Jericho's future.'

'Viv swapped places?' Carla felt a rope being put round her. 'What... what are you doing?'

'You'll be fine. I just don't want to be disturbed while I finish my plans.'

He strapped her to a grave, a stone cross covered in moss and decades of grime. Thank God she was used to being among the dead, but the ties that bound her cut into her skin, scouring her flesh.

'How do you know she swapped places?' asked Carla, desperate to keep him talking.

'Old Jerry Tate confessed before he died. It was eating up at him, so his daughter arranged for me to see him. I found not only had Viv been driving but she was hungover after a party the night before. She'd never have passed a breathalyser test. That's why Jerry swapped.'

'When was this? When did you find out the truth?'

'Just under three years ago.'

Around the time Stella King was killed, the first of the murders. 'Couldn't you have spoken to Viv? You could have had her investigated through traditional channels.'

'That precinct is as corrupt as the college. You really don't understand how things work around here, Carla.'

'Do you think Albert knows?' Carla remembered his silence when she told him Max might be involved. *Of course, Albert knows*, she thought.

'Those poor girls. If you were so determined to have your revenge, why not just target Viv?'

Max tested her bonds for a final time. 'Life can get a bit boring in Jericho and those from the right families rule this town. You'll realise it if you stay long enough, and I had a glimpse of it when I helped Franklin with the design of his mall. It got me thinking about spiritual middens and I decided to have a bit of fun with it. It's bad enough the men having power over this town, worse to watch a woman such as Viv lord it over Jericho too.'

'You're a monster.' Carla couldn't help herself, but he took her words calmly.

'My advice to you, Carla, is to go home.'

'I'm asking you to let me call an ambulance,' she shouted after him as he walked away. 'There's a way out of this that doesn't involve another death.'

The frozen ground glittered as Max disappeared out of sight. Viv must be somewhere close – Max had told her she was nearby. She wasn't making any noise, which was a bad sign.

'Viv,' she shouted. 'Help is coming.' Where the hell were reinforcements? 'Perez,' she hollered. 'I'm tied up. I need you to free me.'

'I'm here.' Perez came over the hill, her gun unholstered. 'Where's the lieutenant?'

'Close. I can't see them but she's not responding.'

'Shit.' She felt Perez pull at the rope, trying to prise the knot free. 'I need a knife. Wait here.'

'Don't leave me like this.' She thought of Iris's last moments as a noose was placed around her head and of Madison's terror as she fought for her life.

Perez's radio was a cacophony of sound. Help was coming, but it would be too late.

'Get away from the lieutenant,' she heard Perez scream. The beam from the detective's torch illuminated Max, who was bending over Viv. For the first time that evening, Carla had a good view of him. It was odd to see him out of his work clothes. Max had more of a chameleon personality than she'd given him credit for. With his dark woollen hat and short gabardine jacket, he resembled a construction worker en route to work. He also matched the description of the man who had walked into the woods with Iris Chan.

'Don't come any nearer.'

The knife in his hand glittered in the light. Perez had her gun trained on him. 'Put down your weapon,' she screamed.

Max bent over Viv. Whether to place the knife on the ground or to finish the job he'd started, Carla couldn't tell.

'Put down—'

A shot rang out and Max fell to the floor. Confused, Carla strained against the rope. 'Where did the shot come from?' Perez swung the torch, illuminating Baros on one knee, his face streaked with blood.

The dispatcher on Perez's radio was shouting into the night. 'I heard a shot. What's going on there?'

Perez spoke into the handset to reassure their colleague. 'Suspect down, officer injured. We need ambulances here as soon as possible.'

A wall of lights was coming up the hill. 'Where's Viv?' shouted Carla, but Perez and Baros had gone. 'Will someone untie me?' she shouted. 'Please.'

She continued yelling out until she heard movement. She didn't know who had a knife to cut through her binds. All she saw was a bright light and a pair of hands supporting her as they removed the rope. They deposited her on the ground and left her there, pushing on to help a fallen colleague.

Carla vomited onto the grass, immediately feeling a little better, although her head began to pound. In the distance, she could hear Albert shouting. 'Where's my wife?'

She lay there until she felt a presence at her side. At first, she thought it was Dan come back from the dead among these graves to give her comfort, but it was a living being who crouched over her, pulling her gently up. Jack.

'What are you doing here?'

'I got a panicked call from Albert looking for Viv. He thought Anna might know, but I rang her and she hasn't spoken to Viv for days. When I called Albert back, he was on the way here and he let me hitch a ride.'

She took in Jack's appearance. He was wearing a dinner suit and no overcoat. He must be freezing in this frosty night. A paramedic handed her a foil blanket and she passed it over to him. 'Have it. My jacket will keep me warm.'

He shook his head. 'You take it. I'll be fine. I'm used to the cold.'

She nodded, pulling the blanket around her. 'Is Viv OK?'

'It seems they're trying to stabilise her condition so they can move her. I don't think she's well at all. How did you know she'd be here?'

In the darkness, Carla couldn't see the Miller plot, but she pointed towards it anyway. 'There are a family of graves with the last name Miller. There's a hexafoil on the top of each of them. The Millers go back to the early settlers and they'd been using a daisy wheel to ward off evil for generations.'

'And what's the connection to Max?'

'The object of Max's hatred was Viv, who he held responsible for his wife's death. You were right about the centre of the hexafoil holding all the energy. The graves are common knowledge among those who know the cemetery well. When Max decided Viv had to die, he constructed this elaborate plan based on those daisy wheels. They're both from old Jericho families. Max of course knew Viv was a descendant of the Miller family.'

'But your first suspect was Franklin. What was his connection?'

'Once Max had the centre of his daisy wheel, he needed to decide on the six points on the surrounding circle. He could make that circle as big or as small as he wanted, but he needed to make six equidistant points. Starting at the mall with its daisy wheel design was important as everything had to fit the pattern he'd started. He'd had a hand in its design and it was perfect for a place to start. It explains why he targeted the harder to reach sorority house and why it was important Tiffany was killed at Silent Brook rather than the Lake House. The flower beds at Suncook must have just been a nice touch – it's possibly why the pattern wobbled a little when I was drawing it.'

'All to get a message to Viv.'

Carla shivered, hugging herself to keep off the chill. 'It's not just that. He has a deep-rooted hatred of women. I wonder what his marriage was actually like, but his wife's death clearly devastated him. Viv wouldn't have picked up the reference immediately, but once I mentioned hexafoils, it was at that point she clammed up. She knew it was a possibility she was being targeted.'

'You think she knew it was Max?'

'Unless she's got other skeletons in her closet.'

'And the witch bottles?' asked Jack.

'Max having a bit of cerebral fun, I'm afraid.'

'You know, if you'd asked me the right question, we might have got here a lot quicker than this. I remember Max telling me he'd advised local architects on the New England vernacular for one of Franklin's developments. I thought he was talking about the exteriors – narrow sidings, large chimneys – but I might have made the connection. Maybe next time don't play your cards so close to your chest.'

Carla stayed silent as they watched Viv lifted onto a stretcher and carried off into the waiting ambulance. Albert was by her side, holding her hand.

'Where is Max?' she asked.

'He was the first to go in the ambulance. He's not doing so good.'

'God, I hope he survives. So many affected by this case deserve their day in court. Madison Knowles' mother, and Dallas, who does so much to advocate for those girls.'

'You know, you gave me a fright.' He pulled her towards him, but she froze.

'What about Anna?' Carla struggled to her feet.

'I don't know.'

At least he was honest. He could have told her that he and his wife were getting that divorce, and she might have believed him.

'That's fine,' she said finally. 'I don't know either.'

54

'Just the person I need. A professional in the midst of rank amateurs.'

Erin, whose nerves had been shredded by the evening's events, felt her heart leap in her chest. She'd been sitting in the empty facility, worrying about Carla, who wasn't answering her phone. Baros's sarcasm might have been true to type, but his appearance wasn't. His usual suit was replaced by a high-vis jacket and jeans, and he needed a shave. A wound across his temple had been patched with tape and gauze. It had been a long day for everyone and investigations were likely to go on into the night.

'Are you trying to give me a stroke? Who let you in at this time of night?'

'Showed my badge to security. It's not exactly the first time I've been here.'

Erin sank into her chair. She was on edge and asking stupid questions. Of course, Baros would have been allowed to enter.

'How's Viv?'

Baros's face set. 'In surgery. She took a knife wound to the stomach.'

'Christ.' It had been a fraught evening after she'd dropped Ethan off at his father's, interrupting an intimate evening between her ex and his new girlfriend. She must have looked like a ghost as she threw Ethan out of the car without explanation and sped off to find Carla. She'd have to make it up to her ex when she next saw him, although maybe not. His girlfriend had looked disappointingly young.

They'd not allowed her through the police tape at the cemetery. There were no bodies, so she had no jurisdiction and police were combing the area for evidence. She managed to find a friendly cop, who'd told her the essence of what had happened and Viv Kantz's deception ten years earlier in a car accident that had left a member of the public dead. Stunned, Erin had got back into the car and driven to the only place where she'd get some peace. Her office had been deadly quiet, only the night security guard reading a newspaper.

'Why've you come here?'

'You're going to be needed. Max Hazen died of his injuries this evening.'

'Shit. Are you OK?'

Baros shrugged, tapping the filing cabinet with his fingertips. 'There'll be an inquiry. I've made a few enemies inside the station, so I'm not counting on coming out smelling of roses.'

'They'd be fools to let you go.'

They regarded each other for a moment without speaking.

'So,' said Erin, finally. 'I know what I'm doing for the rest of the evening. Prepping for tomorrow's autopsy. You can trust me on this one.'

'Thanks, doc.' He looked round. 'Doesn't look like there's much work to do here. How about you come with me and I'll show you something you might want to bear in mind when you're writing up your report?'

'Look, Baros. If there's going to be an inquiry, I need to do this by the book. Believe me, it'll be in your interest to let me get on with things.'

'It's work and not just to do with Max's shooting. I don't want to show Carla this. I've got Doctor Caron to take her home.'

'What the hell was he doing there?'

'Albert called him. Don't give me that look. He slipped through the police tape before we could stop him. It's a benefit of privilege; you just go ahead and do what you please. So, you coming?'

'OK, but can you give me a clue where we're going?'

'Nope.'

His Mustang smelled of coffee; he must drink endless cups of the stuff. The drive took them past Lawrence Hill where patrol car lights continued to flash, catching outlines of stone angels and lopsided crosses. He turned off the highway towards one of the more affluent parts of town, pulling into the driveway of a house set back from the road.

'Is this where Max lived?'

'Sure is.'

Erin looked at the immaculate lawn without a single fallen leaf. 'Looks well kept. The gardener must come every day.'

'Wait until you see inside.'

He pushed past a couple of cops, one of whom patted him on the back. He might have his detractors at the station, but Max had tried to kill a serving cop. Erin had a good idea how an inquiry into Baros's shooting might end. She passed a living room which had an unlived in feel. The furnishings were a little old fashioned, probably purchased by Linda over a decade earlier. Powder-blue velvet drapes hung at the windows, blocking out the night.

'We'll start in the library.' He took Erin into a room where books lined all four walls. Some, she saw, were stacked two deep. 'We've only just made a start, but we've got access to his laptop already. Take a look at this.'

In his email browser, a technician had called up the history of messages between Iris Chan and Max.

'He didn't even use an alias,' said Erin.

'They must have met while Iris was still a student. We knew Iris had a boyfriend after her relationship with Michael Lines fell apart, but we never got into her emails to discover who that might be.'

'Looks like Michael Lines is going to walk free sometime soon.'

'You can bet Larry Foster is working on it as we speak. We're looking for a link with Tiffany Stoker, but that might be harder to pin on him. We're talking super casual about that relationship.'

He took her up the stairs into a front bedroom, passing a technician on the stairs who was examining the carpet. The room smelt of a spicy soap and Erin wondered if this was the smell Carla had recognised when he'd attacked her. The sparsely furnished room was dominated by an old wood-framed bed with a thick mattress, but it was the headboard which drew Erin's gaze. Into the cherry-red wood were carved fifteen or twenty daisy wheels.

'Jesus. He slept on that every night.'

'Weird, isn't it? The thing is, he didn't carve them himself. They're not fresh marks. He must have purchased the bed at auction. Sleeping here must have started the process that led to the idea of the killings forming the hexafoil.'

Erin reached out to trace the pattern with her fingertips. An unbroken line, Carla had said. To her, it felt nothing more sinister than putting a horseshoe over your door.

'I thought he and Lauren were lovers, even if it didn't last long. These markings wouldn't have passed her by.'

'Maybe he never brought her home. Max Hazen was a man who valued his privacy.'

'You know...' Erin had to say what had been gnawing away at her. 'What Viv did was unforgivable. Her partner might have swapped places with her for the best intentions, but she lied from the start of her career. Law enforcement has to uphold the highest standards of integrity. Viv failed to do that.'

Baros turned his face away from her. 'She paid a high price,' he said, finally.

55

The Christmas lights of Jericho glittered in the distance against the pitch-black sky as Carla shrugged on her coat. The town was a stickler for tradition and the seasonal decorations hadn't been installed until the third week of advent. It was typical that Jericho was behind with its preparations. The town, Carla suspected, was always a little late to the party. Max's victims had been denied justice because, rather than investigate the essence of Jericho itself, Viv Kantz had focused on finding a link between the victims when there was none. That, Carla supposed, was fair enough. What was unforgivable was, once she realised that the hexafoil was meant as a message for her, she had tried to shut everything down. Albert's reprimand still came to haunt Carla at night, his questioning of her professional competence a hard act to forgive.

Albert, however, now had other preoccupations. He was on a leave of absence and the rumour was that he wasn't coming back. It left the department rudderless and reeling from the revelations of Max's killings, and that made Carla more determined to stay to help rebuild the reputation of a once-revered archaeology school. Jack would be there too. She would try not to think too much about him during the break, although no doubt her mother Sylvia would want to know the details of every man she'd encountered in Jericho. Well, that would be an interesting conversation.

The zip snagged on the lining of her coat as it reached her collarbone. It was the padded jacket she'd purchased on her first visit to Franklin Mall back in October. She'd worn it a few times but, like most impulse buys, it was an expensive mistake. Not smart enough for college, too pristine to wear in the field. She missed her old dig jacket but couldn't bear to wear it after the night in the cemetery. When she got back to England, she would get herself a replacement and bring it back with her. She'd been warned January in Jericho was bitterly cold.

Patricia had arranged for her meagre possessions to be transferred to her new lodgings over the holidays. Carla had wanted to do it herself – leaving her stuff for strangers to move had disturbing echoes of Lauren's effects languishing on campus. As a compromise, she took all her books and papers and locked them in her desk. Patricia's son would simply be moving her clothes and toiletries. The whereabouts of Lauren's notebook would remain a mystery. Baros was convinced that Max had taken it, but a search of his house had revealed nothing of Lauren's. Carla had another theory: Max had lured Lauren to Suncook Park somehow and what better way than to say he'd an idea of his own as to the pattern that the killings were forming and to bring her notes from visiting Madison's house. The notebook, once it had entered the water, had been worthless. It had been carried away downstream while Lauren had not.

Her new home, when she returned, would be a small apartment not far from Penn Street where Jessica Sherwood had lived. She could walk to her office at college and settle down to another term where this time her students would know her. Her classes would still be second to Jack Caron's in popularity, but that would be OK. Or maybe it wouldn't. Time would tell.

The sound of a horn from the driveway warned her Erin had arrived. Carla picked up her case and hand luggage and walked down the steps. To her surprise, she saw Ethan in the back seat, his goofy grin aimed at her.

'You're honoured,' said Erin, opening the trunk. 'I can't usually get him away from his PlayStation. He's even vacated the front for you.'

Carla opened the door and slid into the passenger seat. The car had the familiar antiseptic smell she'd come to associate with Erin's work. She wondered if her friend even noticed. Erin jumped up beside her and started the engine.

'Your luggage is light. So you are coming back.'

'Never was in doubt.' It was a lie and they both knew it.

Carla was booked on the Boston to London red-eye and Erin had offered to drive her to the airport. Carla was glad of the offer. It allowed her to watch Jericho from the comfort of the car among this small family she had grown to know and like. Erin had gone above and beyond the call of duty as her mentor. She had played devil's advocate and challenged Carla's wilder guesses, but she had ultimately allowed her to tease out the pattern Max had been plotting out. The tragedy was that Lauren had got part of the way there. If only she had turned to Jack rather than her former lover Max. Jack. Carla turned her face out of the window and thought of Anna. She suspected there was unfinished business between the couple despite the divorce proceedings. Carla would heed Erin's warning and tread very carefully next term.

The route took her past Jericho College where people were thin on the ground. The library was staying open for the holiday period, but most students were going home to their families. Albert's empty office was hidden from view. Carla wondered if she'd ever see him again or if she'd return to news of his replacement. She suspected the college would move fast to protect its reputation.

The car slowed to a crawl at lights. In the distance, she could see the church of St Luke's next to Suncook Park. She wondered if Franklin would ever learn of her suspicions that he was the killer. She suspected, in this town, it was inevitable the rumours would reach his ears. Baros was a talker and he'd relish telling everyone that Carla had, once again, got it wrong. Their brief camaraderie outside the Kantz house had evaporated as soon as the emergency services arrived, although Erin had thawed towards the belligerent detective. It was just as well Viv was unlikely to be using the archaeologists as expert consultants in the future.

As the lights turned green, Erin turned onto the highway out of town. The route took them past Silent Brook and through the underpass where she had spoken to Dallas and learnt the story of Stella King, Max's first victim. As they approached, Carla looked out for the woman, but a lone girl, probably no older than fifteen, stood in the glow of a yellow streetlamp. Perez's appeal here had at least done some good. Lighting had been provided and it didn't look like the girls had moved on elsewhere. Stella King had been a victim of chance. It was the shopping centre that had been key, not her profession. Any one of the women standing beneath the concrete roadway would have been at risk.

Traffic was heavy and the car slowed to a crawl as they passed the girl. Behind her, in the side mirror, she could see Ethan gawking.

'Mom.'

'Yes, I know,' murmured Erin. 'Avert your eyes, please. No need to stare.'

'But Mom, look.'

Both Carla and Erin turned to the girl, who looked indifferent at their scrutiny. But Ethan wasn't pointing at the sex worker but the pillar behind her.

'What—?' Carla frowned at the column. Amongst the graffiti and car registration numbers was a daisy wheel spray-painted in violent purple.

'Maybe one of the girls painted it on. Protect them from evil spirits,' said Erin. 'The story has been all over the papers. I'm surprised there haven't been more instances of it popping up around town.'

'I sincerely hope so.' Carla looked at the crude image. Would the girls have appropriated such a violent symbol for themselves? She would call Dallas from the airport and ask her.

The traffic sped up as they drove away from the underpass and the town. Ethan put on a local radio station and Erin hummed along to the Foo Fighters. Still the daisy wheel continued to niggle at Carla. She would definitely call Dallas from the airport. Because, if the girls hadn't put it there, who had?

Acknowledgements

How I loved writing about all things witchy. This book has had a long genesis and began with a conversation between myself, Sarah Tarlow, Professor of Historical Archeology at the University of Leicester, our agent Kirsty Mclachlan and the late film producer Ileen Maisel. I later discovered the history of hexafoils and witch bottles, and once I'd fallen down that rabbit hole, there was no return. New England, which I've visited many times, was a wonderful setting for my fictional Jericho College, but I've also drawn inspiration from my hometown of Lampeter, the site of Wales's oldest university, and also my time as a Royal Literary Fund fellow at Sheffield University.

Thanks as ever to my agent Kirsty Mclachlan at Morgan Green Creatives, who has kept this book on track and to my editor Siân Heap at Canelo for her enthusiastic response. Thanks to the other Canelo staff – Thanhmai, Kate, Alicia – for the work on my books and to my witchy writing friends – Sheila Bugler, Julie-Ann Corrigan, J. M. Hewitt, Rachel Lynch, Marion Todd. Tony Butler, as ever, has provided invaluable input into the finished book and I'm grateful for his continued support and that of his wife Judith. Thanks too to Julie Conlan who gave me lots of witch ideas and a leaving present of door charms. They seem to be working their magic in Wales.

I'm lucky to have the support of my family including my father, Stuart, and I'm especially grateful to my husband Andy, without whom writing would be no fun at all. Finally, heartfelt thanks to Sarah Tarlow, a great writer in her own right, for the chats and inspiration, and to whom this book is dedicated.

CANELOCRIME

Do you love crime fiction and are always on the lookout for brilliant authors?

Canelo Crime is home to some of the most exciting novels around. Thousands of readers are already enjoying our compulsive stories. Are you ready to find your new favourite writer?

Find out more and sign up to our newsletter at canelocrime.com